To Tempt a Lady

BARBARA RUSSELL

trigger warnings

Trigger warnings: mention of a child's death; mention of suicide; emotional abuse; mention of a child having been beaten, prostitution, visit at the mortuary, death of a parent, sexual propositioning, rough sexual advances. This book is written in British English.

one
London, 1879

Marcus was at his happiest when he was alone, but he wasn't a solitary person; he was simply very selective about the people he wished to spend time with.

In the crowded, bright ballroom, he stood in a quiet corner, holding a glass of cordial and searching for his father. They'd arrived on time, paid their compliments to the host, and chatted with many of the guests about things no one cared about. Surely, he could return home now. He would need a week of solitude to recover from that social event.

After all, Father was the person people wanted to talk with, not Marcus—an almost graduated civil engineer with no title or particular achievement to boast about.

He exhaled in relief when Father walked over to him, smiling and bowing at the passing ladies.

"Are you enjoying yourself?" Father asked.

"May I go home?"

Father angled towards him. "Don't you like it here? Good music, great food, and many people your age."

"I'm a bit tired." He gripped the glass harder.

He didn't have anything in common with those people. They

were interested in parties and other activities requiring large gatherings.

"The day you're at the head of our company, you'll learn that mingling with potential clients during social events is a vital part of the job. Just tonight, I've received a commission to strengthen the beams of a bridge in Hertfordshire and another to restructure an ancient mansion in Oxford." He gave a pat to Marcus's shoulder, bursting with happiness. "Smile, ask a lady to dance, and make new friends."

"So I can't leave."

Father cocked his head. "Not until you enjoy yourself."

"I would spend the summer here, then."

"A little enthusiasm has never killed anyone."

"I might be the first one."

"Good Lord." Father tapped a foot briefly. "You are like your grandfather. The life and soul of the party he was!" he said sarcastically. "He left my wedding reception because he felt there was too much fuss."

Marcus took a sip of his drink just to do something. He wouldn't attend any wedding receptions anytime soon. Maybe never.

"Sir Albert!" A gentleman shook Father's hand with energy. "I was talking with Wiscombe about the excellent work you did on my estate. He's interested in working with you on the renovation of his castle in Devonshire. Come with me. Wiscombe is eager to meet you."

"Absolutely." Before leaving, Father gave him a pointed look as if to say, '*That's what I meant.*'

A castle was thrilling, but Marcus was alone again.

No, that wasn't correct. He wasn't alone, but he was lonely, which was ironic, considering that when he was really alone, he never felt lonely.

Since he couldn't leave and he had no intention of dancing, he would at least take a walk and admire the architecture of the building.

No one would notice his absence. He would quietly slide out of the ballroom and take a breath of fresh air that would last for a few hours until Father decided to leave.

"Excuse me." He brushed past a group of young ladies. At the centre was Lady Emma, the daughter of the Earl of Pembroke. They'd been introduced earlier that night, but he doubted she remembered him. Her friends laughed out loud at something she said. Every gaze was on her. Including his. She was a golden jewel with a smile spreading beauty. Everyone would look at her. But she wouldn't look at everyone. "Excuse me."

He walked past a group of young men laughing and chatting and ignoring him. "Excuse me." Finally, he squeezed himself through a group of matrons, watching the ballroom with sharp eyes, and arrived at the end of the room. He sped up once he was in the corridor.

Peace at last.

When the chatter and music died down behind him, he heaved a sigh. His mind was already clearer, thanks to the dim lights and the muffled sounds.

He barely reached the set of double doors opening to the garden when someone called.

"Mr. Kingston?"

So someone did notice him leaving the ballroom. Just his luck. No one paid the slightest bit of attention to him except when he needed to pass unnoticed.

He turned around. "I was—"

Lady Emma was running towards him, leaving him speechless. Her blonde hair formed a golden crown around her head, and as she closed the distance, her large hazel eyes turned green in the gas lamp lights. She looked beautiful when she was still, but when she smiled and ran, she was as captivating as a shooting star. Her sparkling white and yellow gown with golden flounces completed the picture.

"May I have a word?" she asked.

His tongue was in a knot as her brightness overwhelmed him.

She stopped in front of him, but her gold drop earrings kept moving back and forth right under her lobes, catching the light. He wasn't even sure why he noticed those things. A whiff of her refined honeysuckle scent teased his senses.

Being in a crowded room or alone with her was the same for him. He felt lonely. Terribly lonely. And he didn't even know why. Maybe because Father hadn't always been wealthy. His family had survived on potatoes and hope for years before Father's construction company had become huge. And Lady Emma made him painfully aware of his humble origin and gloomy character.

"My lady."

"Your father told me you're particularly good at repairing devices." Her angelic voice matched her golden appearance.

"My father exaggerates." Telling her he studied engineering at King's College and that mechanics was one of his favourite subjects would likely bore her. Silence was more appealing, wasn't it?

"Perhaps you could help me." She took out a small, heart-shaped metallic box from her purse. Porcelain roses adorned the pink lid. "This is my mother's carillon music box. I think it's broken. Would you be so kind as to take a look at it?"

Carillons weren't exactly his speciality. In fact, anything under the size of a building wasn't. She would have more luck with a clockmaker, but he opened his palm anyway. Her hopeful expression tugged at his heart.

"Thank you." She smiled, and he remained quiet for a moment, wanting to enjoy her smile.

"I need the light." He walked to the end of the corridor where a gas lamp burned over a table.

"I don't want Papa to know the music box is broken. He would be upset. I'm upset, but I swear it wasn't me. I didn't do anything. One day, it simply didn't work, but Papa won't believe me. I often break things, you see. Not that I want to. These things just happen." She inched closer as he examined the box in the light, and he couldn't deny a flutter in his chest.

"It means a lot to me." She was so close that her breath touched his skin.

He cleared his throat, studying the tiny screws. "I need a hairpin, please."

Her arm brushed his when she raised her hands to search through her hair. "I find it fascinating, the fact you can repair something with a hairpin, I mean. I once destroyed a mirror with a hairpin. Can you believe it? I was dancing in my bedroom when a hairpin flew out of my chignon and hit the mirror. Seven years of bad luck. How horrible. Have you ever broken a mirror, Mr. Kingston? Dreadful noise. Although Papa told me the mirror was old and likely corroded. So I don't count the broken mirror among the many things I have broken."

Her chatter was calming. He didn't have to fill the uncomfortable moments of silence while she chatted so lively, and it helped him focus on the work. And it made him smile.

He lifted the cover of the case to reveal the inner cylinder and vibration plate.

"Goodness." She edged closer to him until her chin touched his arm, and he trembled at the contact. "That's the secret thingamabob that makes the music. Lovely."

She sounded so enthusiastic he couldn't help but release the tension in his shoulders.

"The crank is blocked." He used the hairpin to point at a golden hair wrapped around the crank. "A hair stopped it."

"Oh, the crank is being cranky." She laughed. "Sorry, I'm just being silly. I think it's my hair. I carry the music box with me often, and it stays in my purse with my comb and spare hairpins. I need to be more careful."

It was amazing how she could point out her carelessness and scold herself in the same speech.

He gently worked on the crank. "I would need a pair of tweezers to completely remove the hair, but the music box should work now."

He put the case back in place and rolled the handle. When he released it, a sweet song sounded.

"Heavens. You're a genius!" She hugged him, and he couldn't breathe. His pulse spiked, and his skin tingled. She stepped back, giggling. "Apologies, Mr. Kingston, but you have no idea how happy I am."

No, he had an idea. She was radiant and contagious. Even the marble floor was jubilant.

"Thank you. Thank you." She stared at him as if he'd invented music in his spare time.

"You're welcome."

"Emma?" a young man called from the other side of the corridor. "The cotillion is starting. You promised to dance it with me."

She waved at the man. "Yes, of course." She slid the music box into her purse. "Are you free for the next dance, Mr. Kingston? It's a quadrille."

"I don't dance."

Her smile dropped. "Just the quadrille or anything?"

"Anything. Dancing isn't my cup of tea."

He'd disappointed her if the way her shoulders stooped was any indication. Somehow, it hurt.

"Then I'll see you after the cotillion, so we can talk and have a drink. Thank you again." She briefly touched his arm before rushing down the corridor.

As she ran away in a flutter of silk and a cloud of perfume, Marcus remained in that quiet corner with his heart beating in his throat, wondering what the hell had happened.

two

Emma breathed hard after finishing the cotillion. Her pulse pounded, and her head spun, but she would dance again in a moment. She clapped at the musicians with the other dancing couples in the ballroom, excitement bubbling within her.

What a pity that Mr. Kingston didn't like dancing. He was a serious gentleman but gave her a sense of safety she rarely experienced with other men. And he was brilliant. Papa had told her he was one of the best students of his year.

She searched the crowded ballroom for him. He'd been wonderful to her, repairing her precious music box in a moment, and she wanted to repay his kindness somehow, but he'd vanished.

Trevor, her elder brother, handed her a glass of fruit punch. "Aren't you tired? You have danced one set after another."

"I love dancing." She accepted the glass. "A day without dancing is like a day without sunlight."

"Which is called night." He sipped his drink.

She chuckled. "Do you see Marcus Kingston anywhere?"

"No. I didn't realise he was here until I saw his father. He has the uncanny ability to disappear when he wants to. Why are you searching for him?"

"He did me a huge favour, and I want to dance, or sit the dance out with him as a thank you." She rose on her tiptoes to take a better look at the crowd.

"What favour?"

She lowered her voice. "He repaired Mama's music box for me."

"You broke it!"

"I didn't. It stopped working, but it works now thanks to Mr. Kingston. Hence the thank you."

He slanted her a sceptical look. "I can't claim I know him extremely well, but we've spent some time together, and I gather he feels out of his depth in a fancy ballroom."

"I can understand why he feels intimidated," she said.

"I can't." Trevor sipped again, gazing around. "I personally find these gatherings of the wealthiest and most powerful people in the kingdom rather subtle and subdued. Look at Lady Beaumont's giant diamond necklace. If you stare at it for longer than ten seconds, you'll get a splitting headache."

"Ha ha." She poked him with an elbow.

"There." He nodded towards the other side of the ballroom. "Marcus, next to that Grecian column."

"Thank you." She handed him her half-full glass.

"Wait. I should come with you as any good elder brother would do."

"But you aren't."

He tilted his head right and left. "I suppose you're right."

"I'll see you in a moment." She weaved through the crowd, speeding up when Mr. Kingston slid out of the room again. "Mr. Kingston."

As it'd happened earlier, he came to a halt and turned around in the corridor. His grey eyes held a metallic quality she couldn't decipher. While he'd been kind and polite to her, she didn't understand if he was trying hard not to yell at her or if he found her nice.

The lack of certainty bothered her. She was used to feeling

confident about people's reactions towards her, either in a good or bad way. Understanding what other people thought of her had always been easy. But Mr. Kingston was as enigmatic as the sphinx. She preferred to know what he thought of her. No matter how harsh, the truth was always better.

"My lady." He bowed, stiff and formal.

"You may call me Emma."

"I don't think your father would approve."

"You're friends with Trevor, and your father knows my father. I'm sure Papa wouldn't mind."

He bowed again, and she didn't know how to interpret the bow. Why was it so difficult to understand him?

She stepped closer, and he drew in a breath, which she failed again to understand. It could be anything from annoyance to relief. "How can I repay your kindness? If you don't want to dance, would you like to be my partner in a game of whist?"

He lifted a shoulder. "You don't have to feel obliged to repay me in any way. I did nothing."

"Would you like some company? Apologies, but I noticed you seem to avoid people in the ballroom. I guess because you don't know anyone aside from my brother, but Trevor can be averse to people, too. So he isn't good company sometimes. Not that I think you're averse to people or that Trevor is, for that matter."

A little crease appeared between his eyebrows as if he wanted to frown but thought it would be rude and restrained himself. Her confidence diminished to a spectacularly low level. Talking with him was a challenge.

She feared Mr. Kingston was judging her. Or worse, he didn't want to talk with her at all.

His brow didn't smooth. "I would like some company."

He sounded as if he meant the opposite. Maybe he'd agreed only to be polite.

"Excellent. I'll introduce you to my friends." She took his arm and started to walk towards the ballroom, but he didn't move an inch, and her slippers screeched against the polished floor. "Don't you want to meet my friends? You'll have the opportunity to talk with new people. My friends are very nice."

"I'm afraid I'm not fond of large gatherings."

"Oh." She slid her arm out of his. "So when you said you would like some company, you didn't mean to return to the ballroom."

"No."

Was she doing something wrong? "I can keep you company if you want."

A sad smile lifted a corner of his mouth. "My lady, you don't have to worry about me. Please return to your friends, dance, and enjoy your evening. I'll be fine. I appreciate your effort."

"But you said you would like some company."

"Yes, I did, but you obviously want to spend time with your friends, and I don't want to keep you away from them."

She was at a loss. It was the first time she'd met a young person who didn't want to meet new friends or dance. Maybe he truly preferred loneliness. Whatever the reason, she wouldn't insist.

She dropped a curtsy. "If you change your mind, let me know, Mr. Kingston."

He bowed. "My lady, enjoy your evening."

She would, but she wondered what it was about her he didn't like.

three

Newport-on-Tay, 1879—Six months
later

Anxiety never failed to torment Marcus every time he was about to see Lady Emma, but he discovered that, if he drank gallons of strong black tea, he became anxious a lot faster and a lot harder while needing the water closet more often.

The motion of the carriage driving him to her house didn't help calm his nervous state. He shifted on the seat and glanced out of the window, dreading the moment he would see her, but at the same time, looking forward to it.

He would spend a few days in her house in Newport-on-Tay as Father and his associate, Sir Horace, did business with the earl, and Marcus had no idea how he would survive being so close to her. He would end up saying the wrong thing, and she would think he was an idiot.

What was worse was that from now on, he would meet peers more often than before. Social gatherings would be his life.

Father was the technical genius of the company, but Sir Horace had the connections, which the company needed to grow. He might not be as talented as Father in engineering, but he had many friends among the peerage and the House of Commons.

As part of the business, Marcus would need to mingle at balls and parties more often.

The mighty Thistle Hall was already visible at the end of the road. The house of the Earl of Pembroke rose in all its Jacobean beauty—red bricks, shapely gables, oriel windows, and pediment doors. As a civil engineer, he found its imposing style challenging, but the people living in it, one lady in particular, were more daunting.

"You're too nervous," Father said from the opposite seat. "What's the matter with you?"

"I'm not nervous."

He wiped his clammy hands on his trousers; his best pair of trousers, that is. He was wearing a brand-new dark blue suit with a matching fine waistcoat. The clouds were reflected in the shine of his shoes, so polished they were.

Father gave him a sceptical look. "You were fidgety on the train, but now you're pale. You should talk to her."

"Who?" He loosened the collar of his shirt, only to tighten it again, lest it give an untidy impression.

"Lady Emma, of course. Every time you see her, you seem to lose the ability to speak, move, and look human."

"Do I?"

"She talks and talks to you, and you just stand there immobile and silent. She'll get discouraged soon if you don't talk to her."

"I remember having a conversation with her about..." He drummed his fingers on his knee. The last time he'd seen Lady Emma, she'd talked most of the time.

"If you keep staying silent and brooding when you're with her, she'll think you don't like her at all."

Which wasn't true. But it was true that he never spoke when he was with her while she never stopped talking. The result was that he knew a lot about her, but she didn't know anything about him.

There were too many reasons to be nervous around her. She

was the daughter of an earl, and he didn't find himself comfortable among peers; he would take a group of rowdy builders any day. Also, she wouldn't be interested in a recently graduated civil engineer whose ancestors had been farmers and serfs.

The shadows of the trees lining the drive blocked the view of the countryside and cast darkness in the carriage, turning his shoes pitch-black. Thunder roared in the distance as clouds gathered in the sky. Exactly what he needed, a dark omen.

The carriage slowed down once close to the entrance to Thistle Hall. Fuelled by the black tea, his heart gave a strong thump.

Father cast a glance at the sky. "Horace should already be here. I need to leave with him and the earl," Father said. "You'll stay here until I return."

Staying at Thistle Hall alone was as appealing as paying bills. "But I want to come with you."

"Not this time." Father gazed up at the darkening sky. "I want you to write those bills to pay." He patted his leather bag.

"Wonderful."

"I couldn't finish them all, and we won't be discussing anything technical, only financial. You would be bored."

He was about to protest when the carriage rolled to a stop.

A few words were exchanged between the coachman and the footman, and he wished to stay seated longer. He wasn't ready to see Lady Emma.

"We'll go together tomorrow morning when I inspect the Tay Bridge," Father said. "You'll enjoy yourself more if you stay here. And talk with Lady Emma."

He would love to, but he wasn't sure she would be interested.

The hedgerows and bushes in the front garden were so well trimmed and tidy that he instinctively ran his fingers through his hair to comb it. The entry hall was a masterpiece in elegance and balance, resembling the beauty of the Pantheon's dome, likely built when his great-great-grandfather was a baby, judging by the style. Just a further reminder of how ancient Lady Emma's family was.

His skin pebbled with goose pimples as another round of thunder boomed. He had to be allergic to aristocracy because he wasn't such a coward when he was with commoners.

He checked that the soles of his shoes didn't leave mud on the carpet.

"Sir Albert, Mr. Kingston, welcome. His Lordship and Sir Horace are waiting for you." The butler showed them to a warm sitting room.

The temperature difference caused his blood to shoot to his face. His cheeks turned so warm he could fry an egg on them. He had to be the colour of a strawberry.

"Welcome." The Earl of Pembroke shook Marcus's hand. "I trust you had a pleasant journey."

He bowed his head. "Very comfortable, my lord." Aside from the knot of anxiety in his stomach and his constantly full bladder.

Sir Horace gave him a strong pat on the shoulder. "It's good to have you here. Learning the trade on the field, aren't you?"

"Yes, sir." Marcus craned his neck, searching the room for Lady Emma, but aside from them and a footman, there wasn't anyone.

He had no choice but to sip yet another cup of tea as his father, the earl, and Sir Horace discussed the technical challenges of maintaining a bridge like the Tay Bridge. The earl had been one of the investors who had financed that prodigy of modern technology, and Father's company was responsible for the maintenance of the bridge's structure. That was what Marcus wanted to do—build safe and modern bridges, railways, and houses for the kingdom.

"The gusts of winds are so strong in the bay," Father said, "and the sea currents add considerable weight to the structure."

Sir Horace nodded. "The traffic of trains on the bridge has increased five per cent in the past two months."

On other occasions, Marcus would pay complete attention to the conversation, but knowing Lady Emma was close started an annoying tingling on the back of his neck. Not to mention, he was going to burst if he drank one more sip of tea.

"Are you all right, Marcus?" the earl asked.

He shifted on his chair again. "I was wondering if I could leave for a moment, my lord. I need the lavatory."

The earl nodded at the footman. "By all means."

Marcus rose, a hand on his belly.

The footman opened the door for him. "Last door on the left side of the corridor."

The corridor was a wide, long hallway, and he feared he wouldn't make it to the last door. He sped up but stopped when a French door overlooking the garden opened and Lady Emma slid inside, accompanied by the roar of thunder.

His anxiety spiked. Her light green gown had the colour of budding leaves in spring and exalted her hazel eyes, making them look like amber jewels. But her smile upon seeing him was the most precious thing. It held the essence of her lively, happy personality.

He couldn't recall a single time when she'd been sad or defeated. Surely, she had those moments, but with a bubbly energy like hers, she only spread happiness. He'd been greedy in taking her happiness.

"Marcus." She bowed her head gracefully, and her blonde curls bobbed on her heart-shaped face. "How lovely to see you again."

"My lady." He bowed but not too low, lest his precarious situation turn unmanageable.

"You can call me Emma, as I told you the last time we met."

He made a gesture with his head halfway between a nod and a head shake, not sure what to say.

"It's getting cold." She closed the door, blocking a cold gust. "Would you like a cup of tea?"

"Heavens, no!" Hell. He squeezed his eyes shut for a moment.

He wished he'd been less harsh, but the simple mention of

anything liquid to drink increased the pressure on his about-to-explode bladder. Not something he could mention to a lady.

Her smile turned into a flat line. "Fine. No tea then."

He pinched the bridge of his nose. "I apologise, but I need to go."

"Don't let me keep you. I'll see you later." Back straight, she marched towards the other side of the corridor.

Damn. "My apologies. I didn't mean to be rude."

"Do not worry." She paused and gave him a graceful nod that could mean anything.

He strode to the bloody water closet, cursing the idea of drinking a lot of tea to calm his nerves.

After he finished, mentally kicking himself for his rudeness, he found Father, the earl, and Sir Horace in the entry hall with their coats on.

"Marcus." Father wrapped a scarf around his neck. "We're leaving. We should be here for dinner."

"Make yourself at home," the earl said as the footman handed him an umbrella. "Stewart will serve tea in the drawing room."

Bloody tea again. Marcus bowed. "Thank you, my lord."

A quick, cold gust whistled past when the footman opened the front door. The treetops swayed against the backdrop of a stormy sky.

"I could come with you," he said.

Father donned his hat. "Stay here, warm and dry, and finish those bills. I'll see you later."

After the footman shut the door, Marcus made his way to the drawing room. Without Father and after his brief, disastrous encounter with Emma, he should go to his bedroom, but that would be rude. He looked out of the window, studying the weather.

Bolts of lightning slashed the sky in the distance. No drop of rain fell, but judging from the direction of the wind, the storm would soon hit Newport-on-Tay.

"Marcus." Trevor entered the room, wearing his riding habit. "Welcome."

"Trevor." He shook hands with him.

"Care for a repast?" Trevor sat on the sofa, crossing his arms behind his head. "I've been out riding all day, and I'm famished."

"The new purebred?"

Trevor's face brightened. He looked like Emma—same blond hair and hazel eyes—but with an air of mischief she lacked.

"You should see him," Trevor said. "Such strong muscles and perfect lines. I love that horse more than people, and I'm not ashamed to say it."

"There aren't many things you're ashamed of."

Trevor laughed. "You're right."

Not even with Trevor, did Marcus find himself completely at ease, and it wasn't Trevor's fault. He'd been nothing but kind to Marcus.

"Have a seat." Trevor gestured at the armchair. "And tell me something scandalous."

He shifted his weight, wondering how much that armchair cost. "I don't know anything scandalous."

Trevor popped a raspberry into his mouth from a silver tray filled with fresh fruit. "You worked in the houses of the most famous peers in London. You must have learnt a secret or two."

"Only that Lord Cleath-Smith hasn't renovated the plumbing in twenty years."

Trevor threw his head back. "Boring. You're a nice fella, but you're too..." He selected another raspberry. "...too innocent and pure. Go out there, steal something, get slapped by a woman, live a little."

"Getting slapped means to live?"

"Experience, that's what I mean. Life isn't only about books and physics. Please sit down. You're making me nervous."

He perched on the edge of the armchair. "But physics makes me happy."

"See what I mean? Who would ever say that? You need to do things you'll regret later in life. Or the next day."

"You mean mistakes."

"Exactly. The currency of a full life." Trevor smirked.

Feeling so open and outspoken had to be good.

"Hello everyone." Emma entered the room. Her lovely smile returned as if the exchange in the corridor had never happened.

He stood up and bowed. "My lady."

She gave him another graceful nod before sitting on the armchair next to him. "Tea?"

Trevor nodded, selecting another raspberry. Marcus nodded, too, before regretting it. There. He regretted things, too.

Stewart served tea and sandwiches, and Marcus couldn't escape another round of drinking. Served him right.

Emma was watching him but didn't make any comment on the fact he was drinking tea.

"I was thinking about you the other day, Marcus," she said.

Trevor frowned and munched on a raspberry slowly.

Marcus couldn't say anything. She'd been thinking about him! He swallowed hard a morsel of a sandwich.

Emma smiled again. "Papa told me you and your father took care of the renovation of Hart House in London before we met, and that you worked on the window of my bedroom personally."

"Did I? I mean, I remember working on a bedroom window, but I had no idea it was yours." Had he known, he would have paid more attention to every detail.

She lifted a shoulder. "Unfortunately, I broke it."

It shouldn't hurt, but it did a little.

"I was distraught," she said. "The window was pretty. An unfortunate incident."

Trevor arched his brow, eating a sandwich. "Incident?"

Emma flushed a little. "Well, actually I was playing cricket in my bedroom despite Father forbidding me to play. Trevor gave me a fright, and I struck the ball so hard it cracked a corner of the window frame."

"I had nothing to do with the *incident*," Trevor said. "Your fault."

"My conscience is clean," Emma said in a playful tone.

"A clean conscience is only a sure sign of bad memory, as Mr. Twain said." Trevor wiggled his eyebrows.

"Have I ever told you that you're unbearable?"

"Every Tuesday."

"I'll be happy to repair it when I'm in London," Marcus said when the two siblings stared at each other.

So that was why she'd thought about him. A broken window. He ought to blame himself though. Obviously, nothing about him was sufficiently memorable for her to remember him without breaking something. Their acquaintance had started with a broken music box, after all, and it wasn't improving.

"That would be lovely. I have my second Season this year..." She lowered her voice. "Papa promised to give me more freedom. I'm nearly twenty. It's already quite late for a suitor. So I want that crack to go away."

"What does a crack on the window have to do with your next Season?" Trevor asked.

She brushed a curl from her face. "I want everything to be perfect. And Papa hopes I'll find a good match. He said the Season is too stressful for him."

"Because he has to deal with all your suitors," Trevor said.

Marcus's stomach churned. He was certain this Season would be her last. She would have a crowd of suitors from the best families in London, ready to propose, and she would be married within a year. He had more chances of having tea with the queen than courting Emma.

If only everything were as easy to repair as a window.

four

If every gentleman was as difficult to understand as Marcus was, then Emma's Season would be a challenging one. Her first one had been disappointing because Papa hadn't given her much freedom, and she hadn't attended all the events she'd wanted to. But the next one would be different. She had every intention of having fun, something Marcus didn't seem to have often.

They'd met several times in the past six months, what with Papa being interested in working with Sir Albert and Sir Horace's construction company, Kingston & Sindall. Sir Albert worked with several of Papa's friends, too. So she'd had plenty of opportunities to meet with Marcus.

On those occasions, Marcus had never spoken more than a handful of words, remaining stiff and serious whenever she talked to him. Only his eyes had lit and focused on her, but she hadn't known if it had been in a good or bad way.

Trevor claimed Marcus was as stiff as a barge pole, but at least he talked to him about boxing and cricket.

She'd asked him to dance, and he'd refused. She'd wanted to

introduce him to her friends, and he'd seemed horrified. She'd offered him tea, and he'd nearly shouted at her.

Her conclusion was that he didn't like her. Perhaps he thought she was too silly and shallow. The spoilt daughter of an earl who knew nothing about the world, which might be true, but he shouldn't judge her without knowing her better.

His eyes had the same metallic grey colour of a stormy lake and could be so icy cold she worried she might get frostbite. His raven hair and the dark suits he favoured added to his brooding persona.

But as she watched him now talking with Trevor in the drawing room, he smiled and seemed relaxed, the opposite of how he behaved with her.

And it wasn't a case of one of those gentlemen who didn't feel comfortable around ladies because he hadn't had any problems talking and joking with other young women her age. She'd watched him having conversations with maids and seamstresses.

It was *her*.

A mystery, because he had been nothing but polite to her, aside from the tea incident. He'd never argued with her, made rude comments, or made fun of her. It was his being quiet and simply nodding at whatever she said, compared to his more lively attitude with Trevor, that proved her theory right.

Even now, she had the feeling he avoided glancing in her direction.

Marcus stood up after finishing his cup of tea. "I need a moment, if you'll excuse me."

Trevor waved him off before biting into another sandwich.

When Marcus left, she sagged in the armchair.

"You look sour. Is it because of my comment?" Trevor asked.

"Which one? You always make comments about everything."

"A gentleman needs opinions, even the wrong ones. Especially the wrong ones."

She relaxed her facial muscles. "It's Marcus."

"He's odd and stiff, but he's a decent chap."

"With you. He must hate me."

Trevor chuckled. "Don't be silly."

"He remains silent and serious when I talk as if I bore him to death." She sipped her tea.

"Well, maybe you do bore him to death."

She exhaled. "Thank you. I feel so much better. With you, he laughs and talks. I don't know why he dislikes me so much."

"No, he doesn't." Trevor glanced at the door. "He's polite with me but not warm. He's warmer with the footmen. But I don't mind if he feels more comfortable with the servants."

"Then he doesn't like me because I'm an earl's daughter."

He shook his head. "The truth is that people always like you, and that the one time you find someone who doesn't worship you, it bothers you."

She scowled at him. "I don't care about people worshipping me. I just wonder why he doesn't like me."

"He isn't rude to you, I believe."

"No, he isn't. He's just distant and cold, which is the same thing sometimes."

"Try to talk less. Maybe he's intimidated by your being very talkative."

"I will." She regarded him with surprise. "For once, you gave me good advice."

"Don't get used to that." Trevor tilted his head and slanted a glance at her. "Why do you care, anyway? Once you start your Season, you'll have plenty of gentlemen interested in you. You'll have so many suitors that I'll probably have to challenge someone to a duel. As much as I think Marcus is a good man, he's the son of a builder. He won't court you. He works for those gentlemen who will be your suitors."

"Do you have to be so crass? You're jumping to conclusions. I've never said anything about Marcus courting me." And their late mother hadn't come from nobility, either. She rose. "Anyway, I need to change."

"Yes, you do."

She rolled her eyes. "Shut up."

"Stop thinking about him, and everything will be better."

Easier said than done. Thoughts of Marcus filled her mind as she headed towards the stairs.

Talk less. Was she unbearably talkative? She would say no, not with Marcus, at least. With him, she found it difficult to talk about everything that popped into her mind as she did with other friends.

She was at the base of the stairs when Marcus came from the corridor. As usual, he stiffened when he saw her. He barely glanced at her.

"Marcus?" she called when he was about to enter the drawing room.

He didn't turn around towards her immediately. "My lady."

Asking a gentleman a direct question about his liking for her was inappropriate, but she needed to know the answer, and likely, Marcus would never want to court her. She had nothing to lose.

She checked that the corridor was empty. "Why don't you like me?"

There. She'd asked. And she wasn't sorry. It was better to be clear than to have doubts.

His grey eyes widened, enhancing their peculiar colour. For the first time, they warmed with an emotion she couldn't place. Shame, horror?

"Why would you say that?" Even his voice acquired a deep, warm tone that started a quiver in her belly.

"You never talk to me, and when we're together, you look like you'd rather be in the Tower of London than with me."

A corner of his mouth curved up in a charming crooked smile. "No, trust me. I'm very happy to be with you."

The honesty in his voice struck her. It was as if she were meeting him for the first time.

"Then why do you never talk to me?" She lowered her tone.

"Why don't you want to call me Emma? Because you want to keep your distance?"

His shoulders rose and fell with a long breath. "Emma, no. I don't want to keep my distance."

She leant over the bannister. "Then what don't you like about me?"

"I like everything about you." His voice turned into that deep baritone again. It did funny things to her stomach.

She'd received many compliments. People often praised her grace and elegance when she danced, or her complexion. But that '*everything*' said in his intense voice and full honesty beat every other compliment she'd ever received.

He opened his mouth again, but the sound of a carriage arriving cut him off.

The footman rushed to the front door and pulled it open. Papa, Sir Albert, and Sir Horace stepped into the entry hall, talking among themselves. A gust swept through the hallway, chilling the air and the atmosphere between Marcus and her.

"There you are, darling. Are you getting ready for dinner?" Papa shifted his gaze from Emma to Marcus.

Sir Albert seemed not to know if he should smile or remain serious. Sir Horace narrowed his gaze on Marcus.

She straightened, still a bit shocked by Marcus's words. "Yes, I was about to change, Papa." She bowed her head. "Marcus, I'll see you at dinner."

As she went up the stairs, she could feel Marcus's fierce gaze on her. She paused at the landing and half-turned around. He stared at her with an intensity that had nothing to do with the usual frost and that made her feel desirable. It was as if his mask had fallen, and now he was staring at her as he'd always wanted to.

And she was more confused than ever.

five

Marcus didn't focus on the chatter in the drawing room after dinner.

Once again, his father, the earl, and Sir Horace were talking about the Tay Bridge, its strength and its weak points; a conversation he should listen to greedily since Father was explaining why they needed to check the eastern pillars of the bridge, those most exposed to the wind.

But no matter how hard he tried to follow the conversation, his thoughts drifted towards Emma and the short, overwhelming exchange they'd shared in the hallway. If he'd imagined she believed he didn't like her, he would have done something to change her mind. She'd sounded almost offended by his supposed dislike of her.

How wrong she was.

From now on, he would behave differently with her and take every opportunity to show her how much he liked her.

He put down his untouched glass of brandy, too nervous to stay still. Besides, Trevor had retired early, claiming the long ride had tired his muscles, and Emma hadn't joined them in the drawing room.

"My lord, Sir Horace, Father, I'll retire if you don't mind. The journey tired me more than I thought."

"Good night, Marcus," Father said.

The earl and Sir Horace nodded.

But Sir Horace slanted him a curious glance, the same as he'd tossed him when he'd seen Marcus and Emma together alone in the hallway. If he didn't approve of Emma talking to him, it was his problem.

Marcus crossed the wide room towards the door, but Sir Horace followed him.

He took Marcus's arm and said in a low voice, "Leave her alone. She isn't for you."

Marcus slid his arm out of Sir Horace's grip. "I don't know what you're talking about."

"If you ruin our business deal with the earl because you pant like an animal after his daughter—"

"I don't pant after her."

"—you'll be responsible," Sir Horace whispered through clenched teeth.

"Nothing is going to happen, sir." He matched Sir Horace's tone.

Sir Horace glanced at Father and the earl deep in conversation next to the roaring fire. "I understand you. Truly, I do. She has a nice pair of udders to be so young—"

"How dare you!" He closed his fists, raising his voice.

The chatter on the other side of the room stopped.

"Is something the matter?" Father asked, craning his neck towards him.

Marcus didn't take his gaze off Sir Horace. "Nothing, Father. I'm going to bed now."

He strode towards the door before Sir Horace could say anything else that made Marcus want to punch him.

The footman shut the door to the drawing room after Marcus left. He started up the stairs, fuming. Sir Horace was worried that

Marcus might ruin the business deal, but he'd been the one who had disparaged Emma. Bastard.

Footsteps thudded from behind him, and he paused, almost wishing it was Sir Horace again so he could tell him what he thought of his comments.

"Marcus, a word." That was the earl, and it wasn't an invitation. The earl slid into a parlour and waited for him.

Pulse racing with anger and worry, he followed the earl. If Sir Horace spread lies about Marcus and Emma, he wouldn't stay silent.

"My lord."

He clasped his hands behind his back. If the earl wanted to scold him about the conversation with Emma, he wouldn't deny his interest in her.

"I won't keep you long. I just wanted to have a quick chat. I gather you were an excellent student." The earl lit a cigar. "Best of your year."

"I was, sir."

"King's College, right?"

"Yes, sir."

"What do you plan for your future?"

Marcus had no idea where the earl was going with those questions, but at least Sir Horace wasn't involved. "Work with my father, expand the company, and take more work for the railways. They are the future."

The earl nodded. "Good. You're a clever man, and Kingston & Sindall is growing at incredible speed. You'll find yourself rich and busy pretty soon."

"Actually, sir, my mission is to develop safe buildings and structures to help ameliorate people's living standards." He winced inwardly at the dry, formal way he talked about his dream. But that was his thought. "Of course, I need to make a living, too, but I wouldn't say making a fortune is my first goal."

"Noble sentiment." The earl blew out some smoke. "Has any lady caught your fancy?"

He raised his eyebrows. "With due respect, sir, may I ask what the purpose of this question is?"

The earl chuckled. "I couldn't help but notice the way you look at my daughter."

Damn.

Emma believed he didn't like her; Sir Horace thought Marcus was only interested in Emma's body, but her father was the only one who understood the truth. He had no idea what that meant about his behaviour. It certainly said something about the people around him.

The earl didn't wait for an answer. "See, Emma is going to have another Season this year. She went out a bit late, but after my wife died, I became a lot more protective towards her, and I confess the idea of her leaving my house and starting her own family frightens me." His tone became sad. "I can't keep my children home forever, but I can't stop worrying about them either. I postponed Emma's first Season for as long as possible, and now I have to come to terms with the fact that one day she'll leave me. And your interest in my daughter is pretty obvious to me."

He cleared his throat, wondering why his interest hadn't been obvious to Emma. "I am aware of my position."

"I wasn't clear." The earl put down the cigar. "My dear wife didn't come from aristocracy, but her family was fairly wealthy. My mother didn't approve of our union. She wanted me to marry higher than a trader's daughter. But I loved Lucy dearly, and our marriage was a happy one. Uncommonly so, I would dare say. She was pretty much like Emma, spirited but kind, lively, and clever." He paused to touch his wedding ring. "I've never remarried because I can't."

Marcus didn't know what to say. He'd always seen the earl as a rich toff who lived an expensive life, but at the moment, he was a widower who still missed his wife.

"My point is," the earl said, lifting his gaze from the ring, "should Emma show interest in you, I won't oppose her choice. I want her to be as happy as I was with my Lucy. She often told me to let our children choose."

It took him a moment to understand what the earl was saying. He had the opportunity to court Emma should she wish so.

"Thank you, sir." His voice didn't betray his happiness. Perhaps that was why Emma had misunderstood him.

"Should Emma agree," the earl narrowed his gaze, "I expect a one-year-long engagement, at least. No less. That's what my Lucy would have wanted, too. You're a brilliant man with a bright future in front of you. I think you would make her happy."

"I will do my best." Marcus stretched out a hand. "Sir, should Lady Emma give me the honour of choosing me, I won't disappoint you."

The earl shook his head. "It's more important that you don't disappoint Emma."

"Right. Of course." He winced inwardly again.

"Whatever happens, my opinion of you will always be high."

He bowed. "Thank you, sir."

Marcus walked out of the parlour feeling as if the floor were made of cotton. He would have never imagined the earl would give him his blessing. That changed everything.

The clouds hid the moon and the stars as he went upstairs. Distant lightning ripped the sky with white fire, and he stared out of the window at the thick flashes. No rain pelted the ground. For the whole day, the weather had taunted them with the threat of a tempest that had never come. But the angry storm promised to hit Newport-on-Tay sooner or later, a monster waiting for the right moment to strike.

"It's frightening, isn't it?" Emma came out of the library, holding a book against her chest. "We're on the edge of a heavy storm. The air is charged with energy, and yet it doesn't rain."

The scent of honeysuckle wafted from her bright red gown. In the light of the storm flashes, her skin looked translucent and seemed to glow from within. She was an ethereal creature, made of light and surrounded by silk.

Courting her was up to him then. If he showed her who he really was and how much he cared about her, she might accept him.

"The storm will hit us tomorrow," he said, looking at her regal profile. "It's gathering momentum. The sea is already roiling."

She shivered. "I wish it would just vent its anger now."

"The longer it takes to hit us, the stronger the blow."

They watched the bolts crossing the sky like arrows of light, and for the first time since he'd met Emma, no uneasiness caused his skin to itch. Maybe the conversation with the earl had reassured him. Or maybe knowing the storm would crash against them soon helped him control his inner turmoil.

The wind howled as if to warn them about the promise of a huge battle.

"I really like you, Emma," he said in a low tone. "Do not think, not for one moment, that I don't like you. Giving you the impression of the opposite wasn't my intention. I feel overwhelmed when I'm with you."

He stopped there. Being more open was one thing, but completely showing her his heart was quite another.

The soft sound of her inhaling filled the silence between the booming of the thunder and the thumps of his heartbeats.

She moved closer, and the air between them was charged with energy stronger than the storm.

"Trevor has an excellent opinion of you," she said, "and my papa often remarks how brilliant you are. I don't doubt their opinions, but I know so little of you."

"My fault." He forced himself not to avert his gaze as he stared at her large hazel eyes. "I hope you'll allow me to start over. I would be honoured if we knew each other better."

His heart skipped a beat when she smiled.

"Of course, Mr. Kingston." She curtsied.

"Lady Emma." He bowed formally. "Enchanted."

"I hope we'll be friends. We're going to see each other often."

Being friends was a start. Not exactly what he was aiming for, but better than nothing.

She hooked her arm through his. "What would you like to do?"

He escorted her to her bedroom, blood pumping in his veins. "We could play cricket together, and if we break something, I'll repair it."

She laughed, as charming as a songbird. "Excellent. Which makes me think, can you fix knobs?"

"Knobs?"

She rose on her tiptoes to crane her neck right and left. "Would you come in a moment?"

"In your bedroom?" He wished he didn't sound as shocked, as prudish as his Great-Aunt Anne.

"Shush!" She searched the hallway. "Only for a moment. I broke the knob of the nightstand. It's a Thonet nightstand and costs a fortune and a half. Papa will punish me if he learns I broke it."

Thank goodness his father had always insisted that he worked alongside the builders to learn new things.

"I can take a look at it tomorrow."

She pouted. "It'll be too late. Papa will realise I broke it. He never misses anything."

"I don't believe it's appropriate for me to enter your bedroom at night, alone." He wasn't a prude, but the earl trusted him, and entering Emma's bedroom sounded like a huge breach of that trust. Not to mention, Sir Horace might produce another crass comment if he learnt about that.

"Nothing will happen. You're harmless."

"Excuse me? What is that supposed to mean?"

"Shush!" She waved him in her room. "Come here. You'll alert the entire household."

He did as told, muttering, "Harmless," under his breath.

She gingerly closed the door. "I just meant you're a gentleman. It's a compliment."

My arse. He folded his arms over his chest. She didn't see him as a probable suitor then. Not even close. A friend or a brother was harmless. A person she was attracted to wasn't.

He would have to do a lot of work to earn her respect as a suitor. A challenge he was happy to accept.

"Over there." She lit a few lamps and showed him the golden knob lying on the top of the nightstand. "I must have pulled it too hard."

He crouched to inspect the damage. "It's not broken. The screw holding it went loose." He picked up the handle. "See this pilot hole? The screw fell out. Did you see it anywhere?"

"Bother." She searched the drawer. "Nothing here."

She knelt on the carpet and touched around. He did the same until a glint of gold flickered from a corner.

"There!" they said together.

Their hands clamped on the screw at the same time. He wasn't ready for the touch of her soft hand on his. They remained still for a moment. Even in the dim light, her flush was visible. Her emotions could be anything from embarrassment to interest. But since he wasn't sure, he'd better stop the contact.

He moved first, slipping his hand out of hers. The last thing he wanted after the conversation with the earl was to ruin his chances with Emma. He had to do everything by the book. As much as the earl showed his support, he wouldn't be impressed by Marcus's presence in his daughter's bedroom.

"Sorry." She took the screw. "I didn't..."

"Emma? Are you still up?" Trevor's voice came from the other side of the door.

"Bloody hell," Marcus whispered.

And here his chances with Emma vanished.

six

Emma swallowed, staring at the closed door of her bedroom. What was Trevor doing here? He'd gone to bed a long time ago. He shouldn't still be up and about.

"Emma," Marcus whispered. He sounded both panicked and angry.

"One moment," she said aloud, dropping the screw again. "Quick, under the bed." She waved at Marcus.

He scowled. "Seriously?"

"You shouldn't be here."

"Now we agree," he said.

"Go, go." She stood up and straightened her gown as Marcus squeezed his large build under the bed, scoffing. When he disappeared completely, she opened the door. "What is it?"

Trevor walked in, hands in the pockets of his dressing gown. "Nice to see you, too. Why do you say that in such a rude tone?"

"I'm not being rude."

Trevor sat on the bed and bounced on it once. "I just wanted to know how you were faring."

"Spectacularly." She picked up the blasted screw.

"You broke something else." Trevor tsk-tsked. "Your touch is a curse."

"It's not broken. It's the pilot that...the screw that left the hole."

He frowned. "What?"

"Nothing." She sat next to him. "Really, what troubles you? Boring conversation? Your conscience doesn't allow you to sleep?"

"No. My conscience is fine." He worked his jaw. "And I find it interesting when Sir Albert and Sir Horace talk about the technical part of their work. It's something else."

"What?" she prompted.

"Promise me you won't be upset."

"How can I? I have no idea what you're talking about."

He lay down, crossing his arms under his head. A soft sound came from under the bed. Likely, the mattress lowered and Marcus got hit by Trevor's weight. She hid the noise with a cough.

"I had a chat with Father before dinner," Trevor said. "He asked me a lot of questions about Marcus."

"Did he?" She propped herself on an elbow. "What did he want to know?"

"My opinion on him, mostly. I told him the truth. Marcus is a bloody good chap, but Father has ideas."

She stiffened, thinking of Marcus under her bed. "You usually don't stop talking. Now I have to pull each word out of you. If you don't want to tell me, don't."

"I think Father is considering him as your suitor."

She sat upright, her face warming. Marcus was right under her bed, listening to every word they said. Did he know that Papa saw him as her suitor?

She wrung her hands. "Maybe we should talk about that another time."

"I knew it." Trevor sat up as well. "You're upset. But don't worry. I don't believe Father will make an arranged marriage with Marcus without telling you."

"No, I'm not worried about that. I'm surprised. That's all." And embarrassed.

"I told Father it wasn't a good idea."

She gave him a shake of her head to signal him to stop talking.

"I'm glad you agree." He patted her hand. "Marcus isn't a good match."

"No, I..." She rubbed her forehead. What a mess. He'd completely misunderstood her intentions. Although she wasn't sure what to make of Papa's idea. "You just said Marcus is a great chap."

"And I stand by that, but he comes from a different world."

"Papa doesn't care. And Mama wasn't from a noble family."

"Yes, and see what happened." Trevor pressed his lips together. "Grandmother didn't speak to Papa for years. She missed our birthdays. The first time I'd met her, I was five. And some peers, like Lady Eve, didn't invite us to her parties until I was twelve. I don't want the same thing to happen to you. Different worlds, as I said."

A flare of annoyance bothered her. "You were supposed to marry Ophelia before she broke the engagement."

It was unfair of her to mention lovely Ophelia, the daughter of a rich trader who had been Trevor's bride-to-be for a short time. But Ophelia came from *a different world* as well.

Trevor's face transformed from slightly concerned to angry. His usual cocksure expression vanished. "Exactly because of my experience with Ophelia, I can tell you that Marcus isn't right for you."

"She was lovely."

"But she broke the engagement. What does that have to do with anything?" He scoffed. "Ophelia and I were different," he said in a softer, sadder tone.

A few moments of silence passed, and she didn't want to press her brother further about Ophelia. Thunder roared in the distance, and the bolts of lightning flashed across the room.

"You're exaggerating," she said, to break the silence and end the conversation so that Marcus could leave. "Listen, the Season hasn't started yet, and Papa hasn't talked to Marcus."

"When you start a conversation with *listen*, I get worried." He frowned. "But if Marcus should propose, what would you say?"

She opened and closed her hands. "It's too early. I don't know."

"Do you fancy him?" Trevor asked. "This morning, you believed he hated you. If I'd asked you about him then, you would have said a resounding no. Why are you so uncertain now?"

"I think I'm tired, and I should go to bed."

Trevor didn't stand up. "Would you be happy if he became your suitor? Aren't you worried about his position in society? Do you want to face what Mama had to?"

"No, I don't." She regretted the words immediately; they'd come out unbidden. But they were true.

Mama had suffered from being shunned by many ladies and lords, hurtful comments, and silly jokes. She'd never complained, but her pain had been clear, and gossip had been brutal for a while. Emma didn't want the same fate, but Marcus was hidden under her bed, and he shouldn't listen to that conversation about himself.

"I'll do my best to protect you," Trevor said.

That warmed her heart. "Thank you, but I want to choose by myself as Papa did. He was happy with Mama, no matter what."

He lowered his gaze as if ashamed, although she wouldn't know about what.

"Happiness is for fools," he said. "All the clever people I know are miserable."

She chuckled. "My brother is back."

He kissed her forehead before standing up. "Good night."

She closed the door behind him and exhaled.

"Marcus?" she whispered. "He's gone."

Slowly, he slid out of the bed, wincing as his shoulders and back scraped against the bottom side rail. He straightened his jacket and brushed some specks of dust from it.

She stepped closer to him. "I'm sorry for what Trevor said."

His grey eyes were as stormy as the sky. "There's no need to apologise, and Trevor cares about you. I understand his worry."

"It wasn't nice. You didn't need to hear that."

He stood tall and proud in the middle of the room among the booms of the thunder. She had never noticed how majestic his bearing was.

"Think nothing of that." He bowed formally. "Good night, Emma."

"Wait, what about the knob?" She didn't care about the knob at that point, but letting him go while he was so upset didn't seem right.

"I'd better go before someone else comes here and I hear something I shouldn't."

"Please."

He remained silent for a while, shoulders stooping. His pose was one she'd seen many times, but now she understood its meaning better. What she'd thought to be boredom or annoyance was a sense of defeat, resignation. He had to feel as if he truly came from a different world from her, but that wasn't true. The only difference between them was her father's title.

"I really want to be your friend," she said. "I want to know you better. Don't let the chatter of my papa or Trevor change that. Unless you don't care about me and want to leave."

A flash flickered across his gaze. He was handsome, and that determined gaze suited him.

"I do care," he said in that strong voice she liked. "Do you have a pair of small scissors or a letter opener?"

"Here." She took a letter opener from her escritoire and handed it to him.

He efficiently fixed the knob, using the small point of the letter opener as a screwdriver. She watched him as he focused on the work, his dark eyebrows drawing together. She'd never noticed how a muscle of his jaw tensed when he concentrated on a task.

"Done." He tugged at the knob. "It might get loose again. It needs to be fixed with a proper screwdriver. This is a temporary solution."

"Thank you. Really."

He pulled at his collar.

"We make a good pair," she said to lighten the mood.

"How?"

"I break things. You fix them."

He flashed a charming, lopsided smile, but it held sadness. "There are delicate things that can't be mended and for which a temporary solution isn't enough."

"Then I'll be very careful not to break those things."

He placed the letter opener on the nightstand. "Good night."

"Good night."

He nodded and walked to the door silently.

"You know," he said before leaving, "I might be harmless, but you're more dangerous than you think."

She wasn't sure what he meant by that, but she was certain their friendship hadn't started on the right foot.

seven

There was little to no difference between the night sky and the daylight when Marcus finished breakfast in the dining room the next day.

The thunder had boomed through the night, sometimes sounding more distant than others. Now the storm kept teasing them, roaring on the outskirts of Newport-on-Tay. The wind had picked up during the night, but still no rain. Strong gusts shook the tree branches, curving them at odd angles. He worried they might snap.

The sea was so enraged its sprays of foam in the firth could be seen from the window. The Tay Bridge appeared dark and thick against the backdrop of the stormy sky.

Father stood next to him, studying the clouds. "The wind has been blowing for hours. The bridge is under a lot of stress."

"Are you worried?"

Father scratched his chin. "Horace was the last one to inspect the bridge, and he didn't find any faults. So no, I'm not worried. I shouldn't be."

"May I come with you this morning?" After the conversation

he'd overheard between Emma and Trevor, he would rather face a day under the rain than see the two of them.

Not that he expected Trevor to consider him good enough for his sister, but the way they'd talked about him had left a mark. Although if the earl approved of Marcus's suit and Emma was happy as well, Trevor's opinion wouldn't matter.

He exhaled. Who was he fooling? Emma wasn't interested in him.

"I didn't expect the weather to get worse when I said you could come." Father averted his gaze from the bridge. "The inspection is a dangerous business, especially in this weather, and we can't delay. Besides, this weather is ideal to test the strength of the beams."

"The earl isn't going to be in danger, is he? He'll probably watch the bridge from his carriage while you do the work. I'll do what he does."

"Then there would be no point in you coming. You won't see anything."

"I want to come with you. It can't be more dangerous than walking up and down the scaffolding."

"It can."

"I can't stay here."

"Why? Did something happen?"

He couldn't tell the whole truth without mentioning Emma inviting him into her bedroom. She would be in trouble if he told everything. And telling Father about Sir Horace's crass remark about Emma wouldn't be a good idea either. Father might start an argument with Sir Horace.

Father put a hand on his shoulder. "Tell me. I can't help you if you don't speak."

"I don't have a lot in common with Lady Emma and Lord Trevor."

"Nonsense. You're friends with them. You always say you don't have anything in common with anyone, but it can't be true."

"Let me come with you."

Father drummed his fingers on the windowsill. "Fine, but if I think it's too dangerous because of the wind, you'll get back here immediately."

"I'll be ready in a few minutes."

He rushed up the stairs, only to bump into Emma coming down. He hitched a breath. She looked like a rose glittering with morning dew in her pink gown.

Last night, she could have lied, knowing he'd been there, listening, but she'd chosen to tell the truth about not wanting him as her suitor. He appreciated her honesty. That didn't mean he wasn't hurt.

He mumbled, "Good morning."

"Trevor and I are going to the town. Would you like to come with us?" she asked.

Those large eyes would be the death of him.

"I'll be joining my father to inspect the Tay Bridge."

"Oh." She looked genuinely disappointed. "In this weather? We wanted to have tea at the Peacock Tea House. It's warm and cosy."

"I've never inspected a bridge with my father. And bad weather is part of my job."

She lowered her eyelashes. "I'll see you later, then."

"Enjoy your morning." He went to brush past her, but she stopped him by touching his arm.

"Are you upset about last night?" She waited for a footman to pass before continuing. "We decided to be friends. You would tell me the truth if you were upset, wouldn't you?"

He wouldn't lie, but he wouldn't talk about how hurt he felt just yet. He needed to clear his head and think about something else for a while.

"I promise we'll talk later. If you'll excuse me, I have to get ready."

He hated the look of disappointment on her face, but the earl had been clear. Emma had the last word on whether she would accept him. The fact he kept changing his mind about his feelings, shifting between hopeful and desperate, bothered him to no end. If only he could choose a frame of mind and stick to it.

When he finally left Thistle Hall in a carriage with Father, Sir Horace, and the earl, his chest became lighter. Not even the howling of the wind and the flashes of lightning concerned him.

"Nervous, Marcus?" the earl asked.

"Eager, sir. I'm looking forward to seeing the bridge and working with my father."

Sir Horace grinned. "I'm happy you chose to come with us. It shows your commitment to the work. Priorities are everything in life."

He closed his fists on his knees. "I would say that manners come first."

The earl glanced from one to another. "I agree with Marcus. What would we be without manners?"

"Pigs," Marcus said.

Sir Horace cast him a hard glance before turning towards the window.

The thunder shook the carriage as they drove along a bumpy road.

MARCUS'S RELIEF about not having stayed at Thistle Hall didn't last. The rain finally hit Newport-on-Tay in the early afternoon. Once at the firth, they'd barely had time to make a general inspection of the beams before the weather turned for the worse.

Sheet after battering sheet of pelting rain had convinced his father to send him back to Thistle Hall, no matter how vehemently Marcus had protested.

By the time the carriage stopped in front of the house, the wind was so strong the footman had trouble holding the door.

Marcus walked the short distance between the carriage and the front door with his head low and a hand on his hat, lest it fly away.

Walking was difficult with the wind and rain battering his back. It was as if a whole team of rugby players were shoving him backwards. Rain had drenched his coat and trousers, and a pool of water gathered at his feet when he stepped into the entry hall.

Stewart and a maid fussed around him to remove his wet coat, hat, and scarf.

"You'd better change into something dry, sir," the maid said. "I will send up hot water, sir"

He removed his muddy shoes. "Thank you."

"Did His Lordship say when he returns?" Stewart asked.

He ran a hand through his wet hair. "No, he didn't. I asked him to come with me, but he wanted to stay with my father and Sir Horace."

The butler and the maid both looked at the inclement storm battering the earth. He could almost hear their thoughts. Staying outside was sheer madness.

He went up the stairs and reached his bedroom when Emma called to him as she was coming out of her room.

"You're back. I was worried." She gave him a long glance. "The weather is wild. Trevor and I came back earlier from the town. Did Papa return?"

"He decided to stay at the bridge."

"Why would he stay?"

"He chose to stay. Perhaps he didn't want special treatment."

Her shoulders stooped. "Oh. Will you join Trevor and me for tea downstairs? Or is tea a problem?" There was a challenging note in her voice, which he deserved.

"I will join you. Thank you." He resumed walking to his room.

"I'm happy you're here. Truly."

He paused to nod at her.

"You promised we would talk," she added.

"We will."

She gave him her star-bright smile that never failed to give him a flutter in his chest.

So far, he'd never had problems understanding what she was feeling, but after last night, he wasn't sure anymore of his ability to interpret her mood. She seemed apologetic, but for what reason? Because he'd listened to a conversation he shouldn't have, or because she liked him, too?

eight

After Marcus had washed and changed into dry clothes and towel-dried his hair, he went downstairs. Thunder reverberated through the house as if a giant were punching the roof and the walls. Two days of that constant shaking and booming started to grate on his nerves.

Trevor and Emma were drinking tea in the wide drawing room in front of the large window. A blazing log fire warmed the air and spread the scent of pine resin; it was a cosy view, a stark contrast to the chaos outside.

"The storm is getting worse," Trevor said.

"How can it get worse?"

On cue, another crack of thunder boomed loudly enough to rattle the diamond-paned window. From that spot, he had an unobstructed view of the Tay Bridge, a paragon of modern technology battling against the ancient power of nature.

"It's terrifying. I've never seen anything like that." Emma sat in front of the window in a froth of fabric. "But I love watching a storm. It's fascinating. Do you like watching a storm, Marcus?"

"This is more than a storm. It's an unleashed monster."

She stared up at him, shivering. The impulse to caress her

cheek and reassure her was so strong he had to clench his fist not to act on it.

He quickly averted his gaze, focusing on the tea. A bolt of lightning lit the room while heavy rain battered the windows and the earth as if wanting to punish it. The lights of the trains crossing the bridge were hardly visible through the storm.

Another crack of thunder caused Emma to jolt. "Goodness. It's getting closer."

"The wind is picking up speed again." Trevor lowered his cup of tea. "What is Father doing there? Isn't it too dangerous for anyone to be on the bridge?"

Marcus agreed. The sea was foaming and roaring under the bridge, fuelled by the strength of the gusts. He frowned, wondering where Father was and if the speed of the wind was truly a concern for the safety of the bridge. Father hadn't had time to inspect the beams properly that morning, and Sir Horace had carried out the last inspection.

The rain hit the glass harder, obscuring the view.

"If Papa wants to return home, I doubt he'll be able to." Emma draped a shawl around her shoulders.

Tension charged the air as the wind blew harder; it howled and screamed, slapping the sea waves this way and that. Snapped tree branches were whipped by the gusts across the road or got stuck against the fence around the house.

A train approached the bridge, its tail lamps flashing through the storm. Then there was a sudden, bright flash of light, followed by total darkness. The tail lamps, the sparks, and the flash of light disappeared at the same instant.

"Did you see that?" Trevor stood up.

Marcus sucked in a breath because what had happened couldn't have been what he feared. He shot up and got closer to the window, trying to see through the rain.

"What happened?" Emma walked over to him.

"Bloody hell." Trevor ran a hand over his face.

They stood in front of the window overlooking the River Tay. The rain diminished enough to allow them to see that the bridge had vanished; piers, abutments, and beams had been swallowed by the monster storm, wiped out into oblivion.

"It's gone." Marcus didn't know if he'd said that aloud or whispered, but his throat hurt as if he'd screamed louder than the wind.

"Good Lord." Emma clamped her hands over her mouth. "The bridge disappeared."

"Is it possible?" Trevor asked.

"It is." Marcus strode towards the door. "I must see my father."

"Papa." Emma followed him.

"Marcus, Emma." Trevor held her back. "You'd better stay here."

She shifted her weight. "No, I want to go. What if something happened to Papa?"

"We'll waste more time arguing than driving there," Marcus said. "We'll all go."

"Terrible idea. We should stay here." Trevor shook his head.

Emma called Stewart. "Get a coach ready."

"My lady?" Stewart looked horrified.

"I want to make sure Papa is fine. Marcus and I will go to the bridge."

Frowning, the butler bowed and left.

"This is madness." Trevor scowled. "You're going to die out there."

She paced, glancing at the window. "I don't want to leave him alone."

Trevor put a hand on her shoulder. "I'm sure they're all safe. The storm is too strong. They must have found shelter somewhere."

"My lady," Stewart said to Emma, "the gale is too strong. The coachman said leaving is too dangerous, and the horses will be difficult to control in such weather."

"Finally some sense," Trevor said. "If something happens to you, you'll make things worse for Father, and someone will have to come and rescue you."

"I can go alone," Marcus said. "No carriage. I'll walk to the bridge."

Trevor narrowed his eyes so similar to his sister's. "Did you look outside? Did you see the uprooted trees, the strong gusts of wind, and the torrential rain? This bloody storm brought down a bridge, for Pete's sake! You won't make it far, and if you get lost or hit by a falling tree, no one will come and find you. You'll lie in the rain for who knows how long."

"Trevor is right." Emma slouched. "We'd better wait here, at least until the weather changes a little."

Every instinct inside him urged him to leave, but then again, Father had to be preoccupied with the incident without adding the worry of knowing that his son was out in the storm.

"It would be a sensible choice, sir," Stewart said.

"All right." Reluctantly, he faced the window again.

The view of the storm only grew more terrifying with the sea boiling and the wind howling.

Oddly enough, that was the first time he could be completely himself while with Emma. In the oppressive space of the drawing room where she was sitting next to him, worried about her father, his heart didn't stutter. His thoughts were for his father only and the implications of the incident.

The train had gone down into the sea in the blink of an eye, which meant the bridge hadn't simply cracked but collapsed altogether. There would be dead people, missing people, and many wounded, and Father would be in the middle of the aftermath. Because Marcus couldn't contemplate the possibility that Father was dead.

The maintenance of the bridge was Kingston & Sindall's

responsibility. A different type of storm would smash Father's company.

Complete darkness fell on Newport-on-Tay like a black pall, but for the glow of the lightning. There was nothing to look at, only a pitch-black chasm and desperation. Yet he couldn't avert his gaze.

Stewart came and went to bring a repast and tea, which Marcus ignored.

Hours passed. Trevor dozed off in the armchair, and Emma fell asleep next to Marcus on the sofa, resting her head on his shoulder.

On any other occasion, he would have been elated to be so close to her and hear her soft breathing next to him. But at that moment, worry was the only emotion in his heart. He draped a blanket over her shoulders and allowed himself a moment to admire the gentle curve of her cheek and the way her lips parted as if she were about to speak. Even in her sleep, she didn't stop being talkative.

The soft light from the fireplace and the gas lamps turned her hair into spun gold. It was cruel that the first, and maybe only, time she was so close to him had to be in a moment of pure dread.

She snuggled closer to him and put her head on his chest. Two different emotions tore at his heart—worry for his father and the urge to stroke her hair. The scent of honeysuckle was intoxicating.

He didn't resist and brushed a golden curl from her cheek, trembling as he touched her silky skin. Feeling like a thief, he dropped his hand and resigned himself to endure the torture of having her flush with him without touching her. But he would rather suffer in silence than wake her up and ask her to move.

The storm finally died down before dawn. It didn't go away quietly, but it kicked and screamed until the end, lashing out at the sunlight trying to break through the clouds. Squalls of heavy rain made him fear the storm would start again.

The red fingers of the sunrise streaked through the sky like bloody claws, as a reminder of what had happened. When finally the sun won the battle, the view was horrifying.

In the sunlight, the missing bridge was a gaping mouth. The pillars and steel had been ripped and were now jutting out of the sea like sharp teeth. But nothing was left to fill the space between the two shores.

Emma stirred next to him. She blinked, her long eyelashes fluttering.

He stared at her, for once simply enjoying her presence without worrying if he was good enough to be so close to her. He could get lost in the depths of her hazel eyes; they gave him a moment of respite and beauty from the horror outside.

"The storm has passed," he said.

She rubbed her eyes and pulled back from him. "I hope Papa will be back soon." She hid a yawn behind her hand. "Did I sleep on your shoulder?"

"You did." And it'd been wonderful.

"Heavens, sorry."

He cleared his throat, not to let her know how much her closeness affected him. "I'm going out."

"I'll come with you." She reached out and shook Trevor's arm. "Trevor, wake up. I want to go."

Trevor raked a hand through his dishevelled hair. He stared at the devastated bridge for a few moments. "Bloody hell. It's a nightmare."

"Hopefully, the road is passable." Marcus rose from the sofa. "Will you come or stay?"

Trevor rubbed his eyes again. "If the coachman agrees to go, I'll come with you."

Voices and footfalls came from the hallway. Stewart called someone in a booming tone.

"Papa." Emma flung the door open.

Lord Pembroke stood in the middle of the entry hall, wet, covered in mud, and with wide eyes. The footman and Stewart fussed around him, removing the wet outer garments and asking him questions he didn't acknowledge.

"Papa." Emma rushed to hug him.

"Father." Trevor hugged him as well.

"I'm fine." Lord Pembroke patted Emma's back, sounding weak and tired.

Marcus craned his neck to search for his father, but the footman had shut the door behind the earl. "Where's my father, sir?"

Stewart helped the earl to the drawing room.

"At the firth with Sir Horace." The earl sagged on an armchair. "An utter disaster. The Tay Bridge collapsed, and a North British Railway train full of passengers dropped into the river."

Marcus heaved a breath. "As I feared."

"Heaven." Emma sat next to her father.

"We saw the bridge going down," Trevor said.

"Any chance of finding survivors?" Marcus asked.

The earl shivered, and drops of rain dripped from his hair. "That's why your father is at the firth."

"I'm going then," Marcus said. "If a coach isn't available, I'll walk."

"I want to go as well," Emma said. "There must be something we can do to help."

Lord Pembroke massaged his forehead. "Yes, I came home to tell you the news. I'm going out again to join the search parties. They need every able hand at the firth."

Emma nodded at Marcus. "We'll go together. You won't be alone."

Those were the best words he'd heard in a while.

nine

Emma was thoroughly impressed by Marcus's behaviour as they worked at the firth of the River Tay. From the moment they'd arrived, he'd rolled up the sleeves of his shirt and jumped on a boat to join the search parties scouring the water for survivors.

No one believed any of the passengers could have survived the fall or the raging river for the whole night, but the search had to be done, and Marcus hadn't backed down from the gruesome work.

The view of the bridge's broken parts torn apart by the wind was horrifying. The jutting pieces of metal looked like the broken spine of a giant snake. The sea beyond was deceivingly calm, blue and flat in the sunlight, all innocence.

She stood on the inlet, watching the river but at the same time trying not to. Ripped pieces of fabric, hats, and shoes floated on the surface, carried gently by the current. Each item was a life that had been lost. A chill took her when a ragdoll washed ashore.

Marcus and Trevor were on the same boat with Sir Albert and a man she didn't know, while Papa and another group were searching the other side of the river. Sir Horace had retired, claiming to feel indisposed. But who didn't?

As she waited for her turn to join a search party, she wondered if she had the courage to go through with the job.

Behind her, volunteers served tea in a large tent. The relatives of the train passengers cried and sobbed on the benches as bodies were recovered, tearing her heart.

She turned around when a boat landed, only to allow the rescuers to deliver a body to the shore. A bitter taste filled her mouth as someone started crying loudly.

Trevor moved his boat into the inlet close to her and tied the rope to the cleat. "Emma, we have a free spot. Mr. Drummond wishes to take a break. Do you want to help us?"

Shaken and pale, Mr. Drummond hurried to disembark so quickly he almost tripped on the edge of the boat before speeding towards the tent.

"Yes." Her voice sounded scared to her own ears.

Marcus offered her his hand to help her onto the boat. His palm had calluses that scratched her skin. His serious expression held its usual composure laced with sadness, and his quiet desperation weighed her down.

Sir Albert looked worse for wear, seemingly aged a decade in a night. He rowed the boat to the middle of the river without a word.

From that point of view, the damage to the bridge was even more frightening. The fall from the railway to the sea had to be around fifty feet or more. How terrified had those people been? Had they realised what was happening? They hadn't seen much between the storm and the darkness. They must have felt the train falling without reason.

Sir Albert's dark-circled eyes seemed lifeless. Other rescuers on other boats had similar lost expressions.

No one talked as they worked with long wooden rods, turning around bits of flotsam in search of survivors or bodies. The movement of the boat and the endless amount of personal items floating around her made her stomach churn. As her head spun, she had to pause the search. She lowered her rod and took deep breaths, inhaling the scent of the sea and death.

"Are you all right?" Marcus dipped his head to stare at her.

She shook her head, a hand on her stomach.

"Maybe she's seasick," Trevor said. "Can we get her to the shore?"

"I don't want to cause trouble." She closed her eyes. "It'll pass."

"No trouble at all." Sir Albert rowed back towards the shore. "I understand. It's hard to watch."

Marcus helped her out, and she leant against him shamelessly, her legs quivering. He stiffened immediately though.

"Marcus, would you please stay with Lady Emma and escort her to the tent?" Sir Albert asked. "She's very pale."

"I'm all right," she said, but so low she doubted anyone had heard her.

Marcus's eyes flared wide, hard to say if in surprise, fear, or shock. "Of course." It came out forced.

Trevor opened his mouth but didn't say anything.

"I'll take care of Lady Emma," Marcus said.

"I'm fine." But she wasn't.

On a cart, the rescuers had piled up the bodies recovered so far, and a sob escaped from her. Her head spun again, and she grabbed Marcus's arm for support.

He held her up. "Don't look at the cart."

"I'm trying not to."

He helped her to a tent where the police officers, medics, and volunteers scanning the river could have a cup of tea and a blanket. She sat on the bench, her legs like rubber. The sky was clear, but the chill clung to the air, and she shivered in her coat.

"Here." Marcus handed her a steaming mug.

"I'm not sure my stomach can handle tea."

"You'll feel better. Trust me." It didn't sound like an order but something similar. He sat next to her and watched the river.

She closed her hands around the mug. At least she would get warm. "I'm sorry you had to stop for me. That wasn't my finest moment."

"I needed a break as well. And seasickness can be debilitating."

"Actually, it wasn't seasickness, not exactly." She took a sip, forcing herself to swallow the sweet, lemony tea. "It was the view. So many people."

He regarded her in a new light. "They said that at least fifty people died, maybe more. Some passengers didn't have a ticket, so their presence on the train left no evidence."

"What exactly caused the collapse?"

He raked a hand through his midnight hair. "The wind might be the culprit, or the train might have derailed, and the impact caused the collapse. The deck spans are still standing while the high girders broke, so that would point to a structural failure, but if the train hit the posts, the impact, combined with the force of the storm, might be the cause. But whatever happened, an incident like that should have been avoided. Bridges are built to endure storms and strong impacts, or at least they should."

"Your father didn't sleep or rest."

He scratched his chin where his dark stubble grew. "I'm worried about him."

So was she.

He hunched his shoulders and exhaled. "He's everything I have," he whispered, staring at his hands. "After my mother died, we both had a hard time dealing with her passing. He hasn't recovered yet, and this tragedy will weigh him down further."

She put her hand on his, and he tensed. "I know how you feel. We both lost our mothers. I wouldn't know what to do without my papa."

"My father is a good man and an excellent engineer. He would never..." He took a deep breath. "He would never be negligent about his work."

"Try not to think of the worst." She closed her hand around his, feeling the rough skin on his knuckles.

He didn't react though, and she slowly withdrew her hand, but he took her fingers gently.

"Thank you." He stared at her with his solemn gunmetal grey eyes.

She'd stared at them other times, but that moment was different. She knew the man behind them better. He hid his emotions well behind those deep pools although little signs belied what was happening in his mind.

"I'm sorry if I hurt you the other night," she whispered.

He sucked in a breath and held her fingers more tightly. "You were honest."

"I didn't mean to say you aren't good enough to be my suitor. That's not what I think at all."

His Adam's apple bobbed up and down as he swallowed, and for some reason, she was fascinated by it. "Please," he said without looking at her, "can we not talk about that now?" The pain in his voice was a punch to her stomach.

"Of course." She held his big hand in both of hers.

She wanted to tell him she would do anything to help him and that, after that moment passed, they would discuss his suit. He wasn't as she'd imagined. He wasn't arrogant but shy, not cold but contemplative, not distant but careful with her emotions. Yes, she wanted to spend more time with him.

If there was one thing she'd learnt about him in the past few days it was that he appreciated the silence more than too many words. She would talk to him when he felt better. She shouldn't have brought up the subject in a moment like that to start with.

"Thank you." His hand was warm, warmer than hers and radiated safety. They held each other's hands for a long time, staring at the river.

She finished her tea. "I'm ready to face the water again."

"You can stay here if you want."

"No, let's find a boat and keep searching. I want to help you."
Now and in the future.

ten

A week had passed since the Tay Bridge disaster, but to Marcus it felt like only one endless, exhausting day.

He'd spent the days and good parts of the nights with Father in Newport-on-Tay, either on a boat searching the shore or discussing the load the bridge had endured before collapsing. His sleep had been short and riddled with nightmares of the train vanishing from sight.

The police had asked them the same questions over and over, and a barrister had been involved.

The exhaustion was taking its toll on his energy and mind, making it difficult for him to understand what Father and Sir Horace were telling him in the drawing room.

Father was as pale as he'd been a week ago, while Sir Horace fidgeted nervously whenever he sat.

"It's not possible," Marcus said. "You always do a thorough job. They can't blame you. The maintenance of the bridge was Kingston & Sindall's responsibility, but not exclusively yours."

Father bent his shoulders as if he were being crushed under a heavy weight. "That's where the preliminary inquest seems to be going. We'll receive the final judgement tomorrow."

Anger washed away his fatigue. "You didn't carry out the last inspection of the bridge. Sir Horace did."

"Marcus," Sir Horace said, "your father is the only one who claims that. I didn't perform any inspection of the bridge. This is the first time I've even been to Newport-on-Tay."

"You did inspect the bridge one year ago," Father insisted, eyes flashing. "But for a bureaucratic mistake, my name is on the latest inspection papers. But it wasn't me."

"Albert." Sir Horace's nostrils flared. "Your attempt at blaming me is despicable."

"How dare you talk to my father like that?" He leapt to his feet, heartbeat thudding. "My father would never lie!"

"I will not stay silent while I'm being offended or worse, accused of a crime I'm not responsible for." Sir Horace stood up as well.

"And I will not stay silent while my father goes to prison instead of you."

"You bloody rat!" Sir Horace clenched his fists and leant closer to Marcus. "Your father is responsible for that inspection, and he will take his responsibility."

"You're a cheat and a liar!"

Sir Horace lunged. Marcus raised his fists.

Father jumped between them before any blow could be exchanged. "Enough! This isn't helping anyone." He stretched out his arms to keep them separated.

When Sir Horace stepped back, Marcus did the same, ready to defend himself.

Father straightened his jacket. "It's early days. There will be another inquest when Her Majesty's Railway Inspectorate starts its investigation. Too many people died. And to be honest, right now I only feel sorry for them."

"You can't take the blame for something that isn't your fault," Marcus said through his teeth.

Father exhaled slowly as if breathing was too much of a chore for him. "I don't mean to, but I'm tired and not thinking straight. Don't mistake my lack of anger for defeat."

"What is that supposed to mean?" Sir Horace said. "I didn't inspect the damn bridge. Your only evidence of my involvement is an entry in your register with a note about me travelling to Newport-on-Tay for the bridge inspection, but I didn't go anywhere. The workers don't remember having seen me; many of them have changed jobs, and your name is on that bloody paper."

"Can you prove where you were on that day?" Marcus asked.

Sir Horace groaned. "I don't remember where I was. It's not me who has to prove where I was. It's your father who has to prove I was here."

"If Father said you did it, then you did it!"

"Careful, Marcus." Sir Horace matched his tone. "Don't talk about things you don't understand."

"I understand very well."

Father was always precise and meticulous in recording every activity of the company. If he'd recorded that Sir Horace had gone to Newport-on-Tay to inspect the bridge, then that was what had happened.

"Father, say something." Marcus didn't want to raise his voice at Father, too, but he looked worryingly dejected as if he had already accepted his fate.

"I'm sure every misunderstanding will be cleared up, and that's everything I have to say for now." Father left the room, dragging his feet.

"The misunderstanding will be cleared up as long as people tell the truth," Marcus said.

"You aren't as clever as I thought." Sir Horace stepped closer, regarding him as if Marcus were a stain on his brand-new suit. "If I were you, I would take a good, hard look at the situation and decide on which side you want to stay."

"Go to hell."

"I'm offering you a safe future." The hard glint in Sir Horace's eyes offered slavery rather than safety.

"My place is next to my father."

Sir Horace strode to the door and paused. "When you fall with your father, don't worry. I'll take good care of Lady Emma for you. Has she rejected you yet? Or are you still waiting like a beggar for a scrap of her attention?"

"If you hurt her, I'll kill you." His honesty and determination must have come through in his voice because Sir Horace lost his cocksure attitude.

"I warned you. Your choice." Sir Horace left.

Marcus couldn't breathe. *Cleared up my arse.*

If Father's name was on those papers, he couldn't prove he hadn't been the examiner of the bridge. He couldn't prove Sir Horace was lying.

Marcus rushed up the stairs, not wanting to meet anyone while he was so furious. He headed to the window at the end of the corridor, which opened to a balcony and stepped onto it, letting the cold air cleanse his lungs.

Moonlight flickered in the puddles left by the storm, and he focused on the glittering light, not to think about the bad news.

Because of a stupid mistake, Father risked going to prison, or worse. Sir Horace was the only one who could spare him that fate, but Marcus had no hope in that swine's honour.

He bent over the handrail of the marble balcony, and even though he was shivering from the cold, he stayed there. The scent of pine resin and wet soil filled his lungs.

Her Majesty's Railway Inspectorate would need a culprit and would need one quickly. He didn't have much faith in a thorough investigation. Not when the evidence pointed at his father. Besides, however the inquest went, Kingston & Sindall would be closed and broken.

"Marcus, how are you faring?" Emma stood behind him, with

a thick shawl wrapped over her yellow afternoon gown, looking like a ray of sunshine.

He straightened, not wanting her to see him so distraught. "I'm well." He couldn't say more, but his tone belied his fears.

"I'm sorry. Of course, you aren't well. Silly question. I'll leave you to your thoughts, then." She was about to leave, but he called her.

"Apologies. I didn't mean to be so rude."

"Do not worry." She stepped closer. "Papa told me about the inquest. But if it can be of solace, my father will do his best to help you and your father. And I'll do whatever I can to help you, too. Just tell me what you need."

A hug. But he couldn't say that, could he? "Thank you, but I don't need anything." He shivered as a cold breeze blew from the firth.

"You certainly need to get warm. It's freezing out here. You'll catch a cold." She held the French door open for him.

He stepped into the warm corridor, but the shivers continued.

She closed the door. "Would you like a cup of tea?"

"No, thank you." He stood next to the window, thinking about going out again.

A little smile tugged at her lips. "Tea seemed a sore point for you."

He let out a short chuckle. "I have a complicated relationship with tea." He released a breath, suddenly exhausted.

She put her hand over his, and the touch was worth an entire speech; it was all the encouragement he needed to speak.

"I'm scared and worried," he said in a low voice. "No matter how I look at the situation, the outcome is never good. The evidence points to my father, and Sir Horace doesn't want to take his responsibility. I don't know how to help my father. He seems so defeated, crushed. Had Mother been alive, he wouldn't have been so distraught, and I fear I'm not enough for him to fight for what is right."

She cupped his cheek, causing him to suck in a breath. "Of course you're more than enough for him. He's probably overwhelmed and saddened by the incident. We could sit in the sitting room and talk if you want."

His heart melted under her touch. If she knew how much her touch affected him, how deeply, she would run away from him.

He swallowed hard. "No. I want to feel cold."

She removed her hand, and he missed its warmth immediately. "What do you mean by that?"

"I want the cold to punish me and make me feel pain because I can't do anything to help my father. He gave up. He didn't say that, but I felt it. He thinks there's nothing he can do to clear his name, and I don't know how to convince him to fight. He isn't risking only his company. He could be hanged." He leant against the wall behind him as a lump swelled in his throat. "And I can't do anything. I'm useless."

"Nothing has been decided yet, and there will be another inquest." She took his hand, and once again, the contact was ridiculously comforting. "If you give up as well, what will be left?"

He could breathe better with her soft hand on his and her beautiful voice in his ears, which made him feel selfish as if he were one of those people who trapped a beautiful bird in a cage only to hear it sing.

She inched her hand away, but her stunning stare stayed on him. "Don't give up. I promise you we'll help."

"Thank you."

"I didn't do anything." She lifted a shoulder, and the shawl slid an inch.

He pulled it back up to cover her. She'd shared her light with him. That was more than she thought of.

A moment of silence stretched between them as it'd happened before. They were close to a point where their *friendship* was about to change, but he wouldn't know in which direction, and none of them wanted to take the first step.

Voices sounded from downstairs, breaking the fragile spell.

She tugged at her shawl. "I have to go and change for dinner. Will you join us?"

"No. I'll have a small supper with Father in his room. We aren't a good company, I'm afraid, and we have taken advantage of your father's hospitality for too long."

"Don't lose hope. Please." She rose on her tiptoes and gave him a kiss on the cheek before hurrying away towards her bedroom.

She was fast. Instead, he couldn't move. Her lips had left a trail of fire going through his body, making him forget his worries for a brief, wonderful moment.

eleven

Emma should learn not to make promises she couldn't keep, especially if the promises were out of her hands. She'd told Marcus that Papa would help him. How wrong she'd been. She'd been wrong about many things.

The verdict of the preliminary inquest wasn't in Sir Albert's favour. He was considered the only one responsible for the bridge's collapse. Sir Horace had left his hotel in Newport-on-Tay to return to London immediately after the pronouncement of the inquest, leaving Sir Albert alone to deal with angry people and journalists ready to pillory him. No one seemed to care that the inquest wasn't definitive. Everyone had already condemned and executed Sir Albert.

She paced in Papa's study after he told them he'd asked Sir Albert and Marcus to leave.

"Papa, we can't abandon Marcus and his father in a moment of need," she said, glancing at the window.

Marcus and Sir Albert had ordered a coach to take them to the station, and it should arrive soon. Too soon. A choking sensation wrapped around her chest at the thought of Marcus being disappointed by her lack of help. She'd promised, and instead he'd been thrown out of her house.

Trevor stood next to the fireplace, an elbow on the mantelpiece, and his silence worried her. Why didn't he take her side?

"We can and we must take our distance from Sir Albert," Papa said. "His negligence caused the loss of many lives. I can't let him drag me into a scandal."

"A scandal?" She stopped in front of him, chest heaving. "Sir Albert was wrongly accused. He needs help to clear his name in the next inquest."

"Help I can't provide." Papa shook his head.

"Is that why you told them they must leave Thistle Hall before dusk?" Her voice cracked at the injustice.

"I had no choice." Papa's eyebrows knit together. "One day, you'll understand that having responsibilities means making difficult decisions. I'm sorry for what happened, but Sir Albert and Marcus need to leave. Besides, they must return to London anyway and talk with their solicitor. So must I, actually."

"Papa, please." She tried once again. "At least talk with the journalists and tell them you believe in Sir Albert's innocence. Your public support will change how people see him."

He rubbed the bridge of his nose. "Emma, you must trust me. I can't get more involved than I already am in Sir Albert's problems. I have messages from my solicitors urging me not to do anything until I speak with them."

She turned to Trevor, desperate to find a compassionate voice in her family. "Marcus is your friend. Don't you have anything to say?"

Trevor scrubbed the back of his neck. "I believe Sir Albert when he says Sir Horace did the inspection. But—"

"But what?" she said.

"But there's no evidence!" Trevor raised his voice. "It doesn't matter what or whom we believe. What matters is what Sir Albert can prove. And there's nothing, not a shred of evidence, to support his claims, aside from a generic entry in his journal. His name is on official papers."

"I can't believe you're so heartless." She held her tears with effort.

"This is business!" Father's angry tone reverberated in the wide room. "I have employees to think of, as well. What happens to me affects them."

"What would Mother have done?" she said. Silence thickened in the room. "She would have wanted us to help Sir Albert, to stand for what was right, no matter the consequences."

Father's harsh expression softened, but only for a moment. "Sir Albert is accused of killing more than seventy people. In the best of cases, he'll be imprisoned for life. I can't have the name of our family associated with him. And that's all. Had there been hope to prove Sir Albert's claim, I would have helped him. This is a lost cause."

Clamping a hand over her mouth, she hurried out of the room. How could Papa be so cold when Sir Albert's life was at risk? Sobs shook her chest. Papa refusing to help him hurt too much. Never would she have thought that Papa could be so heartless. He'd married a woman his family and society had disapproved of, but now he cared about his reputation more than a man's life. He'd raised her with principles of justice and fairness, and they'd been a lie.

She waited in her bedroom to collect herself before seeking Marcus. The least she could do was apologise to him.

The house was quiet, but in her ears, the thunder of the storm still echoed. She paused on the threshold of his bedroom. The door stood ajar, and she took a peek inside.

He was finishing packing his luggage. Even across the distance separating them, she could tell he radiated anger and sorrow so strongly she might choke on them.

She took a tentative step into the room. "I'm sorry, Marcus."

He gazed up from his bag, and for a moment, his features softened. "It's not your fault."

"Papa doesn't want to see reason. His reputation is the only thing he can think about."

"I understand." His tone was flat, but a muscle of his jaw ticked.

"I don't. He defied society by choosing to marry my mother, and now he's a completely different person."

He gave her a sad smile. "Now he's a father and is worried about you and Trevor."

A weak excuse, in her opinion. "May I help you?"

"No, thank you. I've finished anyway." He paused, watching his luggage. "My father feels responsible for the tragedy because he didn't go to inspect the bridge and sent Sir Horace instead, and because no one believed him. He thinks he deserves the punishment."

"Why is Sir Horace lying about that?"

He squared his shoulders, looking outraged. "He's a coward. Because of his cowardice, my father risks being hanged."

"I hope..." She couldn't finish the sentence as another sob broke her voice.

He straightened to his full height, but instead of looking imposing, he gave her a sense of protection. "I understand. Truly." His tone said otherwise as if he only wanted to reassure her.

On instinct, she hugged him, squeezing him tightly. His response was immediate. He hugged her back with desperation. A sound like a stifled sob reverberated in his chest.

She'd never realised how comforting his arms could be or how much she wanted him to be happy. Although it should be the other way around. She should console him, but she had no words of comfort for him. Not after her papa disappointed her.

He held her gently but firmly, reassuring her at the same time.

He released her slowly, and she missed his warmth. "Goodbye, Emma."

"Goodbye? We'll see each other soon, won't we?" She stepped away from him as panic spiked her pulse.

He fastened the flap of the bag with a snappy gesture. "I don't know. It wouldn't be good for you and your reputation."

"I'm not like Papa."

He flashed her favourite crooked smile. "Thank you, Emma."

Her heart stuttered at that moment.

She followed him as he went down the stairs in silence. His father was waiting for him in the entry hall, pale and slouching.

She couldn't speak, not even to wish them a safe trip.

Trevor and Papa came to the entry hall, sad but as implacable as executioners.

"I wish you all the best." Papa shook hands with Sir Albert and Marcus.

Anger swelled with a few comments she had to keep for herself. Papa wished them the best when he could do something to make that wish come true. He'd become a stranger to her.

Trevor did the same but with less vigour than Papa.

She waved at Marcus from the threshold as he climbed into the carriage that would take him to the station. He raised a hand in farewell and smiled only for her. She wanted to see him again.

She wasn't like Papa. Not at all.

MARCUS DIDN'T LOOK out of the window during the drive to the station, not wanting to catch a glimpse of Thistle Hall or the front pages of the newspapers lynching his father.

He'd been so close to realising his dream and courting Emma after the conversation with her father that the pain of having lost the opportunity was too big to ignore. It was selfish of him, considering his father's predicament, but in the midst of everything that had happened, the missed opportunity with Emma didn't help his morale.

And he doubted he would see her again.

Father didn't say a word. He didn't even shout or vent his anger against Sir Horace. He didn't seem to care about what the journalists said. He'd retired into his own pain as it'd happened after Mother's death.

When they boarded the train for London, Father barely talked. He sat in their compartment with his head hanging, staring at his hands in his lap.

"You must react," Marcus said as the train sped up towards London. "I'm sure that once we talk with our solicitor, the situation will look better."

"Better?" For the first time in days, a hard glint flickered in Father's eyes. "People died. I retrieved the body of a child from the water. I held him in my arms before delivering him to the undertakers. He was a small, precious thing, no older than one. Do you know what I thought at that moment? I hoped his parents were dead, too, so they would be spared the pain. How can it look better?"

"I understand what you're going through, dammit!" He thumped the seat.

"Don't use that tone with me." The scolding was worth it just to hear Father's tone strong again. "I feel responsible for those deaths. I *am* responsible for those deaths."

"Sir Horace is responsible."

"Don't you understand? Horace and I share the company, but I'm responsible for everything. When he returned from the inspection, I should have been more insistent and asked him more questions about the bridge's condition and to see the papers to check that everything was right. Instead, I was so busy that I accepted the scant report he handed me. I didn't care about the fact my name was on the official document, and that was it."

"Because you trusted him."

"Because I didn't do my job, which was to check everything,

every detail. Had I done that, that child would be alive." Father's voice shook.

Emotion swelled in his throat, ripping his heart apart. "It was a tragedy, and it shouldn't have happened, but getting yourself hanged won't bring those people back, and it wouldn't mean justice either."

Father didn't say anything.

"Sir Horace is responsible for those deaths," he said again. He would say that over and over until Father agreed. "And if they hang you, he'll be free to do more damage and cause more death."

"I can't prove he's the culprit."

"There must be a worker, someone who remembers seeing him."

Father exhaled and rubbed his eyes. "I put my trust in the new inquest. The royal inspector will establish who is responsible."

Marcus didn't share his optimism.

twelve

In his father's study, Marcus read for the third time the final technical report on the bridge from Her Majesty's Railway Inspectorate. A structural failure had caused the bridge to snap. No doubt about that. The train hadn't derailed and hit the posts, triggering the collapse.

The wind had played a huge role in the incident, but the structure had shown signs of quick degradation, and an inspector should have caught them. If Father had inspected the bridge, he would have found the faults. Marcus was sure of that.

If they'd completed the second inspection, had not the storm caught them off guard, Father would have ordered the bridge closure, and the tragedy would have been avoided.

Now their solicitor would be decisive to save Father's future.

Two weeks had passed since the tragedy. Emma and Trevor had sent word of comfort but no help. He understood why and wouldn't blame them. Besides, the newspapers had already sentenced Father to death as the only one responsible for the incident. Sir Horace had been quiet, not accusing but also not defending Father, blissfully ignored by the press. Thanks to some legal loops Sir Horace's solicitor had found, he wouldn't receive more than a slap on the wrist.

He reclined on the chair, listening to the fire crackling. The cosy room had always been his favourite refuge. With its walnut wainscoting and the rich brown curtains Mother had chosen, it had the atmosphere of a library.

He touched the oak wood desk. He'd learnt the basics of physics at that desk and had tea with his mother, despite Father's lukewarm protests about using his working desk as a tea table. More than once, Marcus and Mother had stained a technical drawing or a book on mechanics with cocoa and tea.

He smiled, remembering Mother's horrified face and her attempts at covering up the disaster while smearing the cocoa further.

Your father will never notice the stain, she would have said.

But Father had always noticed.

The doorbell ringing pulled him back from the sweet memory. It couldn't be Father. He was in his solicitor's office. Marcus had wanted to go as well, but Father had categorically forbidden him to come for whatever reason.

The butler's footsteps sounded from the hallway, then voices came.

"Sir." The butler opened the door to the study. "You have a visitor."

He exhaled. "Not another journalist. I have nothing to say." He stood up and fell silent as a police officer came into view.

"Mr. Marcus Kingston?" The officer removed his hat. "I'm Police Constable Parker."

"What is it?" The inquest was over, and the police had no business knocking on his door.

The constable shifted his gaze. "I'm afraid I have some terrible news for you. There's been an accident. Your father fell on the railway at Victoria Station when a train was coming. He died before he could receive help. I'm sorry."

Marcus clenched the edge of the desk, struggling to make sense of what the constable had said. "There must be a mistake. My father had no reason to go to the station. He's at Spencer & Associates, his solicitor's firm."

"Your father is Sir Albert Kingston, isn't he? There's no mistake. Witnesses saw him slipping off the platform right when an express train was coming."

"But no, he—" The room tilted. He rubbed an aching spot on his forehead. "I want to see him."

The constable hesitated. "He's at the city mortuary, but I must warn you. Many people find the mortuary rather shocking."

Marcus nodded, or maybe he didn't. He couldn't make sense of his life. He must have been a pitiful sight because the officer cleared his throat.

"I shall accompany you," the officer said, "so we can have an official identification although a couple of people confirmed it was him, and we found documents in his pockets proving his identity."

A thousand thoughts rushed across Marcus's mind during the drive to the mortuary. There had to be a mistake. Father was supposed to be with their solicitor at that moment, and the solicitor's office was on the opposite side of the city.

He had no reason to go to the station...unless. No, Marcus wouldn't consider that option.

"Are you sure you want to carry on, sir?" the constable asked.

"I am."

"Would you like to inform a friend or ask a family member to be with you?"

"No, thank you." Besides, he wouldn't know whom to call.

He doubted Emma or Trevor would come.

He walked into the mortuary almost without realising he was moving. It was as if his body didn't belong to him anymore. His legs moved forwards without any effort from him.

While Constable Parker talked with the medic in charge, Marcus ignored the voice at the back of his head, whispering dark things. Maybe Father had changed his plan and had to go to the station for some reason. But surely, it couldn't be... He wouldn't have decided to flee London, or worse.

"Mr. Kingston," Parker said, "please follow me."

Marcus did as told. A wide and dark corridor stretched out in front of him, filled with doctors in bloodstained aprons.

The smell of blood and disinfectant spread by a Lister's spray offended his nostrils, but the sight of the bodies lying under the blankets shocked him back to reality. So many people.

The constable stopped at a table, and a few formal words were exchanged, along with the medic's condolences, which Marcus didn't acknowledge. The medic gently pulled the blanket down.

Marcus sucked in a breath as he gazed upon the familiar face. It was Father. The medic showed him only Father's face unblemished and untouched aside from a shallow cut near the temple. The signs of last weeks' fatigue had disappeared. Father looked peaceful and serene as if resting.

"This is your father, isn't he?" Parker asked.

Marcus could only nod. Pain held his throat in a vice, and a heavy weight pressed against his chest. His sight blurred, and no matter how many times he blinked, he couldn't see properly.

"Sir," Parker said, "would you like me to take you home?"

He shook his head and cleared his throat. "May I have a moment?"

There was an exchange of nods, then the officer and the doctor left him alone with the dead.

EMMA'S LEGS shook as she went up the front stairs of Marcus's townhouse with her brother.

The news of his father's death had shocked her deeply, and she needed to see how Marcus was faring in person. She'd sent him messages in the past weeks, and whenever she'd asked him to see him, he'd made excuses.

Father hadn't wanted to come, and in fact, hadn't she insisted, Father would have forbidden her to go.

Trevor took a deep breath before knocking on the polished door. From the outside, the house looked pristine and immaculate, untouched by any tragedy. If not for the black crêpe and white silk ribbon on the knocker, she wouldn't have thought a tragedy had happened.

She shifted her weight from one foot to the other, eager to see Marcus.

The door inched inwards, and a butler appeared. "Kingston residence."

"Lord Trevor and my sister, Lady Emma. We would like to see Marcus if he's accepting calls."

Boxes and trunks crammed the entry hall, and aside from the butler, the house seemed empty.

"My lord, my lady." The butler held the door open for them and showed them to a parlour. "I'll tell Mr. Kingston you're here."

A detailed steel model of a train rested in a box, glinting with a muted light. Photographs of Sir Albert with a young Marcus next to a bridge under construction filled another box. She paused to study the portrait of a beautiful woman with Marcus's same grey eyes.

Only the sound of Trevor's soft footfalls could be heard in the eerily quiet house.

"Marcus must be distraught." She touched the model of a bridge sitting on top of a pile of books and photographs in yet another box.

"I fear the worst has still to come for him."

"What do you mean?"

The door opened, revealing a pale and dishevelled Marcus. A dark stubble covered his jaw. His face didn't show any surprise or pleasure as he gazed at them. No emotion.

He bowed and muttered something that sounded like, "Good afternoon."

"Marcus." She rushed to hug him but stopped when he stiffened.

"We're so sorry for your loss." Trevor squeezed Marcus's shoulder.

"I'm afraid my maid isn't here." Marcus stretched out an arm towards the armchairs. "If you want tea, I'll ask Taylor to brew it."

"Don't worry about that." Emma put her hand on his arm, and a spark of vitality lit his gaze. "How can we help?"

It was hypocritical of her to ask when they hadn't done anything to help him. Maybe, if Papa had intervened, Sir Albert would be alive.

He looked away. Behind him, the butler carried more boxes to the hallway.

"Everything is almost ready." His voice sounded strained as if his throat hurt.

"Are you leaving?" Trevor asked.

Marcus nodded. "I have no choice. The company has been dissolved, and the legal expenses need to be paid. Even dissolving a company is a process that requires money. A lot of money."

Emma sat on the sofa. "Are you in debt?"

Just the thought sent a shiver down her neck. If Marcus couldn't pay, he would be locked up in Fleet Prison.

"Do not worry." He frowned.

"You could have sent for us. We would have helped you." She regretted her words the moment they left her mouth. The last thing he needed to hear was a scolding. And to be honest, he had every reason not to seek her help. She hadn't given him any hope.

Her father could help. She had little control over the family's finances, but she could convince, beg if necessary, Papa to help Marcus at least that one time.

His gaze turned from sad and lost to sharp and angry in a moment. "No, I don't think you would have."

She deserved his doubt, but his situation was different now.

"But seriously. Tell us what you need," she insisted.

Trevor gave her the slightest shake of his head. "Where are you going?" he asked.

"One of my father's friends offered me accommodation for a few days. After that, I don't know." He leant against the wall and tilted his head back. A tear hung on the tips of his eyelashes, and it was the saddest sight she'd ever seen. Even now, he tried to hold back his emotions. "The money, I don't care about it. There isn't much I can do about that."

"There has to be something we can do for you," she said, but he didn't seem to have heard her.

"I'm not sure what happened at the station," he whispered.

She and Trevor had discussed the incident, too. Witnesses had said Sir Albert had walked on unsteady legs as if he'd been drunk and then slipped, but some people had claimed his move had been deliberate.

"He shouldn't have been there," Marcus said. "He had an appointment with his solicitor but didn't go to him."

"With everything that happened to him," she said, "he might have been simply confused, tired, and disoriented."

Trevor nodded. "He must not have slept well in weeks."

Marcus shoved his hands in his pockets. "He was very tired, yes, and dispirited."

The sound of the butler carrying more boxes filled the uncomfortable silence. The fireplace was cold, and the air was frigid.

"Thank you for coming," Marcus said, walking out of the room.

Was he dismissing them? But she wanted to do something to help him. She followed him to the entry hall. "Where are you going exactly? I would like to write to you."

He held the front door open for them. "I'll send you the address."

"Marcus."

"We'd better leave." Trevor touched her arm. "If you need anything, let us know."

Marcus gave him a brusque nod.

She brushed past him. "Please let us know."

He narrowed his eyes to slits. "I promise."

When she walked down the steps to the pavement, Marcus shut the door. She turned around for a last wave, but he wasn't looking at them from the window.

It was another goodbye, and her heart was crushed by its weight.

On the ground littered with paint, sawdust, and discarded tools, Emma held her hat as she tilted her head back to stare at the half-built houses in St. Giles.

Holes opened throughout the street, and piles of logs and tiles were scattered around. It seemed as if the houses were being demolished rather than built.

She and Trevor had started a project to build better, healthier homes for the people in the rookery, and it'd taken almost four years, hundreds of papers, and no small amount of headaches. But finally the result of their hard work was visible. More or less.

They'd come to the construction site to check the progress. Or lack thereof, since they'd visited the site months ago and nothing had changed since then. But then again, Sir Horace, the chief builder, had claimed all sorts of delays had fallen on him, and the building expense had grown exponentially.

Speaking of the devil, Sir Horace strode towards them in a shiny suit that seemed impervious to lime stains. Her skirt had got stained in a matter of minutes.

"He's here." She tapped Trevor's shoulder.

"Curse the day Father hired him," Trevor muttered.

Sir Horace came to a halt in front of them. "Does Lady Emma need to be here?" he asked Trevor in a clipped tone.

She turned towards him. "Yes, I do, and I would appreciate it if you addressed the questions that regard me to me. Thank you."

Sir Horace gave her a half-moon smile that chilled her. "I'm merely concerned for your well-being, my lady. A construction site is no place for a lady. Your late father, bless him, wouldn't have approved."

"But Trevor is the Earl of Pembroke now," she said, just to put Sir Horace in his place. "And I'm old enough to make my own decisions."

He dipped his slimy gaze to her chest, and she fastened the front of her cloak as the revolting sensation of being touched by him slithered down her back.

"Yes, I can see you aren't a girl anymore." His tone sounded mocking.

Trevor shifted his position to force Sir Horace to stare at him. "As my sister said, I'm the earl now."

A sudden heart problem had taken Papa away three years ago. She regretted the bitterness of the last moments she'd spent with him. They hadn't seen eye to eye about his treatment of Marcus, but their most furious fights had been about Papa hiring Sir Horace. He'd claimed Sir Horace had been the best option.

They'd argued and said harsh words they hadn't really meant. Then he'd died. And she missed him, despite everything. Despite the fact she and Trevor were bound to Sir Horace by a contract they hadn't chosen.

Sir Horace exhaled as if gathering his patience to deal with naughty children. "My lord, your sister's presence here is unnecessary."

"My sister is more than welcome to share my interest in the project. This is *our* project, after all. So any news?"

Sir Horace watched the builders going up and down the scaffolding for a moment. "We're on schedule. We had a minor delay due to a supply of wood arriving late, but aside from that, everything is going well."

"On schedule?" She tried to get Sir Horace's attention, but he ignored her.

"We heard complaints about the construction methods you adopt," Trevor said. "A few workers have been injured because of a lack of safety measures, and a part of the construction site collapsed, which has put us behind schedule. Not to mention the growing cost of the buildings."

"Who said those claims?" Sir Horace put both hands on the pommel of his walking stick. His narrowed eyes glinted.

"The names don't matter." Emma gave him a sweet smile. "We care about the truth."

"No need to worry about that, my lady. There isn't any truth in those accusations. Now, if you'll excuse me, I have two more construction sites to visit before dusk."

After the Tay Bridge disaster and Sir Albert's death, Sir Horace had founded his own company, Sindall Building Co., and had become rather popular, being involved in several projects, which didn't please her in the least.

Besides, since the Tay Bridge disaster, there had been rumours about a few townhouses built by Sir Horace's company having structural problems. She didn't understand why he hadn't been charged with negligence, as it'd happened to poor Sir Albert.

She followed him as he hurried towards the cab waiting for him. "Sir Horace."

He pivoted towards her, staring at her with coldness. "My lady?"

"Did you receive any news from Marcus?" Hadn't she been desperate to know if Marcus was well, she wouldn't have asked him.

He gave her another long, slimy glance that made her feel naked. "Don't come to my construction site again. The only thing your presence does is distract the workers."

She stepped back from him, anger heating her face. "I think you're the only one who gets distracted."

He grinned at her shock and resumed his walk to the cab.

She walked back to Trevor, fists closed at her sides. "He told me I distract the workers."

Trevor's eyebrows rose to the rim of his top hat. "The more he speaks, the less I like him." He worked his jaw. "Weeks ago, he suggested we visit a house of ill repute," he whispered the last word. "I was so furious I feared a vein in my brain might explode. Disorderly houses. I'm no angel, but I would never exploit women."

She was impressed although Trevor's dislike for gentlemen who attended disorderly houses was nothing new. "Apart from his rudeness, I don't trust him."

"Neither do I. I would do anything not to deal with him."

"His company has grown quickly. Too quickly."

"As long as our houses are safe and well-built, I won't complain. After that, I don't care what my solicitor says. I won't go near Sir Horace ever again."

They climbed into the carriage in a foul mood.

Papa hadn't been the most compassionate of men, but he'd agreed to help the people in the rookery. Help she was eager to provide, as she'd been eager to help Marcus.

He'd vanished. He had never written to her, never sent word of his whereabouts, and never shown up again at her house. If he'd started his own building company, she would know; there would be traces. But nothing. He wasn't in prison. He hadn't left England. He'd simply disappeared.

The only reply she'd received was from his friend, who was supposed to have accommodated him for a while, but that had been a lie. Marcus's friend had claimed he hadn't seen him in a long time.

That was why she'd employed the help of a private investigator to find him.

"Listen," she said.

Trevor shot his gaze upwards. "Please. Every time you start a conversation with 'listen,' we end up doing something outlandish, like hiring a private investigator or changing the curtains."

"Hiring that detective wasn't outlandish but necessary, and you agreed. And the curtains needed to be changed. I thought you liked those I chose."

"I was being polite, like every Englishman."

"I prefer honesty."

"What bothers you?" He removed his hat and ran a hand through his hair.

She huffed. "The usual. Sir Horace. I would like to ask for a second opinion. Ask another civil engineer to take a look at his work."

"I'm not sure it's a good idea."

"Listen—"

"Again." He rubbed the bridge of his nose.

"I want to ask another expert."

"All right, but I don't believe we'll find any answers. Sir Horace's company is essentially the only one working at the moment in London. Everyone else is fighting for the scraps of small projects. No one will go against him. Sir Horace isn't an easy monster to slay."

"I want to try."

He scoffed. "Why do you ask for my opinion when you end up doing what you want anyway?"

"Because I'm polite, like every Englishwoman."

"Honestly. You should have married that baron and moved to Bath."

"I didn't like him, and that was a low blow."

"Low blows are all I have right now."

"You rejected one lady after another, too."

"Because I don't want to have a child a few months after I'm married. The ladies I met were all eager to give me an heir. One promised me I would be a father exactly nine months after the wedding. What happened to being romantic? No, thank you. Besides, I'm not fond of children. Too noisy and smelly. And I want a wife, not a broodmare." He tilted his head. "No, actually, I'm looking for a broodmare for my beloved stallion."

"Does Ophelia have anything to do with you rejecting every lady?"

He turned serious. "Don't start."

"I don't mean to upset you. I want to know if you're still thinking about her after all these years."

He seemed to shrink as he hunched his shoulders and slouched on the seat.

She touched his arm. "I saw you the other day staring at the locket with her photograph. You looked so sad."

He scowled. "Do you spy on me?"

"I just happened to see you, and I'm worried about you."

"And I'm worried about you. You've rejected one suitor after another for ridiculous reasons. At least my reasons to reject ladies are moral."

She slanted him a glare. "I want to spend the rest of my life with someone I like and respect."

"You rejected Lord Carlton because you didn't like his laugh."

"It gave me a headache."

"What about Viscount Apley? You didn't like him because he said he doesn't read books."

"What better reason than that?"

Trevor tilted his head as if in agreement. "You look for excuses, and that's fine by me," he hurried to add when she opened her mouth to protest. "If you don't want to marry now, it's all right.

Just say it and be honest. But grant me the same freedom, thank you very much."

She folded her hands on her lap and stared out of the window. She wanted to get married and have a family. But with a man who made her heart race and her mind thrive.

And she hadn't found anyone.

fourteen

In Lady Beaumont's sumptuous bedroom, Marcus pocketed the banknotes she'd given him, forcing himself not to appear too eager to get the money although he was trembling with anticipation, thinking of how to spend it.

"Thank you, my lady," he said.

Lady Beaumont tied the silk garter at her thigh, her gown still half opened on the back. "It's always a pleasure to be with you."

For her, certainly; for him, not so much.

"I want to see you next week as well," she said, turning around to show him her back. "My husband is away, and I want to have fun."

"Of course." He buttoned her dress, already thinking about the next payment. He could pay a physician to visit Jesse, buy fresh food, and put something aside to find a better flat. "Done."

She faced him and wrapped her arms around his neck to kiss him. His first reaction was to tense and step back, as usual. Compared to other clients, she was a stunner, young, and relatively easy to please—at least in bed—but he didn't feel an ounce of attraction for her.

She was just a job, a necessity to survive. Once he put aside enough money to leave London and start afresh somewhere else, he would find another means to survive.

Life was just that to him—survival.

In the past years, he'd tried every sort of job, and the result had been that he'd worked hard for long hours and meagre pay. And the job had lasted until his employers had found out that he was the son of the engineer who had killed the passengers on the Tay Bridge. Then he'd been mocked, scorned, and eventually sacked.

The ladies paid better, but that life was taking its toll on his dignity.

He had to end that life of slavery for himself and Jesse as well. The child was his responsibility now.

Lady Beaumont released him, only to drag a hand down his half-naked chest. "How many other clients do you have?"

"A fair few." Apparently, London brimmed with unhappy, rich ladies who had odd requests in bed, but he met only a handful of them regularly.

A crease appeared between her eyebrows. "And who are they?"

"I can't tell you. I don't mention you to them, so it's only fair I keep quiet." Just business.

"But what if I want to be your only client?" She ran a hand through his hair, making him feel her sharp nails on his scalp. "Be my secret mister?"

Tempting, in terms of income. But as long as he kept multiple clients, he had the excuse to arrange the appointments as he pleased. If he became Lady Beaumont's mister, he would be at her beck and call all the time, completely dependent on her whims, and he wasn't sure he liked that.

Cutting off the ties with her would be more difficult. She was already a demanding and possessive client, always asking him personal questions. He didn't want their relationship to become deeper or more exclusive.

"It's not possible now." He stepped away from her, looking forward to returning home to Jesse.

She glowered. When she had that sour expression, she lost some of her beauty. "I would give you a nice flat in Mayfair or Bloomsbury, perhaps. So many artists live there."

Why artists would be relevant for him was a mystery he didn't care to solve. Although a flat in a nice area wouldn't be terrible. And it would be better than seeing the ladies in their houses, less risky.

Lady Beaumont met him in a discreet flat she owned in Marylebone, but one lady met him in her main house. The subterfuges to sneak in and out of her aristocratic house were what he hated the most. He had no idea how the lady kept her maids and footmen quiet. Maybe she bribed them or threatened them with dismissal, but no servants blabbered about their mistress. He had to endure their smirks and jokes though.

"Thank you, but I must decline for now." He kissed her hand, but she didn't soften.

"I want to see you next week, same time."

He bowed. "Of course."

She sat on the bed in a froth of silk. "You're so handsome, Marcus. Those eyes, those sharp cheeks, and that jaw are stunning, and your body is a work of art. When I met you, you were a scrawny thing. Now you're magnificent. You were too skinny, and only dogs like bones."

He had no idea what to say to that, so he bowed again and put some distance between them, lest she grab him for another round.

"Do you want to start again?" she asked.

"I have another appointment." It wasn't true, but he couldn't be honest and tell her that he'd reached his daily limit of spending time with her.

She pouted. "Go then."

She wanted him to kiss her and tell her she was his best client, or something similar, but he'd had enough of her whims, and he was too tired to keep going.

"Good night."

When he finally left her room, he closed his eyes and breathed in the coal-smelling air of London, just to cleanse his senses from her strong, flowery perfume. The fragrance got stuck on his skin, clothes, and hair, even if he scrubbed himself.

He hated smelling her perfume on him, too. Her perfume on his body made him feel as if she'd marked him and branded him as hers.

It was a job. Nothing more.

He'd been doing it for a year now, and it was easier than stealing.

He was terrible at picking locks, and lifting wallets had never been his forte. He'd been caught by his supposed victims more times than he cared to admit. Instead, the ladies paid well.

He made more in a single night with one of his ladies than in a month of stealing. Although angry husbands weren't less dangerous than underpaid and overworked police constables.

He pulled up the lapels of his coat to fend off the chill from the Thames. The worn fabric didn't hold his warmth though, and cold drafts sneaked through his clothes to bite his skin.

He sped up, not wanting to spend precious money on a cab, and walking would keep him warm. As he left the wealthy area for more unsavoury streets, the smell changed from coal to desperation.

The dark alleyway in Seven Dials where he'd found a place to stay was slippery with fresh rain, and he lost his balance in his hurry to get home. He hit the wall hard and winced, but the pain passed soon because he was familiar with feeling it.

Lady Beaumont had a point. Before starting to work for her and other women, years of scarce food and unhealthy places to sleep had nearly broken his body. Every time he'd hurt himself, he'd felt every possible ounce of pain multiplied by ten.

Thanks to her generous pay and the food he could buy with it, he'd recovered his strength. Most importantly, he'd recently extinguished all the debts he'd accumulated after Father's death.

There were still days when the food was scarce, and the gangs in Seven Dials demanded protection money regularly. He barely saved any coins, also because there were days when he couldn't force himself to be with one of his ladies, no matter how hungry he was. But his current situation was better than last year, and now that he'd finished paying off his creditors, he would save more. Thanks to Father's solicitor, Marcus had avoided languishing in prison for debts.

He opened the door to his flat, wincing again as it screeched on its hinges.

"Marcus?" Jesse said from the bedroom.

Less than a bedroom, it was a large cupboard, barely wide enough to fit the bed, but better than nothing.

"It's me." He lit a candle.

Not even in the semidarkness did the flat pass as half decent. The smell of humidity would kill an elephant, and a chill lingered in the air, no matter how many logs he burned in the stove.

"How do you feel?" He put a hand on Jesse's clammy forehead.

"I'm so much better." Jesse coughed, shaking from head to toe. "I think I'm completely healed. You don't need to worry any—" A violent coughing fit shook his thin body.

"Your fever has lowered, but you're far from healed, and you're sweaty again." Marcus tucked the blankets around Jesse. "I'll find a physician to visit you tomorrow and buy some chicken to make a soup."

"Chicken." Jesse eased back on the pillow. "Do chickens still exist? I thought they were gone. I can hardly remember their taste."

"Don't be so dramatic. We had chicken two weeks ago."

Jesse coughed again. "It seems I've been in this bed for years."

He caressed Jesse's head. "You'll get better. I promise."

Perhaps he should accept Lady Beaumont's offer only for the

sake of Jesse. He would wait for the physician's opinion on the boy's health before deciding.

"How was work?" Jesse asked, snuggling under the covers.

"We don't talk about that." He brewed a fresh pot of tea.

"I didn't ask you to tell me—" Jesse coughed again. "Which work you were doing, but how it was."

"It was good money." He showed Jesse the banknotes.

Jesse's brown eyes widened. "Bloody hell!"

"I told you. I'll find a physician tomorrow, and you'll get better."

Jesse turned serious, too serious for an eleven-year-old boy. "You don't kill, do you?"

He poured the tea into two chipped mugs. "I'm not a killer."

"My father did that," Jesse whispered, accepting the mug. "He worked for a gang at the dock. He said it was honest work because he killed bad people."

"Bad or good, I don't kill anyone. I promise." He only killed tiny pieces of his soul.

Jesse put down the mug and hugged him. His weak arms barely squeezed Marcus.

"Thank you." Jesse shivered. "I would be dead without you."

"You're welcome." He kissed the boy's head.

He would be dead without Jesse, too.

fifteen

T he letter Emma was reading in the sitting room was perfectly polite, yet incredibly offensive.

She'd asked no less than ten reputable civil engineers to inspect the construction site in St. Giles, but none of them had agreed to carry out the job. The moment they'd heard Sir Horace was involved, they weren't interested anymore.

Thank you for your consideration, Lady Emma, but please be more careful in the future and don't consider my company or me if Sir Horace is involved.

She tossed the letter on her escritoire over a pile made with the other rejections expressing the same sentiment. Essentially, every engineer in London believed she was insane to ask someone to check Sir Horace's work because it had to be perfect.

Sir Horace had cast a dark spell over London. Everyone was either charmed or afraid of him.

"Bad news, I suppose," Trevor said from the other side of the room.

"I've received another, *thank you but no, thank you*. This is becoming ridiculous."

"I hate to say it, but I told you so."

"You don't hate to say it."

"No, I don't. I quite enjoy it. It's one of those little joys of life." He put aside the document he'd been reading.

"How can Sir Horace be so respected?"

"I have a few theories in mind. None of them pleasant."

"Like what?"

"A secret society of Freemasons? Magic? Secret lover of the queen?"

"Unlike Viscount Apley, you read too many books."

The knock on the door distracted her.

"My lord," the butler said, "this has just arrived." He offered Trevor a silver plate with a letter on it.

"Thank you, Stewart." Trevor opened the letter and read it, yawning.

"I have no choice but to study engineering myself," she muttered.

He straightened. "Good news! The private investigator found Marcus."

"Finally." She shot up to her feet and ran to read the first good letter in a while. "He's here in London."

That hurt. He was in London but had never come.

Trevor grimaced. "The address is close to Seven Dials. He must be going through a terrible period."

"We found him." Emotion thickened her throat.

She'd hoped to see him again, talk to him, and make sure he was fine. Now a combination of happiness, relief, and guilt overwhelmed her. Not a day had passed without her wondering how she could help him. Papa had been horrible to Marcus, but she hadn't fared better.

Would he be angry with her? Happy to see her?

Trevor held her hand. "You were right about the private detective."

"I hate to tell you, but I told you so." She sat on the armrest of Trevor's armchair, an idea swirling in her mind. "Listen—"

"Oh, dear." He exhaled. "What?"

"Don't be so rude. I was thinking that we could find Marcus and ask him to be our impartial inspector of the construction site. We'll hire him. He won't be afraid of going against Sir Horace."

"Likely, the opposite. He won't be impartial at all. He'll destroy Sir Horace out of spite, and even if he didn't, Sir Horace would accuse him of that anyway."

"I trust his honesty and integrity."

"We haven't seen him in years." He waved the letter. "Seven Dials. If he lives there, he won't be prone to show honesty and integrity towards Sir Horace. Hell, I'm not prone to after his comment on you."

"Why are you judging Marcus without even having seen him?"

"Because only desperate people and criminals live in Seven Dials, and desperate people often become criminals. It's the circle of life." He drew a circle in the air with a finger.

"You don't know what you're talking about." She swatted his shoulder. "I still want his opinion. He's likely the only one in London who would take the job."

"And we would..." He glanced at her. "Repair some of the damage Father and I had done."

Not only Father and Trevor. She could have done more, been more insistent, and stood up for Marcus.

She nodded, letting a tear slide down her cheek.

Trevor patted her hand. "There, there. You know I'm terrible at cheering people up. I'm far better at making them mad. I have my faults. Not many, but some."

She chuckled, wiping her tears. "Let's go."

∼

IN HIS FLAT, Marcus took a sniff at the bottle of cough syrup the physician had given him for Jesse. He wasn't an expert, but the medicine smelled of laudanum, yet the label read a list of harmless medicinal herbs and some flavours without mentioning the opioids.

"Does it taste bad?" Jesse asked, shivering.

"It shouldn't. Syrups are usually sweet." He gave Jesse a tablespoon of the drug.

Jesse scrunched up his face, his eyes watering as he swallowed hard. "De-delicious. I feel better already."

"Does your throat hurt?"

"No, I'm fine." Jesse forced a smile, blinking tears away.

Marcus put the bottle aside. "I need you to be honest. If you aren't well, you must tell me."

Jesse fiddled with a corner of the bedsheet. "I don't want to be a burden."

"You are not. I swear. I care about you. We're a family. So when you're sick or uncomfortable, I need you to tell me."

Jesse nodded without looking at him.

"I'll give you more soup later." He touched Jesse's forehead, feeling the boy's skin still too hot. And the chicken soup he'd made wasn't great. It looked like a disease and tasted like disappointment.

The knock on the door caused them both to jolt.

Marcus's clients didn't know his address; they contacted him by sending a message addressed to him at the post office. Aside from an occasional neighbour or the local gang asking for money, he didn't receive any visitors. Desperate people might attack other desperate people.

He stood up. "Stay here and be quiet."

Jesse nodded, his blond curls bobbing over his reddened cheeks. The door to the small, narrow bedroom couldn't be shut properly, thanks to a broken hinge, so he left it ajar.

He tensed, approaching the front door. He listened as a knock came again. "Who is it?"

The person on the other side cleared their throat. "Marcus? It's me, Emma."

Silence.

"Trevor is here as well."

That voice. He'd heard it only in his dreams in the past years. Emma was here. It had to be a trick played by years of starvation and lack of sleep.

"Marcus?" Jesse whispered from the threshold of the bedroom. "Who is Emma?"

"Go to bed and close the door," he ordered in a low voice.

He waited for Jesse to do as he was told.

"Hello, Marcus." That was Trevor. "We're sorry to come unannounced, but we would like to have a word with you if you agree."

For a moment, he didn't say or do anything. Lady Emma and her brother, the Earl of Pembroke, seeing where he lived was humiliating, to say the least. He'd never cared about the poor aesthetic of the mismatched chairs, the paint flaking from the window frame, or the smell of mould until now.

"Marcus? Are you there?" Emma asked.

Hell.

Jesse wasn't visible. Good.

He straightened his tattered shirt. A hole ripped the fabric on his elbow, and the hem of his trousers was frayed. Nothing he could do about that.

Ignoring them wasn't simply rude but counterproductive. He was curious to know what they wanted. He took a deep breath and opened the door.

"I'm—" The rest of his meaningless sentence was cut off the moment he set his gaze on her.

Emma looked like an angel in a light blue gown with a matching hat and a pair of gloves. Her hazel eyes were guarded, and she clenched her purse with both hands, but her beauty hadn't changed. Trevor must have grown a foot since the last time Marcus had seen him. He was broader, too.

Instead, Marcus felt as if he'd shrunk in the past years, becoming insignificant and thin.

Emma was the first to speak. "Marcus. I'm so happy to see you again."

Trevor smiled broadly, but the smile didn't reach his eyes. Behind him, a couple of footmen kept an eye on the alleyway.

He wanted to ask her how she'd found him, but at the moment, his tongue didn't want to work. He gave her a nod and held the door open for them. She brushed past him on her tiptoes as if scared he might snap at her.

Trevor removed his top hat and offered him his hand. "You're a hard man to find. We searched for you. I'm so glad to have found you."

Marcus shook his hand out of habit. "I'm happy to see you, too." His voice said otherwise, and he was too shocked to talk more.

The aristocratic pair in their fine clothes and healthy bodies were a stark contrast to the utter misery of his room.

He offered them the chairs. "Would you like a cup of tea?"

Not that he had fresh leaves. He brewed tea from the same leaves a few times before using fresh ones.

The two siblings spoke at the same time. "Oh, no, thank you," Emma said as Trevor said, "We don't drink tea anymore."

"Really?" Marcus asked.

"No, I was joking." Trevor chuckled.

"Great."

Silence thickened like gelatine. They tried hard not to stare at him, but their gazes roamed the room and his body, surely making a quick assessment of the situation.

Their thoughts could almost be heard: Not a lot to eat. Not decent clothes. Likely he was riddled with diseases like a rat.

"How have you been?" Emma asked, causing a storm of emotions in his chest.

"These have been difficult years." There was no point in denying it. "I moved around the country until I found a job in London."

"Construction?" Trevor asked.

Not quite. "No. Apparently, no one wants to hire the son of a mass murderer, as my father was called."

"That's terrible." She stepped closer, and he caught a whiff of her honeysuckle scent.

It instantly brought him back years when his major problem was to gather the courage to talk to her. Lady Beaumont's perfume sickened him after one minute, but Emma's scent revived him with fresh energy. And he wouldn't mind smelling it on his skin.

He didn't know anything about her life aside from the fact her father had died suddenly. She could be married for all he knew.

"We came here for many reasons." She stared at him with a pleading gaze. "Not only to see how you were faring, but also to ask for your help and offer you a job."

He didn't expect that. "A job?"

"Since our father died," Trevor said, "Emma and I have carried out a series of projects to develop our land and help less fortunate people live in decent homes." He glanced around but didn't comment on the state of Marcus's room. "We're currently building new homes in the rookery of St. Giles, and Sir Horace is the chief developer of the project."

Marcus's blood boiled at hearing that name. It was curious how the mention of Sir Horace changed his mood so quickly. "I'm not surprised. His company is one of the few working at the moment."

"Well, we don't trust Sir Horace's work." Trevor lifted a shoulder. "There were incidents on his construction site, not fatal, and another bridge he was responsible for collapsed, but he was never accused of negligence. We tried to hire new engineers to inspect the construction site, but we didn't—"

"Find anyone," he completed. "No one wants to go against him. He has good friends in Parliament."

"Alas, that's what I feared." Trevor nodded. "So we wanted to ask you."

Marcus folded his arms across his chest. "I haven't worked as an engineer in years."

"But we trust you," she said. "We fear that those homes have some major flaws that will put people in danger."

"I understand, but you should find someone qualified for an inspection."

"At the moment, we only need an expert who can confirm or disprove our doubts. You can stay with us while you work, or we'll rent you a room if you prefer, and we'll pay you, of course." She stared at him with too much intensity. "Thirty pounds to start with."

"Bloody hell!" Jesse was standing at the door to the bedroom, wrapped in the quilt. He coughed. "Thirty pounds! I've never seen that much money."

"Jesse." Marcus frowned. "Go to bed."

"Thirty pounds!" Jesse coughed, his shoulders shaking.

"Who's this boy?" Emma smiled at Jesse.

"My charge." Marcus hauled Jesse up and carried him to the bed. "I told you to stay here."

"Are you going to accept the job?" Jesse coughed again.

That bloody syrup wasn't doing much.

"I don't know." He tucked the blanket around Jesse. "Stay here."

"Thirty pounds. We could buy a whole flock of chickens."

"Stay warm." He took a moment to consider the offer. It was tempting, but the problem was Sir Horace. If he learnt Marcus was inspecting his construction site and meddling in his affairs, he would unleash his wrath.

Sir Horace would destroy him.

Not that it would take much effort to do so. Marcus was already broke financially and spiritually. But the man was capable of anything, and Marcus had Jesse to protect.

He couldn't keep his work as an inspector a secret because, if he found something irregular, he would have to file a report, and without his legal name, it wouldn't have any value.

So accepting the job meant openly going against Sir Horace, which he couldn't afford. And he didn't completely trust Trevor and Emma. They might be well-meaning, but he doubted they would risk their reputation to protect him. He would be better off accepting Lady Beaumont's proposal.

When he entered the other room, Emma and Trevor were chatting in low tones.

She turned to face him. "Is the boy sick?"

He ignored the question. "Lord Pembroke, Lady Emma." The formal tone caused them to tense. "I thank you deeply for the offer, but I'm afraid I must decline."

"Why?" Emma asked.

"Sir Horace would destroy me. He's a vengeful man, and I've tasted his wrath before when he stripped me of everything, and as I said, he has powerful friends. I'm sorry, but I can't risk crossing him again."

"We'll do everything to keep you safe," Trevor said.

Yes, of course, as they'd done years ago. "I'm sorry."

Emma looked about to burst into tears, and he had to suppress the impulse to hold her. "Will you think about it? Please? You're the only one we trust."

"I'll do that." He probably wouldn't, but he wanted to end the conversation.

She came closer again, and he had to ignore the quick thumping of his heart. "I thought about you."

He'd thought about her as well. Every day, no matter how miserable, how hungry or how cold, she'd been his happy thought.

But he never, ever thought of her when he was with his ladies. Bringing Emma into those moments seemed wrong, like soiling her.

"And..." She took a deep breath but didn't add anything else.

"Emma, we should leave." Trevor put his hat back on. "We must respect his choice and give him time to think."

"Thank you," Marcus said.

"But if you need anything, please come to us. I mean it. Do not hesitate." Trevor put an elegant calling card on the table.

Marcus wasn't sure if he would ever use it.

sixteen

Emma couldn't focus on her needlework in the sitting room. She loved needlework. It relaxed her, and creating beautiful compositions of flowers was a form of art. But after the meeting with Marcus, she kept thinking about him; she kept worrying about him.

He was leaner than she remembered but with taut muscles and the wary expression of someone who expected a beating at any moment. And goodness, that house! Damp and dark with cold draughts and the smell of mould.

She wanted to drag him out of that horrible place, make him warm and comfortable, and give him a good portion of stew. But no. Instead, she'd babbled some nonsense about having thought of him. Not very helpful to him.

She tossed the needlework on the sofa and marched to Trevor's study.

"Trevor?" She inched the door open.

He was hunched over his desk, surrounded by documents and papers. "Yes?"

"Listen—"

He closed his fists against his eyes. "No, please! My ears work perfectly. I can't help but listen to every sound, including your voice."

"No, you mean hearing. You can hear everything, but you don't always listen. It's different, like seeing and observing."

"I'm listening," he said, drumming his fingers on the desk.

"Stop being so dramatic. I'm thinking about Marcus. We should have been more insistent with him. Why didn't we insist more?" She paced over the carpet. "Perhaps we should see him again."

He leant back in the chair. "Marcus is an adult with a troubled past. He's used to doing everything on his own. Insisting wouldn't lead anywhere. Let him mull the offer over, and he might change his mind. If he doesn't reply in a few days, we'll see him again."

"He didn't trust us when we said we could protect him from Sir Horace."

"Can you blame him? To be honest, I'm not sure if we can. Sir Horace seems to have friends everywhere. The prime minister is less popular."

She threw a hand up. "I should have told Marcus we would take care of the boy as well. Maybe he thought that, if he worked for us, he would need to leave the boy behind."

Trevor arched his brow. "Take the boy here? You must be bloody joking."

"Oh, Trevor. You wouldn't have to deal with the boy."

"But he would live here. I would hear his screams, hysterics, and tantrums, and he is what? Ten?"

"He looked like twelve."

"That makes the whole difference." He waved dismissively. "No children. We can take care of the boy from a safe distance."

"You're impossible. One day, you'll get married and produce an heir. What will you do then?"

"Pay someone to take care of the child until he's one and twenty."

She shot her gaze upwards. "Never mind. I'll go to Marcus right now."

"Emma, please." He stood up. "Leave him be for now. Let him think our offer through. He has our address. If he changes his mind, he knows where to find us. Don't push him. Please. We'll try again in a few days if he doesn't send word."

She exhaled. "All right. But if Marcus eventually decides to work for us, the boy is going to stay here."

"No." He pressed a finger to the desk. "No children. And that's my last word on the matter."

A WEEK HAD PASSED since Marcus had seen Emma and Trevor, and Jesse hadn't improved. He kept coughing and shivering in the cold flat. The fever had returned, even though Marcus had followed the physician's instructions religiously.

He hadn't recovered from the shock of seeing Emma again and still hadn't decided if it was a good or a bad shock. One smile from her, and his pulse raced, erasing the smiles and touches of all the women he'd been with. Emma destroyed the memories of any other woman with one glance.

But if he'd been beneath her years ago, now he wasn't worthy of polishing her slippers. She was a dream, returned to torment him.

He added another blanket over a shivering Jesse. Thunder and rain battered the house, reminding him of that fateful night in Newport-on-Tay when his life had changed.

"Jesse?" He touched the boy's forehead. It was boiling. "How do you feel?"

Jesse's face was red and sweaty, and his pupils were so dilated the brown irises weren't visible. A gurgling noise came out of him when he tried to speak.

As Marcus rummaged through the bag with the drugs and

potions the physician had given him, a noise coming from the kitchen caught his attention. Water was gushing inside the flat from underneath the front door. A pool gathered quickly in the middle of the kitchen, fuelled by the torrential rain.

Jesse coughed again. The cough was so strong he convulsed in the bed, teeth chattering. Cold gusts swept the room. The water trickled farther into the kitchen, and his fear grew with the rising level of the water.

"Enough." He put his coat on and wrapped all the blankets he had around Jesse before gathering him up in his arms.

Jesse muttered something unintelligible.

He made sure the boy was properly covered before carrying him out of the bedroom. "We're leaving. I'll get you somewhere better."

The water reached his ankles in the short time he crossed the kitchen.

Before leaving, he snatched Trevor's calling card from the table.

seventeen

A storm battered London without pause that night.

Emma was sitting in her favourite bay window in the library, watching the impressive downpour, the flashes of lightning, and the drops of rain pelting the glass. And she couldn't stop worrying about Marcus and the boy.

That decrepit, unsafe house might get flooded. She'd learnt a thing or two about bad houses since she and Trevor had started their project in St. Giles.

Were Marcus and the boy safe? She was warm and comfortable in her beautiful house while he lived in that horrid place. Maybe she should pay him a visit right now, not because she wanted to ask him again about the work, but to see how he was faring and convince him to accept her help.

She shoved off the blanket covering her legs and stood up when the door opened.

Stewart gave her a quick bow. "My apologies, my lady, but there's a man, who claims to be Mr. Kingston, at the rear door. He said that you and His Lordship invited him here. He wants to see you urgently, and His Lordship has just left for his club."

"Marcus!" She ran towards the servants' entrance.

"He's changed a lot." Stewart followed her downstairs towards the rear entrance. "I hardly recognised him."

She rushed past Mrs. Daubney, who wrung her apron and shifted her weight.

"We're worried, my lady," Mrs. Daubney said.

Emma skidded to a stop at the end of the corridor. Completely soaked and dripping water, Marcus stood next to the door, holding a bundle of blankets. A shock of stillness went through her.

"My lady." He sounded breathless. "I beg you. Jesse is sick. I'll do everything you want if you help him. I'll work for you. I'll stay here, but please help Jesse."

"My lady," Mrs. Daubney tilted her head to stare at Emma. "Them boys seem to be starving."

Emma blinked. "Good Lord, of course. Come in." She turned towards Stewart. "Send for Sir Paul immediately and have the blue room ready."

"At once." Stewart left in a hurry.

Mrs. Daubney exhaled. "Thank you."

"Prepare a hot meal for our guests," Emma said to the cook.

Mrs. Daubney beamed. "With pleasure, my lady."

"Thank you," Marcus said in a broken voice.

"We'll take Jesse to my room for now. It's warm and dry. Follow me." Emma went up the stairs, concerned and relieved at the same time.

Marcus's soft footfalls were a contrast with the boy's laboured breathing.

"Is he running a fever?" she asked.

"Yes. It's getting worse."

She opened the door to her bedroom. "Our physician is excellent." She lifted the covers to make space for Jesse.

Marcus discarded the soaked blankets on the floor and laid him gently on the bed. "I'm sorry to have barged in here, but Jesse was burning up, and then water started to flood the flat. I didn't know what to do."

"Marcus." She touched his arm but withdrew her hand when he tensed and drew in a sharp breath. "You did the right thing. You don't need to apologise."

He wiped his wet hair from his face, shivering.

She caressed Jesse's hair. The boy was breathing heavily, and his face was red with fever. "Why don't you go downstairs and ask Mrs. Ferguson, the housekeeper, to have a hot bath drawn for you? Ask her for some dry clothes as well."

"I want to stay close to Jesse."

"You'll catch a cold, too, unless you change. That won't help Jesse. I'll stay with him until the doctor arrives."

He pressed his lips together and nodded. Before leaving, he paused at the door. "Thank you."

"You're more than welcome."

She sat on the edge of the bed once alone. Jesse stirred, scrunching up his face in pain. He muttered something, and she leant closer to hear him.

"What is it, dear?"

"Mama?" He opened his large brown eyes; the pupils were fully dilated. "Where were you when I cried for you last night?"

Emotion tightened her throat. She held his burning hand. "I'm here now, darling. All will be well."

"I was scared." His voice sounded raspy.

"I'm here now," she repeated, caressing his matted hair.

He squeezed her hand tightly and muttered something she didn't understand.

Trevor wasn't at home. He wouldn't be pleased to learn she'd let Marcus and Jesse in. But then again, Trevor was never pleased.

She held the boy's hand until Stewart showed Sir Paul into the bedroom.

"Lady Emma." He gave her a quick bow, glancing at the bed. "Is this boy the patient?"

"His name is Jesse." She stepped aside to give space to the

physician, but the moment she released Jesse's hand, he wheezed and coughed.

"Mama, don't leave me!"

She rushed back to him. "I'm here." She took his hand again. "I'm not going anywhere."

His breathing was laboured, but he calmed when she took his hand.

Sir Paul frowned as he visited the boy, checking his eyes, pulse, and chest. "What did they give him?" He leant closer to him. "It seems the boy had too much laudanum and something else which someone with a running fever shouldn't take."

"But he's going to be all right, isn't he?"

"I'll do my best, my lady. I'll give him some valerian for the pain and salt of tartar for the cough. At least he'll sleep decently tonight, and sleep is the best cure."

The boy squeezed her hand tightly throughout the visit, and her vision blurred a little at the boy's pain.

When the physician left, Jesse was soundly asleep, his breathing already better than before. The nightstand was filled with bottles of potions.

She caressed his forehead, brushing the thick locks from his face. The fever was still high, but he wasn't shivering anymore.

Marcus knocked on the doorframe before entering the bedroom. His hair was wet from the bath, but he wore a brown suit that had to be warm and thick.

"Come in," she said, waving him in.

"How is he?"

"Better. Sir Paul said the syrup Jesse had taken made the sickness worse, but he's asleep now. He needs rest and light food. We'll take good care of him. Don't worry." She kept saying that, but he didn't look relieved.

No matter what Marcus decided to do with her offer, she would make sure Jesse recovered quickly. She hated the fact that Marcus agreed to work for her only out of desperation. She wanted to tell him she and Trevor would think about the boy even if Marcus refused the job.

He stroked Jesse's head with tenderness. "Thank you. I'll do my best to repay your generosity."

No, there was no need for that. "About that. I need to talk to you."

Tension returned quickly to his shoulders. "I thought so."

"You said you would do everything to keep Jesse safe, and I guess you meant it."

"I did." He narrowed his eyes.

"Well, I have a proposition for you. Something between just you and me, if you know what I mean." She would deal with Trevor later. He would bark and grumble, but she wouldn't change her mind.

"I know what you mean. But not here." He was flustered and… angry? "Can we go somewhere else? In case Jesse wakes up."

"My personal study is next door."

He frowned deeply. "The study?"

"What better place?"

His puzzled expression confused her.

Worried by his sudden tension, she opened the door to the study and shut it behind them once Marcus was inside. She sat on the Chesterfield sofa while he took the armchair in front of her.

The sizzling log fire made the atmosphere cosy, despite the lingering tension between them.

"I know you were serious when you said you would do anything for Jesse," she said, trying to find the right words to offer him her help without offending him.

As Trevor had said, insisting would have the opposite result with Marcus, so she would be subtle.

"I understand what you mean," he said in his deep, strained voice.

"Do you?"

He nodded, scrubbing the back of his neck.

That was a relief. Less talk on her part.

"Well, so what do you think?" She didn't fully understand his behaviour though, and he didn't say anything else.

"Are you married?"

The question surprised her, not because she found it improper, but because her marital status had nothing to do with the job offer or Jesse's well-being.

"No." A nervous giggle escaped her. "I don't even have an intended." Why did she add that?

"So we won't be disturbed."

"No," she repeated but more cautiously. Was she missing something?

"What do you like?"

So they were back to knowing each other better. Although since after the tragedy, they hadn't had the chance to do that.

She trapped her bottom lip between her teeth. "I like so many things I wouldn't know where to start."

"Let's start then and see how it goes."

She was speechless for a moment. "Right."

He sucked in a deep breath and clenched his fists over his knees. The fabric of his jacket strained across his shoulders as he tensed further. Perhaps he already regretted having declared his commitment to a job he didn't like with people he didn't trust, but she would reassure him shortly.

When he looked up, it was as if a mask had dropped on his face. Any signs of fragility and worry were gone, replaced by an emotional coldness that left her shivering.

Before she could say anything, he stood up and started unbuttoning his jacket. It was a little hot in the study what with the big stove in the corner, the thick carpet, and the wooden wainscoting. He had to be too warm. But when he discarded the jacket and unbuttoned his shirt, a moment of shock took her.

"What...what are you doing?" She wished her voice didn't sound so squeaky.

He lowered his shirt, revealing his naked chest and fine body although a few thin scars were a testament to the hardship he'd endured.

"Am I allowed to kiss you?" he asked in a cold, professional tone.

She opened her mouth in disbelief. What was happening? Her brain didn't seem capable of doing anything.

"Kiss me?"

"It's your choice." He tossed the shirt on the jacket, standing gloriously half naked in front of her.

But when he started to work on the falls of his trousers, she returned to reality.

"Stop!" She shot up to her feet, chest heaving.

Her tone must have stunned him if the shocked expression on his face was any indication.

He kept his hands on the falls. "Have I done something wrong?"

"Who knows? I have no idea what you're doing." She didn't want to gaze upon his nakedness, but he was the first man she'd ever seen half naked in real flesh, and she was a little curious. And he was a little handsome. Well, more than a little.

"I think there's a misunderstanding here," she said. Alas, she had no idea which type though. "What are you doing exactly?"

He thankfully removed his hands from the falls of his trousers. "You want me to lie in bed with you, don't you?"

"Heavens, no!" She turned around to face the stove. Now, the temperature was indeed too hot. "Please get dressed."

There was a moment of silence. Then the swish of fabric came from behind her.

"I'm dressed," he said.

She faced him again, relieved to find him fully covered. She rubbed her burning forehead. "I didn't mean that you and I...I mean, you know what I mean." Embarrassment had taken control of her speech.

"I'm sorry. I misunderstood you."

Obviously. What kind of people had he met? What kind of person did he think she was? She would never take advantage of him in *that* way.

Her legs quivered, so she sat down again, focusing on her hands. "What I meant to say is that I'm going to take care of Jesse no matter what you decide to do with the job. It doesn't matter if you don't want to work with us. I don't want you to feel forced into doing something you don't want to as if I were blackmailing you. That's all."

"That would be charity. I'll accept wages for a work well done."

"I only want Jesse to be healthy."

He sat down again. "And I want to work for you. It's not only fair, but I thought about your proposition, and I believe Sir Horace's work puts people's lives at risk. People shouldn't get hurt because I'm worried Sir Horace will retaliate."

"Trevor and I will do everything to protect you." She must have said something wrong because his grey eyes suddenly became sharp. "Nevertheless, should you change your mind, we won't force you to do anything you don't want, and Jesse will be taken care of anyway."

Another long moment of silence filled the room. The thunder boomed, offering much-needed noise.

"Thank you," he finally said in a sweet tone that made her sigh.

"I'll tell Stewart to have a room ready for you."

"Do not worry. I'll sleep where Jesse is sleeping. I want to make sure he's all right."

"I'll have a chaise longue carried to the bedroom then."

His eyes remained hard. "I can sleep on the floor. It wouldn't be the first time."

"There's no need for you to sleep on the floor. You're in my house, and I'll do everything to make you comfortable."

"I'm used to living without any comforts."

She pressed her lips tightly. Their awkward conversation had turned into a competition in endurance of discomfort. Of course, he would be the winner.

She jutted out her chin. "You and Jesse are my guests. I'll have the chaise longue delivered to Jesse's bedroom. You decide what to do with it."

"Fair enough."

"Good."

"Good."

eighteen

Marcus didn't sleep well even though the chaise longue —he'd decided to use it, after all—in Jesse's bedroom was better than the bed in his flat, he was warm and dry, and Mrs. Daubney had arranged an excellent dinner for him. Also, Jesse had slept peacefully through the night, never waking up to cough.

He shouldn't complain.

But being in Emma's house and needing her help made him uncomfortable. Not because he was above asking for help, but because it was *her*.

He'd accepted charity from people when he'd lived on the streets, but those had been strangers. She wasn't.

After all those years, his feelings towards her hadn't changed. If anything, they'd sharpened and became enriched with flavours, like fine aging wine in an oak barrel.

She still was the most breathtakingly beautiful woman he'd ever seen. Her eyes held him captive whenever she looked at him, and her lively personality made him feel kissed by the sunshine. But he had made a fool out of himself last night. He'd assumed she wanted to have a tumble with him in exchange for having sent for the doctor. Habit. Tumbles had been his currency as of late.

Her face had been of horror then disgust. Disgust for him.

He was glad she hadn't meant to bed him because, while he still had romantic dreams about her, he didn't want to bed her only to settle a debt. It would be like spoiling his feelings for her.

Knowing she didn't have a suitor had been a sweet relief. Being engaged or married wasn't something he usually cared about a woman who wanted to pay to be with him, but she was another matter.

Sitting on the bed, he put a hand on Jesse's forehead, glad the skin was not feverish anymore.

Jesse's eyes fluttered open. "Marcus." His voice was rough.

"How are you?"

The boy took some time to answer, rubbing his face and chest. "Better. Tired. What—" He sat bolt upright, gazing around. "Where are we? What's this place? Did I die?"

"No, silly. Calm down. Remember the lady who visited us the other day, Lady Emma? We're in her house."

Jesse eased back on the pillow. "Are we going to stay here?"

"For a while. At least until you've fully recovered." He pulled the covers up to Jesse's chin, lest he feel cold.

"This bedroom is incredible." Jesse gazed around. "You can tell it's for a lady."

Another reason to be bothered was that he was in her bedroom. Her honeysuckle scent was everywhere—in the air, on the bedsheets, and even on the chaise longue. It was like holding her. The pretty vanity with the perfectly arranged bottles of perfumes and creams was a further reminder of the intimacy of the room.

"I'll fetch you something to eat," Marcus said.

Jesse's eyes flared wide. "No. Don't leave me here alone."

"I'm not leaving you. I'll go downstairs to the kitchen and come back up."

"This house is probably so big that it'll take ages to go to the kitchen."

"Don't be so dramatic. It's downstairs. This isn't Buckingham Palace."

Jesse nodded, but his bottom lip quivered.

"Why are you afraid?"

Jesse tugged at his nightshirt. "It's a big house, and I don't know anyone."

"I'll be back in a few minutes. You're safe here."

The boy slid under the covers.

Marcus walked down the stairs but came to a stop upon hearing voices coming from the dining room.

"I don't understand why they're here." That was Trevor.

"I had to send for Sir Paul," Emma said. "The poor boy was feverish."

"You could have…" The rest of Trevor's sentence became unintelligible as he lowered his voice to a whisper.

"Honestly, I can't believe we're having this conversation." She sounded annoyed. "You're overreacting. As usual."

"I just want you to inform me when you make decisions that matter to both of us, you know, as if we were a family."

"You make a lot of decisions without telling me anything."

"So this is revenge."

"Oh, be quiet."

Marcus walked down the rest of the steps and made his presence evident in the dining room. If Trevor had something to say, then he should have a normal conversation with Marcus.

"Good morning." Marcus bowed. "My lord, my lady."

The scent of eggs, freshly baked bread, and kippers tickled his appetite. Emma, in a lovely yellow morning dress, was the best cure for his headache.

Her cheeks flushed, and she found her cup of tea suddenly fascinating. He pretended not to notice.

"Marcus." Trevor straightened. "Emma was telling me about your misadventure. I hope you and your friend are well."

"Very well, thanks to Lady Emma and her generosity."

"How's Jesse?" she asked, putting down her cup of tea.

"No fever for now. I was wondering if he could have some breakfast."

"By all means." She nodded at the footman, and Stewart arrived a moment later.

"My lady." The butler bowed.

"Ask Mrs. Daubney to prepare a breakfast tray for Jesse and Mr. Kingston, please."

"Of course, my lady." Stewart gave Marcus a nod. "Mr. Kingston."

He returned the greeting. And then he had no reason to stay in the dining room unless he wanted a confrontation. Thinking about Emma's shocked face when he'd asked her if he could kiss her didn't help him feel better. And Trevor didn't add anything else.

"I'll get back to Jesse," he said.

"Wait. I'll come with you." She folded her napkin on the table.

Trevor slanted her a glare but didn't say anything.

Marcus would make clear he wasn't the same man from five years ago. The loner, the quiet young man he'd been before didn't exist. He'd died on the streets and in the ladies' beds. "Is something the matter, my lord?"

"Not at all." Trevor rose. "And you can call me Trevor, as you've always done."

"And you can be honest with me, as you've always been."

"Are you accusing me of lying?" Trevor's tone changed.

"Yes," Marcus replied.

Instant tension sparked.

"Gentlemen, please." Emma gave a shake of her head at her brother. "What matters now is that Jesse recovers quickly. We can discuss anything else later."

Trevor sat down again. "Fine by me, but I'm not a liar. I'm a gentleman."

"Which sometimes is the same thing," he said.

Oddly enough, Trevor regarded him with interest. "I often wonder if people use rudeness as a substitute for wit."

"If we keep conversing, you might find that out." He could go on for hours.

Emma raised a finger when Trevor was about to reply. "This is not the right time. Please, both of you."

Trevor picked up a copy of *The Times* from the tray, hiding himself.

She beckoned Marcus to follow her and went up the stairs with a nervous twitch in her steps. "Don't mind Trevor."

"I guess he isn't happy to have us here."

"Of course he is."

"I heard your conversation. I didn't mean to, but Trevor's words were clear."

At the landing, she stopped and faced him. "Trust me. Trevor didn't mean anything with those words. I know him. He grumbles about any change at first. I ordered a new carpet, and he had a fit. I changed the menu, and he accused me of hating him. The last time I rearranged the shelves in the library, he refused to talk to me for two days. Being annoyed at everything is his first reaction. Do as I do—ignore him. As I said, I think we should think only of Jesse."

"You're right."

Jesse sat up in the bed when Marcus entered with Emma. He shifted his gaze from him to her as if worried they might take him away.

"Do I need to leave?" He lifted the covers.

"Not at all. Good morning. How do you feel?" Emma smiled, but Jesse didn't smile back.

He said something, but since he pressed the hem of the quilt against his mouth, his words couldn't be heard.

Marcus lowered Jesse's hands and the quilt. "What is it?"

Jesse swallowed. "I'm very well. Thank you, my lady."

Emma touched his forehead, and his eyes fluttered wide. "No fever, but your voice is raspy. Your throat must hurt."

"A little."

Right then, a maid entered, pushing a buffet trolley loaded with food. There was a bowl of soup, rye bread, scones, butter, porridge, and kippers. Marcus's stomach gave a loud roar. Emma glanced his way but didn't say anything.

"Blimey!" Jesse said, following the tray with his gaze. "Is that food all for us?"

"Yes," Emma said. "Mrs. Daubney wasn't sure what you would like."

"I'm not picky. As long as it's food, I'm happy." Jesse shifted his position, his chest rising quickly. "Is it for the whole week? We'll split it carefully, my lady."

"No." Emma frowned. "This is only breakfast. You need your strength, Jesse. A fresh meal will be served for lunch and supper."

Jesse's jaw dropped open. Even Marcus was impressed. He hadn't seen such abundance in years.

"Well." Emma flashed a smile that seemed forced. "Enjoy. I'll see you later."

The moment she shut the door, Jesse shoved aside the covers and threw himself over the tray. "Just in case she changes her mind, I'll finish the lot."

"Not so fast." Marcus took his arm. "You're still recovering and need to eat slowly, or you'll have a stomach ache."

Jesse didn't listen. He stuffed his mouth with a large piece of a scone, a generous spoonful of eggs, and some kipper.

Marcus clapped his back when he started to cough. "I told you. Slowly."

Eyes watering, Jesse sipped some tea and swallowed hard. "When will another occasion like this happen?"

He wiped a few crumbs from the bed with a napkin. "Every

day, if I start working for Lady Emma and the earl. There's no need to gorge yourself."

"Will you work for them?" Jesse paused, halfway to devouring a slice of bread.

"Yes, I will."

"You didn't want to."

"I changed my mind. The salary is too generous to refuse."

Jesse hugged him, saying something unintelligible because his mouth was full. Marcus hugged him back.

He didn't need to live in Emma's house for longer than necessary. With that salary, he could afford a nice flat for Jesse and himself.

And Trevor could keep his opinions.

MARCUS ADMITTED to a spot of uneasiness when he knocked on the door to Trevor's study. The fact he wasn't welcome in the house made him feel no different from when he was with one of his ladies. Except the pay was better, and he didn't have to remove his clothes.

"Come in," Trevor said from the other side.

He took a deep breath and entered. His heart gave a kick when he looked at Emma sitting in front of the desk. Sooner or later, he would get used to seeing her.

With the sunlight lighting her from behind, a golden halo formed around her hair. A familiar shiver he hadn't experienced in years danced on his skin as if no time had passed or nothing had happened since the last time he'd seen her.

His heart still remembered the time when she'd kissed his cheek or when they'd hugged each other.

"I hope Jesse is fine," Emma said.

"Thank you for taking care of him. I believe he would have died without your help."

Trevor nodded and gestured at the stuffed chair in front of his large oak desk. "Take a seat."

Marcus did as told.

Trevor cleared his throat. "So Emma told me you changed your mind about working with us."

"I did."

Trevor took out a leather folder from a drawer and put it on the desk. "This folder is one of the many that contain all the papers and reports regarding the homes we're building in St. Giles. You might want to start reading them before we take you to the construction site." He paused. "I suppose you'll need a week or two before you recover your full strength, too. Enough time for you to read everything."

"Excuse me?" Marcus leant forwards.

"Trevor." Emma squared her shoulders.

Trevor frowned. "I didn't say anything offensive. You're quite pale, Marcus, and with signs of exhaustion. I'm not a physician—"

"I can take care of myself," Marcus said.

Trevor narrowed his eyes. "But even I can tell you need rest. And I would like to ask Sir Paul to visit you."

"Why?" Marcus and Emma asked together.

"Why not?" Trevor rebuked.

"I'm fine." Marcus closed his fists.

"Well," she said. "Marcus will need some time to study the documents anyway. So he'll have the opportunity to rest."

"I'm all right." Marcus wasn't sure why his voice sounded so strained or why Trevor's remark upset him so much, but for some reason, all the fuss about his well-being and the comments annoyed him.

They had no idea what he had to endure in the past years. From starvation to humiliation, he'd survived dark days. His well-being wasn't any of their concern.

"We're worried about you. That's all," Emma said in a low tone. "We don't mean any offence."

He took another deep breath, wondering why the hell he was so upset. Emma had done nothing but be kind to him and Jesse, and he had a good, honest job, thanks to her. His ladies had treated him worse than that, ordering him around and sometimes enjoying humiliating him. Still, he felt as if he were soliciting himself all over again, because he was out of place, and he didn't like the feeling. "I'm grateful for everything you've done so far for me, and I appreciate your concern. But you don't need to take care of me or worry about my health. After all, I've been on my own in the past years and survived." He grabbed the folder and stood up. "I'll start immediately. Thank you, my lord, my lady."

He bowed and strode out of the room, carrying his annoyance with him.

nineteen

Emma winced when Marcus left the study and closed the door behind him. "We offended him. Or worse, we hurt him."

Trevor exhaled and rubbed the bridge of his nose. "I just wanted to show my concern for his obvious fatigue. He has such evident dark shadows around his eyes that he looks like he was punched in the face. He hasn't slept properly in months. Maybe years. And what if he carries a disease?"

"Don't start. I share your concern about Marcus being tired." To an extent. After having seen Marcus shirtless, she was sure he wasn't starving. He was lean and muscular, not as broad and brawny as he'd been, but not scrawny as someone who lived on the streets. Although he wasn't the Marcus she remembered. And she wasn't thinking only of his body. He didn't radiate competence as he'd done before. "You should have been less direct."

"He isn't a stranger."

"In a way, he is. He isn't the same man we knew years ago."

She didn't want to linger too much about what Marcus had gone through those years, but he must have found himself in horrible situations.

"Fine," Trevor said. "But I'm trying to prevent an accident. A construction site is a dangerous place, especially when there might be foul play. I want him to be fit and strong before venturing up the scaffolding. I don't want him to faint and fall from a height. There have been incidents. We don't need another one."

He wasn't completely wrong.

"I'll talk to him."

"Fine by me."

She put a hand on the knob. "Trevor, please be patient. He didn't have an easy life, and we had a hand in that."

He fiddled with something under his hand. "He and the boy won't need to stay here more than a few days, will they?"

"I'm not going to answer that. They're my guests and will stay here for as long as they want. When did you become so heartless?"

"I like my privacy in my home." He lifted his hand, revealing Ophelia's locket, but the moment she glanced at it, he stuffed it in the drawer and shot her a warning look.

Whatever had happened with Ophelia, she didn't want to discuss that now. She had plenty of reasons to argue with her brother.

"Jesse is a nice boy, and you would like him, too, if you took the time to talk to him."

He propped his elbows on the armrests. "I don't like children. Is that a crime? I didn't like myself when I was a child."

"And look at the result." She shook her head and left the study.

The closer she got to Jesse's room, the slower she walked. There was some truth in what Marcus had said. She could have done more to help him because she wasn't like Papa, as she'd told him. As she'd told herself too many times to count.

Or maybe she was.

But she and Trevor had searched for him. Could they have done more? Maybe, but Marcus hadn't bothered sending word to them, either.

She knocked on the door. "Marcus, Jesse? May I come in?"

Marcus opened the door, stiff and cold. "My lady."

She wanted to tell him to call her Emma.

"Jesse is asleep again," he said. "I think he ate too much."

She watched the boy asleep in the large four-poster bed. His breathing was regular and soft, and his arms were spread wide as if he were about to hug someone.

He pointed at the window. "The frame has been repaired, quite nicely, too."

"You remember?"

A smile graced his lips. "I remember everything." He didn't sound as if he meant to reproach her for her lack of help.

A warm flutter started in her belly.

"I hired someone to repair it, but I wish it had been you."

"I'm not sure I'm still good at repairing things."

She was sure he was. "I have a room ready for you and another for Jesse. Follow me." She led him to the guest room and opened the door. "This room has an escritoire in the corner. You can read and study here. The library is downstairs, and Jesse's room is through that door." She pointed at the door on the other side of the room. "You and Jesse can stay here for as long as you want."

"Thank you." His tone was forcibly polite.

"I'm sorry if Trevor and I offended you. It wasn't our intention."

"I understand." But he sounded like he didn't.

"I tried to find you, and I know I could have done more to convince my father to help you. I regret that, too."

His dark eyebrows formed a sharp V. "You don't need to apologise."

"It seems I do have to, if you resent me."

"I don't. I regret what happened." He placed the folder on the escritoire. "And I'm having trouble adjusting to this new reality. For years, I did nothing but survive, worrying about my next meal. And now I'm here, surrounded by wealth. It's a huge change. I'm grateful for your help and offer." He touched the folder. "I won't disappoint you."

"I know. I trust you."

For the first time, a light had flickered in his grey eyes, resembling the spark of vitality she remembered.

"I'm happy to hear that," he said.

Another question lingered on the tip of her tongue, but whether she should ask it was debatable. "I was wondering..."

"Yes?"

"Forget it. It's nothing."

"I insist."

"Well, how come Jesse is with you? Forgive me, but when he was delirious, he talked about his mother, and I wondered if you knew her."

A muscle in his jaw ticked. "No, I didn't. I found him. He was starving and weak, living in the rookery. He begged for help, and I decided to take care of him. Not that I did a good job."

"That's not true. It must not have been easy for you, but hopefully now you won't have to worry about money anymore."

He kept working his jaw, and she was thrown back to those days in Thistle Hall when she'd tried to understand him. She hadn't been subtle back then and asked him blunt questions; she wouldn't be subtle now.

"Marcus." She moved closer to him, and he stiffened further. "I have the feeling that everything I say causes you nothing but pain."

"I'm not the same person I was years ago."

"Neither am I, but we were friends."

He averted his gaze before staring at her again. There was a harsh quality in his stare she couldn't dismiss.

"There are things about me you don't know and that I'm not ready to discuss now."

She had an idea. Living on the streets, he must have survived by stealing wallets and pocket watches when he didn't meet someone who took advantage of him. She wouldn't judge him for that. "I don't care. I know your heart."

Sadness crept into his crooked smile. "You can't be sure of that. Many things have happened since we last saw each other."

"Jesse is proof your heart hasn't changed. You're still the caring man who spent a day searching the river for survivors and who repaired my music box. That's all I need to know. As for the rest, it's your choice whether you want to share your past with me or not."

The grey in his eyes melted like frost in the sunlight. "Thank you, Emma."

She didn't know what he'd done, but she knew she would never, ever blame him.

twenty

Marcus begrudgingly had to admit Trevor had been right.

A week had passed since he had moved to Hart House, and the good meals, plenty of rest, and the warm bed had changed his body and mind for the better. For the first time in years, he felt strong and well rested; his head was clear and sharp, and he didn't get tired after reading for five minutes. At first, he'd had trouble reading the building reports and got a headache whenever he tried to focus. But now he could study and concentrate all day without feeling exhausted.

Jesse had improved as well. No fever or coughing. The only problem was that, despite his improved concentration, Marcus was making slow progress in reading the documents. He had to stop reading often to consult engineering manuals because he didn't remember a great many things.

The late morning sunlight streamed through the window when Jesse entered Marcus's bedroom. Emma had provided them with brand-new clothes, and Jesse wore a fine tweed suit, complete with a waistcoat and bow tie.

"How do I look?" he asked, fiddling with his bow tie.

"Elegant." He straightened Jesse's jacket. "Are you nervous?"

"No. I mean, it's the first time I've left my bedroom to have breakfast in the sunroom, and I don't want to do something terrible."

"You won't." He went downstairs with Jesse.

"I'm happy you taught me how to behave at a fine table."

"You'll do well. Just enjoy the meal."

"I'm starving," Jesse whispered. "But I won't stuff myself. I promise."

The sunroom was particularly bright that morning, especially because Emma wore a lemon gown that brightened the room further. She smiled when they entered, but Trevor frowned.

"Good morning." Marcus bowed his head and glanced at Jesse.

"Good morning." The boy bowed from the waist, his curls bobbing on his cheeks.

"I'm so happy to see you up and about, Jesse." Emma gestured at the chairs at the long table. "You must be bored, staying in the bedroom alone."

"I had a lot of fun," Jesse said. "I like my bedroom."

A pristine white tablecloth covered the table. White daisies filled the vases on the windowsills, and the scent of freshly baked scones teased Marcus's senses. The view brought him back to when he'd had breakfast with his parents in their beautiful townhouse. Mother had loved white daisies.

Jesse walked to the chair as if wearing boots made of lead. He pulled the chair back and grimaced when it screeched against the polished floor.

"Sorry," he said in a low voice.

"Let the footman do that," Marcus whispered.

"Do not worry, and choose what you want," Emma said.

Trevor hid behind an ironed copy of *The Times* as the footman carried plates of bacon and eggs to the table. Jesse groaned.

Marcus served him a not-too-big portion. "Eat slowly."

Jesse nodded, his eyes on the bacon.

"The napkin." He showed him how to properly fix the napkin on his collar.

Jesse copied him but fumbled with the napkin and the long flap of the tablecloth for a moment before getting it right.

"So how's the reading going?" Trevor asked, lowering the newspaper.

"I'm a bit slow," Marcus said, pouring tea for himself and Jesse. "But the project seems solid so far."

Emma buttered her scone. "We want to replace the awful, humid houses in the rookery with proper ones. The project was designed by one of the engineers working for Sir Horace. In fact, the whole venture is managed by his company. Papa chose it."

Marcus glanced at Jesse trying to cut his bacon into tiny pieces for some reason. "I have to give Sir Horace and his engineers credit for the project. We'll see if the execution follows the design." He winced when Jesse elbowed him hard while cutting the bacon.

"Sorry," Jesse muttered. "I was using the knife."

"I'm looking forward to knowing your opinion," Trevor said. "Now that Jesse is fine—"

"We could go somewhere all together," Emma completed, but he had the feeling Trevor had meant something else.

Trevor continued, "Actually, what I meant to say..."

The loud clatter of Jesse's fork against his plate rang out. Then a thick slice of bacon flew out of his plate to slap Trevor in the face and smear grease on his cheek and suit.

Everyone seemed to hold their breaths after a collective gasp. Jesse's mouth hung open as he wielded the knife. The footman remained with a foot forwards and an arm outstretched in the attempt to catch the wayward slice.

Trevor picked up the offending piece of bacon between his thumb and forefinger and deposited it on his plate, an expression of absolute disgust on his face.

"Well—" He didn't finish the sentence before Jesse scraped his chair backwards and darted out of the room.

Or tried to. Somehow, the hem of the tablecloth had got caught in his collar when he'd spread the napkin on his chest and the yank, caused by his sudden escape, thrust the cups, pot, plates, and trays of food forwards.

The cups toppled over. The teapot rattled, and the basket of bread, the plates of eggs, bacon, and the kippers tumbled to the floor.

Trevor, Emma, Marcus, and the footman shot up at the same time, spreading their arms to save the breakfast. In the midst of the chaos, Marcus's hand ended up on top of Emma's, and he sucked in a breath.

Aside from a few rare occasions when he'd touched her hand by chance or when he'd helped her out of the boat in the Tay River, he hadn't held her hand like that in a long time, with his palm fully on the back of her hand and his fingers lacing with hers.

His heart thumped faster, reminding him how little some things had changed in the past years. Her hand was so soft, like a warm petal made of silk and velvet, and he wished he could kiss her knuckles just once.

Her lips parted as she fluttered her long eyelashes at him.

"I'm sorry." Jesse's high-pitched voice broke the spell.

Sobbing, he waved his hands until he disentangled himself from the tablecloth before running away.

"What a disaster," the footman said under his breath.

He hurried to pick up the bread and straighten the tablecloth, but the tea had spilt everywhere, soaking what hadn't been thrown to the floor.

Marcus removed his hand from Emma's, collecting himself.

"What a bloody mess!" Trevor wrung his handkerchief soaked with tea.

"Trevor!" Emma said.

"I didn't say anything to the boy." Trevor wiped his face with a napkin.

"Your angry face scared him." Emma folded her arms over her chest.

"For heaven's sake. A little bit of trust would be appreciated. I wasn't going to scold him." He turned to the footman. "Neil, tell Adam I need a fresh suit."

"My lord." The footman left.

"You should talk to Jesse," Emma said.

Trevor gestured at the mess of food and stained cloths. "He made this disaster. What am I supposed to tell him?"

"That you aren't angry with him for having thrown bacon at your face by accident."

Trevor removed another piece of bacon from his collar. "Oh, I have many things to say to Jesse."

"I'll talk to him." Marcus picked up a few plates from the floor. "And I apologise on his behalf. He was very nervous this morning. He usually isn't so agitated."

"Nothing happened." She smiled encouragingly.

"Nothing?" Trevor slammed the napkin on the table. "Look at me. Look at the entire room."

"Stop being so harsh."

"I'm simply saying that something did happen."

"Listen—"

"No! I don't want to listen!" Trevor closed his fists.

"I'd better go," Marcus said.

Emma flashed him a genuine smile. "Please don't mind us. This is normal for us."

Marcus left the sun room quietly. The voices of the two arguing siblings followed him into the hallway.

He found Jesse in his bed hugging the pillow for dear life. "Jesse."

"I ruined everything. Are they going to kick us out?" His eyes were red and filled with unshed tears. "I don't want to return to that room in Seven Dials. It's cold, and I don't want cramps from hunger again."

"We aren't going anywhere." He sat next to Jesse. "It was an accident, and no one wants to kick us out, and even if they did, we won't return to that room. I promise."

"I wanted to cut the bacon into small pieces to eat it slowly and look more polite." Jesse wiped his eyes with the sleeve of his jacket. "But it was slippery, and I lost control. And then the cloth was stuck to me. And I ran…"

"It's all right."

"No, it's not. The earl wanted to kill me."

"Don't be silly."

Jesse hugged the pillow harder. "I won't eat with them ever again. I'll stay here and be quiet."

"You're exaggerating. I'm sure Lady Emma will want to see you again."

"But not the earl." Jesse shook his head, his eyes unblinking.

Marcus squeezed his shoulder. "Trust me. You won't starve again. That period is over."

One way or another.

twenty-one

After the disastrous breakfast and the endless conversation with Trevor, Emma went upstairs to Jesse's room.

She had no intention of throwing out of her house an orphan who had barely recovered from a serious bout of fever. Trevor was the earl, and the house belonged to him, but she wouldn't stay quiet, and he wouldn't be so harsh as to disregard her opinion entirely.

Another sore point was the ball they'd planned a while ago. After the breakfast incident, Trevor wanted to cancel it, claiming the two guests would cause disruptions. She disagreed. What did Jesse and Marcus have to do with a charity ball? They were welcome to join the guests.

Trevor could argue all he wanted, but she would carry on with her plans and host the charity ball. It was a family tradition started by Mother, and she wouldn't be intimidated by one of Trevor's fits.

She knocked on the door. "Jesse? May I come in?"

"Yes, yes."

Shivering, he shot up to his feet when she entered. His eyes were red and puffy, and her heart clenched for him.

"Lady Emma," he stammered. "I, I'm sorry."

"Don't worry, dear. I came here to see how you were faring."

"I'm sorry," he said again.

"Nothing terrible happened. I want you to understand that. It was an accident."

He nodded, staring at the floor.

"Will I see you at lunch? Mrs. Daubney told me you asked her if you could eat in the kitchen."

He nodded.

"So I'll see you at lunch?"

"No, I mean, I will eat in the kitchen from now on."

"Don't let what happened discourage you. I would enjoy your company during lunch."

He didn't say anything.

She wanted to hug him but wasn't sure about his reaction. "Is Marcus in his room? I would like to talk to both of you."

"He went to fetch some tea for my throat. It burns a little."

Right then, Marcus entered, carrying a tray with a couple of cups and a pot of tea, and her hand—the one he'd taken quite fiercely—felt the weight of his hand. The sudden hand-touching had been a bizarre moment. In the midst of the chaos and the smell of bacon, their hands had found each other, and the world had stopped. A gesture so simple yet so intense.

Marcus cleared his throat. "Emma...Lady Emma."

"I came to reassure Jesse that nothing terrible had happened and to give you both good news. We're giving a ball for charity." She smiled widely. "Isn't that exciting?"

Judging by their serious faces, the answer was a resounding no.

Marcus frowned, and Jesse didn't raise his gaze from the floor.

She didn't desist. "There will be a lot of excellent food and music."

"I'm too young for a ball," Jesse mumbled.

"Yes, but..." *Heavens*. Her plan had backfired. "You could listen to the music in the parlour. And you can enjoy the food, and there will be a cake with whipped cream and strawberries and a sorbet as well."

That got Jesse's attention. "Blimey. I've tasted cream only once."

She heaved a sigh of relief at his interest. "I'll have a special portion of whipped cream and strawberries prepared for you alone."

Jesse smiled. It wasn't a bright, wide smile, but it was a start. Marcus, on the other hand, didn't seem pleased at all.

"Will you attend the ball, Marcus?" she asked.

She knew he didn't dance, but surely, he would enjoy a ball after so many years away from society.

He looked annoyed. "I don't think it would be appropriate."

"Why would you say that?"

He shot a quick glance at Jesse. "I'm not exactly welcome in society. Perhaps it would be better if I remained unseen for now. I can't stay hidden indefinitely, but if I can avoid exposing myself, I will."

"Oh, right." She folded her hands in front of her and unfolded them again.

Jesse was indeed too young, and Marcus had been shunned by society. How silly of her to think they would be happy to attend her ball.

She should leave. "Well, I hope I'll see you at lunch then."

Jesse bowed his head, and Marcus gave her one of his enigmatic, intense stares that made her toes curl.

The more she tried to repair the relationship with Marcus, the worse it turned.

MARCUS POURED a cup of tea for Jesse after Emma left the bedroom, leaving a trail of her flowery scent behind.

She'd sounded so enthusiastic that rejecting her invitation had bothered him.

A ball. That was the last thing he needed. Finding himself face-to-face with his lady clients would be embarrassing, to say the least. Potentially dangerous at worst.

The prospect of whipped cream didn't cheer up Jesse for long. He lay on the bed, hugging the pillow again.

"Why are you sad now?" Marcus asked.

"Whipped cream. Where will I find another lady who gives me whipped cream, even if I'm bad?"

"The important thing is that you didn't do it on purpose. That would have been terrible."

Jesse sat upright, hugging the pillow. "But I don't belong in this house. I'm not a toff. I don't mind staying with the servants in the kitchen. Mrs. Daubney is nice."

There was a knock on the door.

"Boy, are you there?" It was Trevor.

Jesse pulled the pillow up to cover his face and shook his head. "Tell him that I'm not here."

"We have to see what he wants." Marcus opened the door. "My lord." He kept his tone neutral, mostly for Jesse's sake.

Trevor stepped into the bedroom. "There you are, boy."

Marcus signalled Jesse to stand up. The boy obeyed, slightly bending over and still clenching the pillow.

"I'm sorry, my lord," he said. "I didn't mean to cause that disaster. I'll be good. I promise."

Trevor was wearing a fresh suit, but a faint smell of bacon lingered around him. "Accidents happen. I caused accidents when I was a child, too. Not that I remember any of them."

If that was all Trevor had to say, Marcus doubted Jesse would feel better.

The boy twisted a corner of the pillow. "I'm sorry for all the food that got wasted, too. All that bread, eggs, and bacon could have fed a family for a week."

"A week?" Trevor huffed. "Hardly. There wasn't that much food."

Jesse shook his head with energy. "No, my lord. If one is careful and splits the food into small portions, it lasts many days. Marcus and I have done that several times with smaller amounts of food than your breakfast. We still got hungry, but we had enough not to faint."

Marcus rubbed his forehead, wondering if he should tell Jesse to stop talking.

"Faint?" Trevor sounded shocked.

"Fainting is worse than cramps because your head spins before you pass out." Jesse nodded. "And you don't know where you might collapse. A footpad might rob you where you lie. Not that we had anything worth stealing, but once, when I came around, someone stole my shoes. Walking back home was terrible. My feet—"

Marcus cleared his throat. "Perhaps the earl isn't interested in these details." And they felt a bit too intimate to be revealed for some reason.

"I am, actually," Trevor said. "Continue, boy."

"My feet were all cut and sore by the time I arrived home. A lesson for me." Jesse finally put the pillow on the bed. "It's a shame you had to throw that food away because of me."

Trevor's expression was unreadable, like someone who didn't want to tell a person he didn't speak their language. "I'll make sure that nothing goes to waste. Mrs. Daubney will certainly find a way to save the food."

Jesse exhaled. "Good. I was worried. When I had cramps, I would devour everything, even if it was covered in dirt. I volunteer to eat the ruined food if Mrs. Daubney doesn't know what to do with it. A boy who lived next to us in Seven Dials once had a bad tummy because he ate a sandwich he found on the pavement. But hunger is hunger, my lord. It doesn't care about a bad tummy."

Marcus rubbed the spot between his eyebrows. Never would he have revealed those details to anyone.

Trevor regarded Jesse through a narrow gaze that could mean anything. "Well, no need to worry, lad. I doubt you'll have a bad tummy from eating in my house."

"That's good to know, my lord," Jesse continued. "Do you want to hear another story?"

Trevor gave him a graceful nod.

"Once, I found an apple, and I was hungry, but I shared it with a pony."

"Did you now?" Trevor perked up.

"Yes, I love horses, and the pony looked sad, so I gave him the apple." Jesse smiled. "He was a gentle animal, and you don't find that among people often."

Trevor looked surprised, or maybe Marcus didn't understand him.

"Excellent story. Now, rest and enjoy...everything you want. I need a word with Marcus. Your room," Trevor said and strode out of the room without looking to see if Marcus was following him.

Before closing the door between their rooms, Marcus gave a reassuring smile to Jesse who waved back without confidence.

"We'll eat in the kitchen from now on," Marcus said the moment he was alone with Trevor.

"If you feel more comfortable, I understand." Trevor gave a brusque nod.

He didn't expect any other answer from the earl. "What did you want to tell me?"

"As you must have guessed, your presence here wasn't previously discussed with me. Emma made the decision without informing me."

"Jesse was sick, and you weren't here."

"Yes," Trevor said, "but my point is that we didn't discuss the rules."

"Rules?"

"The first rule is..." Trevor scratched his chin.

He closed a fist. "Yes?"

Trevor stepped closer. "You'll keep your distance from my sister."

That shouldn't be a surprise. Trevor hadn't approved of Marcus as a probable suitor of Emma when he'd been an eligible candidate. He wouldn't approve of him now.

"I would never, ever hurt Emma."

"Good. Another thing..." Trevor paused again. "Make sure the boy doesn't faint." He left the room without waiting for Marcus's reply.

twenty-two

By the time the night of the ball arrived, Marcus knew the building papers and reports backwards.

He'd seen Emma very little, and due to her errands and appointments before the ball, he and Jesse hadn't shared any meals with her or Trevor, which was good for Jesse.

The kitchen was perfect for enjoying their meals. They could be themselves in the company of the cook and the servants, and Jesse didn't have to worry about etiquette.

Marcus was ready to inspect the construction site, and a combination of anticipation and anxiety bothered him.

There was another reason to be bothered, particularly that night.

As he watched the endless stream of carriages stopping in front of Hart House from the window in his bedroom, he wondered if any of his lady clients would be present. Lady Beaumont had to wonder what had happened to him. He'd up and vanished from one day to the next, and he hadn't checked the post office in a while. There were other ladies who might be looking for him, and they could be there that night.

"Marcus, look." Jesse waved him closer from the door opening between their rooms. "Look at this beauty."

A large bowl filled with whipped cream and sliced strawberries lay on his table, looking like a soft mountain of snow. Impressive.

"Do you want a taste?" Jesse grabbed the teaspoon, ready to attack the cream. "Mrs. Daubney said it's for both of us."

"No. Enjoy it. But don't eat it all. It's too much. You'll get sick."

"Don't worry." Jesse picked up a strawberry and licked the cream off it. "So good!"

Marcus settled on an armchair in his room to read another report, wanting to be thorough and needing a distraction from his worries.

Muffled violin music and laughter came from downstairs. He wondered if Emma would dance tonight with a gentleman who might become her suitor. She hadn't mentioned anything although he shouldn't care one way or another. That dream was good and dead.

His mind enjoyed tormenting him, and he found it difficult to focus on reading.

The carriages had stopped arriving. All the guests had to be downstairs. He rubbed his tired eyes. He should leave Hart House and—a groan came from the other room.

Jesse shuffled towards him, looking green. "I think I ate too much." He put a hand on his belly. "I have a stomach ache."

Marcus lowered the document. "You ate it all."

Jesse nodded. "I couldn't stop."

"Jesse!" He exhaled. "Cramps?"

"A little." Jesse clamped a hand on his mouth. "The cream wants to come out again."

"You're nauseous."

"I'm sorry," Jesse muttered.

"I'll ask Mrs. Daubney for some ginger brew and rosemary oil."

Jesse dropped himself into the armchair, groaning.

"In case you feel sick." He handed Jesse an empty bowl.

As he went down the stairs, the sound of the music grew stronger, and the scent of vanilla and cinnamon mingled with perfumes and expensive colognes.

He paused in the hallway that led to the kitchen when he caught a glimpse of Emma in the ballroom.

Pearls and gold glittered in her complicated chignon, and her gown was a triumph of white and light green silk. So beautiful.

She laughed at something the gentleman in front of her said. Her pearl earrings swung back and forth, catching the light like two stars on her skin. The layers of silk draped down her body, exalting her waist.

She was so beautiful that watching her hurt.

He had to remind himself he wasn't a respectable gentleman with a good income anymore. If she learnt the truth about his past as a man-whore, she wouldn't let him stay in her house.

He hurried to the kitchen, brushing past maids and footmen in a hurry to carry trays to the ballroom.

"Mrs. Daubney?"

"What is it, dear?" She wiped her hands on her apron and, even though a dozen unfinished plates lay on the table, she smiled at him.

"Jesse ate the whole bowl of cream and strawberries."

Her gaze flew towards the ceiling. "I shouldn't have sent him the whole thing. What do you need?"

"Ginger brew and rosemary oil."

"Over there."

He fetched everything Jesse needed while Mrs. Daubney finished arranging tiny sandwiches on a multi-layered tray.

"I'm glad you and Jesse are here with us," Mrs. Daubney said. "Don't get discouraged by His Lordship. He isn't the same since Miss Ophelia broke their engagement."

"He must have cared for her a lot."

Mrs. Daubney nodded. "After she left him, he didn't go riding for a month, so sad he was."

"That says it all."

To return upstairs, he chose a secondary corridor, not to walk too close to the ballroom and see Emma again. He sped up but skidded to a grinding halt when he rounded a corner and found himself face-to-face with Lady Beaumont in a flamboyant red gown.

"What the h—" The shock froze him for a moment. He went to return to the kitchen, but she tugged at his wrist with surprising strength.

"So it's true." She raked a slow gaze over him. "You live here now."

Hell. He put the tray on a nearby table. "My lady." He bowed his head, searching the hallway for Emma or Trevor. "I don't live here. I temporarily work here." At least that was true.

Her cheeks became the colour of her gown. "You disappeared." She placed a gloved hand on his chest, inching closer. "I searched for you everywhere. Then my maid heard rumours about a handsome man living with bland, boring Lady Emma of all ladies. Other rumours claimed it was you, but I didn't believe them."

He stepped back to get some distance from her, but she hounded him.

"I need to go," he said in a firm tone.

"Go? You vanished without a word, and now you want to leave me again?" She pressed her chest against his. The top of her breasts was pushed up over the neckline of her gown. "I demand satisfaction." She grabbed his crotch with a firm hand.

He winced and took her wrist. "My lady, I must go."

"I'll give you five pounds if we have a quick tumble in the drawing room." She fondled him, and a cold shiver slithered up his neck.

"I can't." He removed her hand, suppressing a groan of pain as her grip hurt him.

"Ten pounds."

"I can't."

"Twenty pounds," she insisted.

"It's not a game. I don't do paid tumbles anymore."

"Fantastic. I won't pay you, then." She went to grab him again, but he blocked her.

He wished anger were the only emotion burning within him, but humiliation won the race. Lady Beaumont's behaviour was the result of his subservience and desperation. He couldn't blame only her.

"No. I'm not interested."

She let out a half-laugh. "You can't be serious."

"Very. Now, if you'll excuse me, I have to leave." Holding her by the waist, he moved her out of his way, ignoring his boiling blood and the sense of shame pressing against his chest.

She was a persistent woman. "But you need me and my money, don't you? We have a deal."

"I'm afraid we don't."

She moved closer again. "You belong to me, Marcus. Whatever sum Emma pays you, I'll double it. I would have never imagined that Emma was like her brother."

"Excuse me?" he asked, curious despite himself.

"Rumour has it Trevor had a relationship with a prostitute."

"That is none of my concern." And he didn't care about gossip. He picked up the tray again and sidestepped her. "I wish you well, my lady, but we can't see each other any longer. Goodbye."

And he didn't belong to anyone. Only his heart belonged to a woman he could never have.

"Think about what you're missing. You'll regret this," she said in a calm, cold tone. "And I don't believe you. Whatever brought you to say something so awful to me, I forgive you."

"You managed to contradict yourself four times in one sentence."

He hurried towards the stairs, a sense of lightness spreading through his chest...at first. Then fear for his future gripped him harder than Lady Beaumont's hand.

If his new venture ended up badly, he would need ladies like Lady Beaumont again. He shouldn't have been so drastic. Living in Emma's beautiful house and eating regularly made him feel absolutely frightened of ever living on the streets again, which didn't make sense. He'd lived hand-to-mouth for years; he should be used to it. But the comforts of Hart House made him weak and bold at the same time—weak because he didn't want to leave the comforts Hart House offered, and bold because he would have never replied in that way to Lady Beaumont.

A groan came from the bedroom when he entered. Jesse was bent over the bowl.

"Here." He gave Jesse a glass of ginger brew. "Drink it."

Jesse scrunched up his face. "It tastes like the water from the Thames."

"Maybe next time you'll remember not to wolf down everything."

Jesse groaned again. "What happened to you?"

Marcus shrugged.

"You look as green as I do." Jesse swallowed hard, squinting his eyes.

"I'm tired. That's all."

Jesse put the glass aside to touch his hand. "I promise I won't do anything embarrassing again. You don't have to worry."

"It's not you." He patted Jesse's shoulder. "I'm worried about something I did in the past."

"Your job," Jesse whispered. "The one you had before coming here."

He neither denied nor confirmed. "Let's say I promise not to do anything embarrassing, either."

twenty-three

Standing in the hall on her sore feet, Emma looked forward to saying goodbye to the last of her guests and going to bed. The event had been a success. Her guests had been generous, and they'd raised a few thousand pounds to donate to a children's hospital.

She pasted a polite smile on her lips as she bowed her head over and over to the ladies and lords filing out of Hart House. Trevor did the same although his smile looked more strained.

"Good night," she said to Lady and Lord Redfern. "Thank you for coming. It was delightful to see you here."

"Lovely night." Lady Redfern paused and seemed about to say something.

"Is something the matter?" Emma worried the lady might start chatting and keep her up for another twenty minutes.

Lady Redfern craned her neck right and left as if looking for someone as her husband walked ahead towards the front door. "Nothing. Good night, Emma, Pembroke."

Trevor bowed without making any effort to smile.

"Who is left?" he whispered after Lady Redfern finally left.

"Only a few people. A bit of patience. I'm tired, too."

"If I smile one more time, I'll need surgery to mend my face."

"Because you aren't used to smiling."

"The night wasn't entirely pleasant. I wanted to punch Lord Wallace, but I forced myself not to. You should be proud of me."

"What did he do?" she asked.

Trevor tensed. "He refuses to sign a bill that will help women working in a disorderly house find a new job. How asinine can he be? He claims fallen women don't deserve our effort. I wanted to smack his pompous face in front of everyone."

She squeezed his arm. "As soon as we finish building those houses, we'll start a project to help fallen women."

He brightened in an instant. "I love you, sister of mine."

Her mouth dropped open in shock, but she didn't have time to say anything.

Lady Beaumont marched towards her as if in a rage. "Emma."

"Good night. Thank you for com—"

"May I have a word?" Lady Beaumont gripped her fan.

"Of course." She exchanged a glance with Trevor who shot his gaze skywards.

Emma walked to a quiet corner and had barely time to smile again before Lady Beaumont asked, "What are you playing at?"

"Excuse me?" She gazed around.

"You can't keep him for yourself only. You don't own him."

She must have had too much champagne because she didn't follow the speech. "Whom are you talking about?"

"Oh, please." Lady Beaumont huffed. "I don't know what you did to him. Blackmail is my guess, which is truly despicable of you, but I'll do everything to have him back and help him. Poor thing. A stallion like that in chains."

Oh, horses then.

"I assure you that Trevor is more than careful with his stallion. If he treated people the same way he treats his horses, he would be more popular."

"You aren't funny."

With those obscure words, Lady Beaumont thrust out her bosom and strode away, her bustle swaying like a cat's tail.

Trevor walked over to her, glancing at the retreating, angry silhouette of Lady Beaumont. "Is something the matter?"

"I have no idea. She said something about me blackmailing someone."

He sighed. "I wish you were that type of person."

"Don't joke."

"I don't."

"She mentioned your stallion. I think. Honestly, I'm not sure."

A shadow crossed his face. "I treat my horse better than I treat you."

"That's what I told her." She pressed her lips together. "I got told off for something I didn't do."

"Lady Beaumont drank too much champagne. Our reserve of Dom Pérignon is dangerously low, and she drank half of it. When we attended her dinner party, she served that horrible champagne made in Saxony. Saxony! Since when did the Saxons know anything about champagne? A bottle of that potion must be no more than a shilling."

"Trevor, I'm serious."

"So am I. Horrible drink." He hid his yawn behind his hand. "I'm too tired. I don't make much sense."

"Not even when you're well rested."

He waved dismissively. "I need to see Stewart, then I'll retire. Good night."

When the footman shut the front door behind the last guest and the house was quiet, she dragged herself upstairs. The soft clinking of the plates and glasses being gathered by the servants came from the ballroom.

Light limned Marcus's door, and she was tempted to knock. The corridor was empty. The servants were busy cleaning up the ballroom. Trevor was with Stewart.

She stood an inch from the door, opening and closing her hands. To knock or not to knock.

There was nothing wrong with asking her guest how he was faring, and he was obviously still up. Or maybe he'd fallen asleep with the lights on. That could be potentially dangerous. She should make sure he was awake or put out the lights. A matter of safety.

She edged closer to listen and pressed her ear to the door. No sound. He could be either reading or sleeping. She bent over to take a peek through the keyhole. Not a ladylike behaviour, but desperate times called for desperate measures.

She could see the armchair and the edge of the bed, and maybe a corner of the fireplace—

An airflow against her cheek was all the warning she had before the door was flung inwards.

"Emma?" Marcus said as she let out a squeal of surprise.

She straightened up so quickly she lost her balance and bumped into him. He caught her easily, wrapping his arms around her waist. A whiff of his clean citrus scent energised her, and somehow, her face was squashed against his chest.

"What were you doing?" He kept holding her.

"I..." The point was, she had no idea what to say. Whatever she said, she would make a poor impression. "Thank you for your hard work."

"My pleasure." Judging from his tone, he didn't believe she'd come to thank him.

Right then, Trevor's voice came from the stairs. "...and put that horrible gift Lord Atkinson gave us in the cellar. Or better yet, destroy it. It'll give me nightmares or bring bad luck."

"Yes, my lord." That was Stewart.

The footsteps were getting closer.

She closed her fists on Marcus's chest to push herself back and get some distance. "I should leave."

"By all means." He steadied her.

She went to dash towards her bedroom, but something pulled her back. To her horror, her gold bracelet had got tangled in the chain of Marcus's pocket watch. In the momentum, he staggered towards her and she towards him, ending up hugging him again.

"Order more champagne as well," Trevor said, pausing on the top step. He didn't face straight forward but over his shoulder to talk to Stewart. "Real champagne, not that potion from Germany that's all the rage just because the queen is half German. I don't even want to hear the word *Saxon* related to food and drinks in this house."

She held her breath. Marcus moved quickly. He pulled her into his bedroom and shut the door silently.

Footsteps pounded closer from the other side of the door, along with Trevor muttering something. When silence dropped, she released a breath.

"Goodness. He almost caught us."

"This is the second time." He pulled at her wrist.

"Don't pull. I don't want to ruin the bracelet."

"It's stuck." He dropped his chin to his chest to look at her wrist. "The chain of my pocket watch is wrapped around the clasp."

"The clasp is delicate. Can't we cut the chain?"

His dark eyebrows knit closer. "It's delicate, too. I like this pocket watch."

"Yes, but repairing a chain is easier than repairing a gold bracelet."

When he exhaled, her wrist followed the rising of his chest. "Come with me."

"I don't have a choice."

He gave her his lopsided smile. "How is it possible that the clasp got caught in the chain?"

"I might have fiddled with it when I tried to fix it after I almost broke it."

He started laughing but stopped with effort, if the way he twitched his mouth was any indication. "I thought so."

To walk together without causing damage to her bracelet, she had to stay flush with his body, and a fluttery tingle started in her belly.

"I should have a small pair of nippers here." He opened the drawer of his nightstand. "What were you doing outside of my door?"

"Just passing by."

He stopped the search to raise a sceptical eyebrow. "You were spying on me through the keyhole."

She laughed nervously. "Don't be ridiculous. Why would I do that?"

"You tell me why." He picked up a pair of nippers.

"I was...relieving my back after dancing." She winced inwardly. She was a terrible liar.

"Do you relieve your back by bending over keyholes?"

"It's not against the law."

"It's not normal, either. Stay still, please." He slowly cut the small links of the chain, lifting her wrist. "How was the evening?"

"Odd. Well, normal until Lady Beaumont, she's married to the Viscount of Beaumont, told me something strange." She tapped a finger to her chin. "Anyway."

He stopped working with the nippers. "What did she say?"

She waved dismissively with her free hand. "Something about me blackmailing someone to force him to do something. I didn't follow the speech."

He clenched his jaw. "Strange indeed."

She had the impression he meant to say something else.

The cutting edges clicked when he cut the links. "Done."

She gingerly removed her wrist. "Thank you."

He clicked his tongue at the broken chain. "Pity."

"My clockmaker will have it mended in a heartbeat."

"You paid for it, after all."

She glared at him, rubbing her bracelet. The playful atmosphere was ruined.

"Is something the matter?" He lifted a shoulder. "Isn't that true?"

"Yes, but the way you said it sounded like you regretted coming here."

"I don't. It's that I haven't had such fine clothes or a fine watch in a long time. If not for your generosity, I would still be on the streets."

"It's not generosity. I can afford it. There isn't generosity without sacrifice, and buying good clothes for you and Jesse is no sacrifice at all."

His expression softened. "I'm used to taking care of myself."

"It's not charity either. I offered you a job, and you're getting paid for it. That's all. You also needed clothes. You couldn't walk around naked." Her cheeks burned. Why had she said that? "I mean, it's a matter of practicality."

He smiled again. "You're right. I'm nervous. I say things I don't think."

"I'm nervous, too. I know the situation here is difficult for you and Jesse as well."

He parted his lips, closed them, and released a breath before saying, "It is."

"I know Trevor hasn't been very welcoming."

"We had a chat." He fiddled with the nippers.

"What did he tell you?"

"Nothing you don't know, I guess."

"I apologise for whatever nonsense he said." She put her hand on his by instinct. "I'm happy to have you here."

He drew in a breath, and his grey eyes pulsated with life. "So am I." He slowly covered her hand with his and rubbed her knuckles with his thumb. It was a slow, gentle gesture as if he were worried she might slap him for his impudence.

Shivers danced down her neck, and she didn't seem to control her breathing anymore. It quickened while her senses sharpened. She could see the blue patterns in his grey irises and the light stubble covering his jaw. And his scent...fresh and heady, caused her toes to curl.

He drew circles over her knuckles with his thumb, staring at her as if she were the most beautiful woman he'd ever seen. It felt as if he adored her, and she would be lying if she said she didn't like it.

"Do you still like me?" she whispered, remembering their conversation in Thistle Hall when he'd reassured her he liked her a lot.

He regarded her with heavy-lidded eyes. "No."

Her heart took a dip to her stomach.

"I worship you," he said with so much honesty that the words became heavy with it and settled on her heart.

What could she ever say after that? Maybe she didn't need to say anything. She only needed to act.

She rose on her tiptoes and kissed him on the lips. He wrapped an arm around her waist and held her close, but his lips didn't yield. Perhaps she was too bold. She was about to lower her heels and step back from him when he tilted his head and parted his lips.

The tip of his tongue stroked the gentlest of touches on her lips, and she couldn't stifle a moan. A burst of new sensations turned her skin sensitive.

She'd kissed other gentlemen during her Seasons, but no one had been so passionate and delicate at the same time. His kiss was gentle but determined, drawing out sensations and thoughts from her she wasn't aware she possessed. She followed her instinct. Besides, in that moment, there was nothing but instinct and sensations within her.

She opened her mouth and expected him to thrust his tongue inside, as it'd happened with other men. Instead, he slid his tongue past her lips smoothly and softly, letting her savour every reaction of her body.

He cupped her cheek and deepened the kiss. The warmth of his body engulfed her in a sweet caress, and her knees weakened. The first stroke of his tongue against hers caused her to sag against him. He welcomed her weight, holding her up as he teased, stroked, and caressed until an ache pulsated deep inside her.

She couldn't contain an involuntary movement of her hips against him, but she needed to do something for her sudden need.

As he kept kissing her, he inched his hand up from her waist. It was a slow climb that fuelled her ache further. She felt on the verge of something big, of a huge change from which there was no return. Energy sparked in her veins, and the ache became unbearable.

He brushed her nipple with his thumb through the satin of her bodice, and all that energy burst like fireworks. And it was fantastic. A pulse started between her legs and spread through her, making her gasp with pleasure. Heat flushed her face as her breathing came out quickly.

Was that normal? Was she supposed to react like that after a kiss and a light touch? Was she too wanton?

"What is it?" He cupped her face. "Did I do something wrong?"

Heat was still coursing through her, and every part of her body was incredibly sensitive. She was aware of his warmth on her skin, the delicious tingle on her lips, and his red lips, swollen by the kiss.

"Emma?" he pleaded. "What happened?"

"Nothing." *Everything.* "I feel very...peculiar."

"In a good or bad fashion?"

"Good," she whispered, afraid of confessing to how much she enjoyed herself. "Heavens. Very good."

He brushed a kiss on her forehead and stroked her back. She let him take care of her while her heartbeat slowed down and the sweet ache petered out, leaving a delicious fatigue in its trail.

Footsteps echoing in the corridor brought her back to reality.

The servants were likely going to bed, and soon her lady's maid would wonder where she was.

She didn't lift her cheek from his chest, needing to cling to that powerful pleasure for longer.

"Do you want to go?" he asked, seemingly reading her worries.

"Yes. I mean, no." She closed her eyes for a moment, trying to collect her thoughts and take control of her emotions again. "I'd better go to my bedroom before someone realises I'm here. My maid will be waiting to help me get ready for bed."

He caressed her head. "Just tell me that you're all right."

How could she? She wasn't all right. But she wasn't unwell either. "I'm all right. Truly. And you didn't do anything wrong. But I need to leave."

He released her face slowly, caressing her cheeks. "Good night."

She brushed past him, sensing another wave of tingling feelings coming to unsettle her body, and it was a good type of unsettling.

twenty-four

E mma awoke agitated and disquieted after a turbulent sleep, or lack thereof.

During the night, she'd awakened several times when her body experienced again the wonderful, special, absolutely powerful kiss with Marcus. She wasn't an innocent debutante anymore. She was aware of how tumbles worked and what they implied or how they ended. Her friends with more experience had told her everything. And she'd read books and novels about the subject. She'd thought she was knowledgeable until last night.

Yet nothing could have ever prepared her for the real experience. He'd barely touched her while they'd been both fully clothed, and she'd reacted as if she were having a full tumble. Her friends hadn't told her it could be that simple.

Aside from all that, she'd kissed Marcus, and that was no small feat. He worked for her at that moment and came from a troubled past—no, she wouldn't think about that. She didn't care about his past. To her, he was always the same man she'd met years ago.

Sitting on the stool in front of her vanity, she couldn't find a comfortable position.

"Are you all right, my lady?" the maid said, combing Emma's hair in a chignon.

"Just a bit tired." She glanced at her reflection in the mirror.

She looked feverish with her cheeks constantly blushing, her eyes bright as if she'd used belladonna eye drops, and her breathing was a little quicker than usual.

When she walked towards the stairs to go to the sunroom, she slowed down in front of Marcus's bedroom. Just knowing he was a few feet away from her made her want to knock on his door and ask him to kiss her again to feel those wonderful, intoxicating sensations.

"Emma, there you are." Trevor's voice surprised her.

She put a hand on her chest. "What are you doing here?"

He frowned. "Going downstairs to have breakfast."

"Of course." She brushed a curl of hair from her face.

"You look flustered. Are you running a fever?" He touched her forehead.

"I'm not." She swatted his hand away.

"Your eyes are bright. Is it the boy? Was his disease contagious?"

She shot her gaze towards the ceiling. "Don't start again." She went down the stairs to the sunroom.

For a silly moment, her heart gave a kick as she expected to find Marcus at the table. But of course, he would have breakfast in the kitchen. Thanks to her brother.

Trevor talked about the latest news at Parliament, but she barely listened. Aside from the kiss, something else bothered her: Lady Beaumont.

The more she thought about the odd conversation, the less it made sense. Lady Beaumont hadn't seemed intoxicated, as Trevor had said. No, she'd been angry and clear-headed. She'd meant every word.

You don't own him.

Unless Lady Beaumont had truly meant to discuss the acquisition of Trevor's latest stallion, the only '*him*' she could have referred to was Marcus, but that didn't make any sense.

Lady Beaumont might have met Marcus years ago when his father's company had been thriving. But would she refer to him in such terms? And why would she care about defending him from her? Besides, no one knew Marcus was in Hart House. His presence wasn't exactly a secret, but she hadn't divulged the news either, and he hadn't been out with her. But that detail was of no matter. The problem was what Lady Beaumont meant. If she'd referred to Marcus, why would she complain about Emma *owning* him?

She didn't own anyone, and Marcus was free to leave whenever he wanted.

She put down her spoon. "I'm not hungry. If you'll excuse me, I have letters to answer."

The footman rushed to help her out of the chair.

Trevor regarded her from over the rim of *The Times*. "Shall I send for Sir Paul?"

"Don't worry. It's nothing that some sleep won't cure."

Or perhaps a new kiss from Marcus.

MARCUS HAD CHANGED his mind about the kiss a dozen times during the night.

The sleepless night.

Not because he regretted it, quite the opposite, but because he shouldn't have kissed her without telling her everything about him. She wouldn't have kissed him if she'd known about his past.

The moment her lips had touched his, all his thoughts had lost meaning, and he'd let his emotions take control.

If Trevor learnt about the kiss, he would throw Marcus and Jesse out without a penny. Marcus should prioritise his job and opportunity over everything else, but he'd wanted to kiss her ever since their conversation in Thistle Hall.

After leaving his bedroom, he walked past the sunroom while heading to the kitchen, but only Trevor was sitting at the table. Since he wasn't hungry, he went back upstairs again. Jesse was still asleep, recovering from his stomach ache, so he went to Emma's study and knocked on the door.

"Come in."

She raised her gaze from a letter when he entered the room, and her cheeks flushed a deep red. That blush told an entire story of a secret kiss shared in a quiet room.

"Good morning." He closed the door behind him but waited for her invitation to step farther into the room. "How are you?"

She shifted her gaze and folded the letter a couple of times. "I'm well."

"You seemed upset when you left my room last night."

"I was a little shocked, yes."

No, he couldn't stand the distance between them any longer.

He walked around the desk and gently took her hand. "I'm aware I crossed a line last night, and if that made you uncomfortable with me, I won't do it again."

Her eyes flared wide and glowed from within as it'd happened last night. She whispered something so low he didn't understand it.

"What did you say?" He dipped his head, getting dangerously close to her plush lips.

She darted out the tip of her pink tongue over her bottom lip. "I said that it would be a pity if you didn't kiss me again because I enjoyed the kiss very much."

"But? Something bothered you."

She reddened again, and her lips turned a dark pink that suited her. "I didn't expect it to be so powerful. I reacted in a certain way when you kissed me and touched me, and I'm not sure it's normal. It was very pleasurable but maybe I shouldn't feel that way."

He drew circles with his thumb over her hand. Even now, he should release her hand and walk away, but he couldn't leave her when she had doubts and felt shame over something so simple and wonderful.

"It's normal. You don't have to feel ashamed."

"But shouldn't it take a bit longer? I thought it required more activity and fewer clothes, not a mere touch."

"Yes, but everyone is different, and you're special."

"I have kissed other men before, but none of them made me feel like that." She sounded genuinely worried.

Her words couldn't be more pleasant to him. He failed to contain a smile. He understood her because a touch from her could never compare to one from his ladies.

"I'm glad to hear that because it's the same for me." He kissed her hand, lingering with his lips on her silky skin.

She released a slow breath that caused his body to tense in anticipation. He'd started to solicit himself over a year ago, but he'd never experienced such a sudden, intense pleasure as he had with her.

"Marcus," she whispered, "Will you kiss me again?"

"Anytime you want." He should tell her they needed to think about the consequences, that she was a lady and he was a ruined man with no prospect of improving his future. He shouldn't touch her.

But his heart screamed louder.

She rose from the chair, deliberately moving closer to him, and all his good intentions were crushed by the desire in her gaze.

"Even now?" She tilted her head.

"Even now."

She drew closer, her soft breath fanning on his skin. Her chest rose and fell, touching his. "We need a more private place. Trevor could come here any moment."

She barely said that before the sound of a door shutting in the corridor jolted her. She stepped back from him, and he released his breath as excitement rushed through him. He felt as if he'd been very close to dropping from a height, only to be rescued at the last moment. Hell, he hadn't even thought about Trevor coming there. He'd only wanted to kiss her.

She cleared her throat and touched her cheeks as footsteps padded. Marcus stepped back as well, putting more distance between them.

Jesse's voice came from the corridor. "Have you seen Marcus?"

"Not yet." That was Stewart.

"He isn't in his room."

"I need to see what Jesse wants," Marcus said.

She nodded, her face still tense.

He was used to the subterfuges and secrecy, but somehow they felt wrong with Emma. But everything else concerning her felt right.

twenty-five

Emma was boiling as the air in her study became suddenly hot. She fiddled with the collar of her high-necked shirt and rearranged the documents on the desk as Marcus opened the door.

She had no idea what she was doing other than piling things up and shifting them again. He hadn't kissed her, but the same tingle as last night tormented her. Her thoughts were scattered in every direction. Her body shook with the fatigue of exercising control.

"Jesse? I'm here," Marcus said louder, opening the door.

"I need to talk to you and Lady Emma," Jesse said.

She straightened. "What is it?" She craned her neck as Jesse appeared on the threshold with his flat hat on and a satchel strapped across his shoulders.

"My lady." He sniffled, eyes red and puffy.

"What is it?" Marcus asked at the same time as Emma said, "Are you going somewhere?"

Jesse removed his hat. His dark blond hair was dishevelled, and his face had a worrying grey colour. "I came to thank you for your hospitality and to say goodbye."

"What?" Marcus said. "What are you talking about?"

She waved him closer. "Come here and tell me what has happened."

Jesse shuffled across the room, his stare on the carpet. "You'll throw me out once you learn the horrible thing I did."

She glanced at Marcus who gave her a quick shake of his head. "I assure you that I won't throw you out, no matter what you did."

Jesse shook his head. "I did something terrible."

Emma lowered her head in front of him, catching his sad gaze. "Tell me."

Jesse's bottom lip quivered. "Last night, my stomach was upset because I ate too much, and I couldn't sleep."

"Why didn't you come to my room?" Marcus asked. "I thought you felt better after the ginger brew."

Jesse wiped his cheek with the sleeve of his jacket. "I didn't want to bother you."

"So what did you do?" she asked.

Jesse took a deep breath. "I tried to sleep, but my stomach was upset, and I...threw up in the bed," he whispered, tears hanging on his eyelashes.

"Oh, dear Jesse." Emma hugged him, and he rested his head on her shoulder.

"The bedsheets are a mess. They smell horrible. I took them off and tried to wash them, but..." He shook his head. "I made things worse."

"You should have called me," Marcus said.

"How do you feel now? Is your stomach still upset?" she asked.

He hiccuped among sobs. "I felt better after throwing up."

"Good. Soiling the bed is nothing of importance. I'm not going to throw you out."

"Really?" He wiped his face again.

"Never. Hart House is your home now. You're going to stay here no matter what you do."

His face brightened. "No matter?"

She nodded. "This is your home."

Marcus's frown deepened, and his grey eyes turned frosty.

Jesse hugged her again. "I'm going to have breakfast then. I was so worried I didn't eat."

"Eat something light. Tell Mrs. Daubney you didn't feel well last night." She smiled. "Off you go then."

He hugged Marcus, too, radiating happiness.

"Next time, if you feel unwell, come to me, no matter the time," Marcus said.

"Yes. Thank you, Lady Emma." Jesse rushed out of the room, shouting, "I'm not leaving!"

She chuckled at the boy's enthusiasm. "He's such an adorable boy."

Marcus's brow didn't smooth. "I'm grateful for everything you've done so far for Jesse and me, but I must ask you not to make promises you aren't going to keep."

"What do you mean?"

"This isn't Jesse's home. Once I finish my job for you, Jesse and I will leave, and it'll be very hard for him to leave if he believes this is his home."

That shook her to the core. If he meant to leave, what about them? She was jumping to conclusions, and they could see each other even if he lived somewhere else, but the way he'd said that sounded as if he knew whatever started between them wouldn't lead anywhere.

"But I mean it," she said. "You and Jesse are welcome to stay here for as long as you wish. I want you and Jesse to be part of my life."

"We must be practical, though." He knit his eyebrows, looking sad. "This is the house of an earl who will marry one day and have a family, and you'll marry as well and move out of here. What are Jesse and I supposed to do?"

She rolled her bottom lip between her teeth, at a loss. She'd wanted to comfort Jesse, but at the same time, she meant everything she'd said. "I didn't think the promise through, but that doesn't mean Jesse shouldn't consider this place home. We'll find a solution when the problem arises."

"That's not what I do. I don't wait for a problem to arise. I try to prevent it." A muscle of his jaw ticked. "With due respect, Jesse is only eleven years old. He's been through a lot in a short time. After he lost his parents, he joined a gang and was beaten by its leader, and he was forced into becoming a thief by the age of eight. I don't want him to suffer any longer, and giving him the hope of having found a home might break his heart. And mine."

She sighed. "You're right, but you have to trust me when I say that whatever happens, Jesse will be well cared for. And I'm not in a hurry to get married." Especially now.

"The earl has a different idea about our permanence here."

"Trevor grumbles a lot, but he's a sensible man. He would never do anything to harm you or Jesse."

"Well, he—" He fell silent, squeezing his lips together.

"What?"

"I'm not at liberty to say."

"At liberty to say? You sound like a spymaster working for Her Majesty. What did Trevor do?"

"Nothing, and I shouldn't have mentioned him." His expression remained unforgiving.

"I want to know if Trevor said something that upset you."

"He didn't." He pinched the bridge of his nose.

"Marcus." She stepped closer. In the past, she'd made the mistake of not being direct with him until the very last moment. She wouldn't do that again. "I know what you're thinking." She paused because speaking her mind was more difficult than she thought. "The kiss complicates the situation between us. But..." She lost her train of thought when he gave her a smouldering gaze.

"But?"

"Can't we just be ourselves when we are alone and not think

too much about the future? Enjoy each other's company for as long as possible?"

"And face the problem only when it presents itself." He didn't sound happy at all.

The shelves around her, heavy with books, and documents and letters to be answered, seemed to close in on her, reminding her that what Marcus had said was true. She would marry sooner or later to someone of her status, but she had no idea what had just started with him, and if there was one thing she'd learnt after the bridge collapse, it was life could change completely in a moment and not always for the better.

"It's selfish, I know," she said. "But I don't want to look back and have regrets. I already have too many. If you don't share my sentiment, I understand. But I believe a solution that will make us happy is possible."

She would help Marcus set up his own company again, and after that, he would feel less unworthy. Because he was more than worthy in her eyes.

He flashed a quick smile that would brighten her day for hours. "So do you still want your kiss?"

She nodded. "Absolutely."

"We should find a private place where no one will find us."

Why was the idea of searching for a secret, safe spot so exciting?

"I will."

He cleared his throat. "Meanwhile, I finished studying the entire documentation of the building site in St. Giles. I'm ready to inspect it."

"Excellent. I'll organise the visit, then."

He bowed and went to leave, but there was something else she wished to discuss.

"Marcus, may I ask you something?"

"Of course."

She fiddled with her hands. "It's probably nothing, but remember what I told you about Lady Beaumont last night?"

A hard glint flashed across his gaze. "Yes, I do."

"Do you know her?"

"A bowing acquaintance. Why?"

"As I told you, she said something odd last night before she left. She accused me of holding someone against his will here, and she said, '*You don't own him.*' I have no idea what she was talking about, and the only person she could refer to is you."

He remained deadpan. "I can't help you. I have no clue what she meant."

"I don't understand. She strode out before I could ask her what she meant. Are you sure something didn't happen with her? Maybe you and your father worked in one of her houses?"

"It's possible, but I have no recollection of any direct contact with her." His voice lowered gradually until the last few words became a whisper. He stared at the carpet, avoiding her gaze.

"I'll have to ask her again then."

"Of course. If you'll excuse me, I haven't had breakfast yet, and I would like to see Jesse."

"By all means."

He left the room in a hurry. The atmosphere between them changed, and she wondered if he'd been completely honest.

twenty-six

Marcus couldn't find a comfortable position in the carriage as he rode with Trevor, Emma, and her lady's maid to St. Giles.

Lady Beaumont confronted Emma about him. Likely, she believed Emma was his sole client and that he'd refused her proposition so that he could be with Emma, which was ridiculous. No lady client would ever let him stay in her home.

Or kiss him with such passion to make him forget who he was.

Cowardly, he'd lied to Emma that morning. He would hate to see the disgust on her face. He would do anything to keep his past secret for as long as possible. She didn't need to know. Kisses were one thing. But he wouldn't go beyond them without telling her the truth.

Lady Beaumont couldn't be completely honest with Emma without exposing herself as well. She wouldn't be reckless enough to blabber about her infidelity, would she?

"Are you all right?" Trevor asked. "You keep twitching. Please don't tell me Jesse's stomach disease is contagious. This morning Emma looked feverish, and now you won't stop twitching. I'm worried."

"Trevor," Emma said in a warning tone.

Marcus released a breath through his teeth. "I'm nervous." That was true.

"Sir Horace is in Bath this week," Trevor said. "You can inspect the construction site without worrying about him."

"That's reassuring." It wasn't, but he had a job to do and was aware of the risks.

Emma's presence distracted him. His thoughts kept going back and forth between engineering problems and kissing her. She didn't want regrets. Neither did he. To an extent. He would satisfy her curiosity about kisses and touches without hurting her.

She smiled at him, a secret smile of companionship for him only, and his heart pounded faster, silencing his dark thoughts.

The smell of coal and horse dung became strong and pungent when the carriage rolled to a stop in front of the construction site.

In the past years, he'd slept in a rookery, and it hadn't been a pleasant experience. Foul smells were only one of the problems. There were desperate people who would literally slit someone's throat for a farthing.

The site was in a good spot, though, in terms of sunny location and proximity to the high road. He tilted his head back to take a look at the scaffolding and the skeletons of what promised to be strong townhouses.

The workers tipped their hats at Trevor and threw sideways glances at Emma. She attracted most of the stares. The advantage was that no one paid him the slightest bit of attention.

"Where do you want to start?" Trevor asked.

"The log to see which materials have been delivered, and then I'll check the foundations."

"Good."

Marcus studied the structures again. He would be lying if he said he hadn't missed the job.

For the first time since moving to Emma's house, he didn't feel like a fish out of water.

EMMA HAD GIVEN up following Marcus's work at the construction site after half an hour.

While she loved the project in St. Giles and wished only to help the people in the rookery, the technical aspect and the terminology were quite boring.

So she'd opted for a promenade on Oxford Street with her maid. She stopped in front of a milliner's window shop displaying a lovely arrangement of velvet hats when Lady Redfern came out of the shop.

"Emma, what a pleasure. I was thinking about paying you a visit."

"Oh, lovely." She smiled although she didn't fully understand why Lady Redfern was suddenly so interested in her.

"I wanted to tell you..." Lady Redfern gazed around. Her lady's maid was a few feet behind, and Emma's maid followed at a discreet distance. Lady Redfern lowered her voice and leant closer. "My husband is away next week. He's going to Birmingham for work."

"I see." Although she didn't. And who cared about Lady Redfern's husband?

The lady gave her a pointed look as if waiting for Emma to say something else.

"Yes?" she prompted when Lady Redfern didn't say anything. Why was she having only awkward conversations as of late?

Lady Redfern raised her eyebrows. "I'll be on my own for four days. Is that clear?"

"Oh, you'll feel lonely. You would like some company."

Lady Redfern smirked. "Exactly."

Yes, but what did Emma have to do with anything? She and Lady Redfern weren't close. Surely, Lady Redfern had other, closer friends she would like to spend her time with. But anyway, she wouldn't refuse her company to a person who felt lonely.

"You're welcome to have dinner with us, or we can arrange an afternoon tea and a walk in the park. Or would you prefer going to the opera?"

Lady Redfern scrunched up her face as if smelling something rotten. "Would that be all? Are you making fun of me?"

"Good gracious, no!" She hadn't paid a lot of attention to which entertainment was in fashion those days, but a nice tea party was always welcome.

"Then?" Lady Redfern asked with the tone of a governess speaking to a particularly difficult child.

"Er…a poetry reading?"

Lady Redfern huffed and inched back. "Truly, Emma, I'm disappointed to learn the rumour is true."

Emma opened her mouth, an apology almost ready to leave her lips, but on second thoughts, she had no idea what she should apologise for. "I don't understand."

Lady Redfern shot her a glare. "Your attitude is rather extreme."

Extreme? "This conversation is just bizarre. I demand an explanation."

Lady Redfern's eyes widened. "You demand? Have a good day."

The shock caused Emma to stand there for a moment. Her attitude was extreme? And what rumour?

The conversations with Lady Beaumont and Lady Redfern stayed with her. She had nothing in common with either woman. Lady Redfern hadn't accused her of blackmailing someone, but the tone and attitude were the same. And the whole story of her husband leaving her alone? Odd.

People gossiped all the time, and she wouldn't be surprised if something untrue was being said about her. Still, the fact she had no clue about what it might be worried her. Marcus was again the only thing that had recently changed in her life.

"Did you hear the conversation, Gibson?" she asked her maid.

"I didn't understand anything, my lady."

"Do you know of any rumours about me?"

Gibson shook her head.

Huffing, Emma hailed a cab, more confused than ever about the two ladies.

When she returned home, Marcus and Trevor were already there and talking excitedly in the drawing room in front of steamy cups of tea.

"Any news?" she asked, still thinking about the odd encounter.

She was so annoyed she hadn't thought about a safe place in the house where she could see Marcus alone.

Jesse was sitting quietly in front of the fire, munching on a biscuit. He smiled when she waved at him. His cheeks were less grey than that morning.

"We have news, and not good, I'm afraid," Trevor said, "not for Sir Horace or us."

"What do you mean?" she asked.

Those odd conversations must have put her brain in turmoil.

"I found several problems with Sir Horace's work." Marcus went through a stack of notes. "First, I found structural problems. The weight of the house isn't well distributed. Also, improper shoring of soil, which again might cause the homes to shift their positions. But above all, I think Sir Horace is committing expense fiddling."

"How?" She poured herself a cup of tea.

"He deliberately inflates the cost of the materials he's buying to pocket the difference, and even worse, he's buying cheap, low-quality material while claiming the opposite."

"Heavens."

"If he's doing that," Trevor said, "then why don't all his buildings collapse?"

"Because he's clever. He takes more risks when he builds houses for the rookeries, as in this case, because he doesn't care about the people living there. They would be less likely to challenge him. The houses might not collapse, but they'll crack. There will be water infiltration and excessive humidity with the health consequences they bring, and other problems, like crumbling walls or even water contaminated with sewage, which may cause a potential cholera outbreak."

"How despicable." She put her cup down. "So he tells everyone he's doing a great job when he's doing the bare minimum while pocketing a lot of money."

Marcus nodded. "I can write a report about the irregularities I've found, but he might claim he's aware of these problems and about to fix them. If we want to put him out of work, we need more proof. We need receipts, documents, contracts, everything he's done so far."

"I'll talk to my solicitor," Trevor said. "Thank you, Marcus. You have most likely saved lives and us with your work."

Marcus's smile was so wide and bright it changed his whole face. "Just doing my job."

No, it was more for him. She was sure of that. It was a mission, redemption for his father, and maybe a revenge, too.

"You seem preoccupied, Emma," Trevor said. "The walk didn't go as you wished."

"Oh, that." She put her cup down, her mood still sour. "I met Lady Redfern on Oxford Street, and we had the strangest conversation. She told me her husband was away and that she was lonely. I invited her here, but she got so upset she left. Absurd."

Marcus lowered his gaze quickly, flipping through the pages of his notes.

"That's odd," Trevor said. "Did she say why she was upset?"

"She mentioned a rumour about me and my disappointing attitude." She huffed. "Nonsense."

"If you'll excuse me, I'll retire," Marcus said, standing up.

"By all means." Trevor nodded and shot a curious glance at Jesse.

"Jesse?" Marcus said. "Mrs. Daubney is waiting for us in the kitchen."

Jesse slid off the chair without making a noise, his gaze on the floor.

"Perhaps we all could have dinner together, as a celebration," she said.

Marcus bowed his head. "Thank you, but we'll be fine in the kitchen."

Jesse bowed and muttered, "Thank you," before following Marcus. He walked almost on his tiptoes as if he didn't want to make any noise.

Emma slanted a glare at Trevor. "What did you do to that child?"

"Nothing! The fact you think I might have done something to him is ridiculous."

"He looks terrified."

Trevor twirled his spoon in the cup. "He asked me, politely I must add, if he could have tea with Marcus and me. I said yes as long as he was quiet and didn't cause trouble."

"Or?" She balled a fist on her hip.

"I wouldn't let him take tea with us again."

"Trevor!"

"You wanted me to be more friendly and welcoming to him!" He sounded outraged as if he were the wronged one.

"Jesse is a scared boy who comes from extreme poverty, and you're treating him like a thief."

"I'm not, and I don't understand why you're so upset. Once Marcus finishes the job, which is going to happen soon, he and Jesse will leave."

"Oh, not this again. The fact they would leave one day has nothing to do with our friendship. I can perfectly visit them wherever they move."

"Emma, please." He touched his forehead. "You understand

the implications of being friends with someone like Marcus, don't you?"

"Enlighten me."

"He wasn't thrown into prison for bankruptcy by mere chance. Somehow, he paid his debts. His father was accused of negligence and murder. He's ruined. How would you explain your friendship with him?"

She folded her arms over her chest. "I don't have to explain anything to anyone, and I believe in him. Once he starts working again as an engineer, his reputation in society will change. I thought you cared about him. I thought he was your friend. Are you?"

He reclined his head and stared at the ceiling.

"Answer me. Do you still consider Marcus a good man with a brilliant brain, as you did before the incident?"

He nodded. "Yes, I still think he's an admirable person."

"Then do something to show it."

"What am I supposed to do?" He closed a fist on the table.

"Help him rebuild his good reputation. Help him get a proper job, instead of disparaging him from your high position."

He said nothing.

She wasn't sure why she was so upset. "You consider yourself a philosopher, but maybe you're just a cynic."

He cradled his chin. "Cynics were ancient Greek philosophers."

"Yes, and they suggested that rejecting social recognition and materialistic desires was the best path. Maybe you aren't a cynic, after all." She opened the door. "I'll have dinner in my room."

twenty-seven

Still upset with Trevor about their last conversation, Emma did her best to ignore him as they were having tea the next morning. It was a childish behaviour, but to her defence, so was Trevor's. On top of that, she hadn't seen Marcus because he and Trevor had kept working on the reports until late.

He scowled at her from over the rim of his cup. "Are you still angry?"

"Disappointed more than angry."

"I'm first and foremost a businessman."

"And a cold-hearted man."

A tendon of his neck stood out. "Business and kindness don't go hand in hand. If I wanted to make everyone happy, I wouldn't be an earl but a Cornish pasty baker."

"You don't like Cornish pasties."

"That's not the point." He gripped the table. "What do you want from me?"

She pushed aside her cup. "I want to see that you care about something other than your reputation or your horses. Why do you still keep Ophelia's locket?"

A shadow crossed his face. "I told you not to mention Ophelia."

"Have you ever cared about her at all?"

He thumped a fist on the table. "So typical of you. You do whatever you want without a care in the world. I asked you not to mention Ophelia, but you do it anyway. Do you know what the difference between you and me is? I have responsibilities."

"So have I."

He pressed his lips tightly.

"I don't understand you sometimes," she continued. "You can be cold and snobbish, but you're eager to help fallen women and people in the rookery. Can't you choose an attitude and stick to it?"

Stewart entered the sunroom. "My lord, Sir Horace wishes to see you. He said it's urgent."

Trevor composed himself and exhaled. "Show him in."

Emma folded her napkin, glad that Trevor didn't ask her to leave.

Sir Horace strode into the room as if he owned it. He hinted at a bow before piercing her with his dark eyes.

"Horace, I thought you were in Bath. I didn't expect you this morning." Trevor didn't stand up.

"I didn't expect you to visit the site in St. Giles without telling me," Sir Horace said. "And I changed my plan and returned earlier."

"Obviously." Trevor didn't flinch. "You work for me. I pay the bills. I don't need your approval to visit the site where *my* houses are going to be built."

Sir Horace radiated fury. "I'm afraid you do, especially if you employ a new engineer to inspect *my* work."

"We only wanted another opinion," Emma said.

Sir Horace turned his head towards her like a bloodhound sniffing a trail. "Pray, my lady, would you be so kind as to remind me when I asked for *your* opinion?"

"Beware of the English when they grow polite." Trevor stood up. "I think that's enough for today. I can do as I please with my money and time, and my sister is free to give her opinion whenever she wants. As I said, you work for me, and I have the right to make sure you're doing a good job. We don't want anything bad to happen, do we?"

"Absolutely not. It would be a pity."

"Then you understand my position," Trevor said. "You're a businessman. It's not personal."

Sir Horace worked his jaw. "I must insist."

"By all means, do insist. I love watching people fighting a lost cause." Trevor smiled.

Emma was glad not to be at the end of Trevor's sarcasm for once.

Sir Horace clenched a fist. "Your attitude, Pembroke, isn't constructive."

"Funny you use that word, constructive, considering I have doubts about your constructive skills."

"It doesn't end here." Sir Horace gave another shallow nod before leaving.

Emma sagged in the chair. "Can't we give him the sack?"

"Not so simple. All those bloody new laws about work regulations and workers' rights." Trevor waved a dismissive hand. "A nightmare."

She touched his hand, her anger from before gone. "Anyway, thank you for sending him away and speaking up for me."

He smiled, and for once it wasn't his smug smile. "No one disparages my little sister."

She hugged him, and he returned the hug. "I don't like fighting with you."

He patted her back. "I love it instead. It's refreshing. No one argues with me."

"I'm never sure whether you're serious or joking."

He winked. "That's my most charming trait."

WITHOUT THE DOCUMENTS TO STUDY, Marcus had been left alone with his thoughts, and there wasn't a worse torture for him, especially since he was trying to sleep.

During the day, he'd tried and failed to distract himself with work. Now sleep eluded him as he tossed and turned.

Between what he'd discovered about Sir Horace, Emma's kiss, and Lady Redfern asking dangerous questions, his mind was racing.

He'd thought his ladies didn't know each other, that he'd kept their names private. How wrong. Obviously, Lady Beaumont and Lady Redfern had talked about him. And that was worrying.

Emma had been busy all day, which actually allowed him some time alone to think. But as night crept over London, he grew more restless.

Since sleeping was out of the question, he dressed and left his room. A herbal tea would be wonderful, and he didn't need to bother a maid to brew it.

He paced in the kitchen as the water heated in the kettle. If all his clients talked with each other, he would soon face a group of angry ladies. But what worried him the most was Emma. He hated that they might vent their anger on her.

When the herbal tea was ready, he went to the library. Just roaming through the shelves would be enough to keep him busy until fatigue came.

He lit a few gas lamps, but the glow coming from the end of an aisle caught his eye. Either someone was still up, or a lamp had been left burning. The glow from his lamp cast long shadows over the leather-bound volumes filling the rosewood shelves. Emma's sweet scent intruded on the combination of smells of old leather, wood polish, and paper.

He drew in a breath when he found Emma bent over a typewriter on a table in a corner.

She gasped, a hand on her chest. "It's you." Her shoulders sagged. "I thought it was Trevor."

"What are you doing here?" He put the mug and the lamp on the table.

She balled her hands on her hips, staring at the typewriter. "I know it'll be difficult to believe it, but I broke this machine."

He chuckled, and just like that, his dark thoughts vanished. "What did you do?"

"A hairpin got stuck between two keys and jammed them. I tried to pull it out with a pair of tweezers, but I used too much strength. The hairpin snapped, and now a few keys are stuck together and don't work."

He took a look. It was a fine machine, shiny black with bright red flowers decorating the case. "Is that a Remington number two?"

She sighed. "It is."

"It cost a fortune."

"Yes, I insisted on buying it, but Trevor disagreed. He said I should start typewriting with a simple, not expensive model, but I fell in love with this beauty, and if he learns I broke it, I will never hear the end of it."

"I'll take a look at it tomorrow morning, but I can't promise anything. I've never repaired a typewriter before."

She smiled. "Thank you. I'm good at creating disasters, am I not?"

No, she wasn't.

"If there were a competition, I would win."

And he wanted to kiss her again. Desperately. That would be a disaster.

"And what are you still doing up?"

"I couldn't sleep."

"Worrying thoughts?"

"Not all of them. Some are more pleasant than others."

She nodded. "It's the same for me. You're my pleasant

thought, but even with that pleasant thought, I can't sleep." She tilted her head towards him. "Perhaps I need a kiss."

He couldn't stop himself and dipped his head to do her bidding. He paused a breath away from her lips and waited for her to be sure.

She closed the distance between them, pressing her lips against his, gently at first then harder. A moment of stillness caught him. Even his breathing slowed. He wanted to remember that moment and store the precious memory of Emma kissing him for when they weren't together anymore, for when he would feel lonely.

He cupped her nape and traced the seam of her lips with his tongue, as he'd done many times with other ladies. The gesture was the same. The emotion wasn't.

She let out a soft moan that urged him to go faster, but he wanted to go slowly and savour her so that his body would remember. When she opened her mouth, he deepened the kiss, caressing her tongue with his. She was a world of softness, silk, and flowery scent.

She ran a hand over his chest, going up to touch his cheek. Again, many ladies had done the same—it was a path others had trodden—but he shuddered with new sensations when she touched him with her inexperienced hand.

He grazed her plush lower lip lightly with his teeth, and she moaned louder. She pressed her thighs together and rolled her hips against him. His body reacted, demanding a release, but he wanted to take care of her first. He'd done the same thing with his ladies, but for once, he wasn't after a good pay; he only wanted her to be satisfied.

He led her backwards, until her back was flush with the wall, and stared at her large eyes. There wasn't only desire in them. So much trust shone through them they could light London's streets for a night. Her chest rose and fell quickly, and her breath caressed his skin. Her trust was a responsibility he would accept gladly.

He dragged a hand from her cheek, down to her slender neck

and her chest. The moment he cupped her breast through the fabric of her shirt, she reclined her head and sank her teeth into her bottom lip, looking stunning.

But he wasn't finished. He'd barely started.

He stroked her waist, feeling her corset under the fabric, and went further down to the flare of her hip and her thigh. Kissing her slowly, he bunched up the skirt and petticoats until he could slide his hand underneath the layers of fabric.

Her breathing sped up again, but he kept kissing her slowly, stroking her tongue with his. He closed his eyes for a moment and pressed his forehead to hers when he touched her silk stocking. Her warm skin was under his fingers with only a flimsy barrier separating them. He couldn't believe he was touching her.

"I feel on fire," she whispered.

"So do I. Trust me." His voice was low and husky. Not once had such a tone come out with his ladies.

A shudder made his fingers tremble when he slipped his hand between her silky thighs. She gripped his shoulders, sinking her fingernails into the fabric of his shirt, and the sensation carried a tiny hint of pain he liked.

They both remained still when he found the slit of her drawers. He watched her as he inched his fingers forwards, both fascinated and worried about her reaction. The first brush caused them to groan at the same time. He slowly rubbed her, but after a few brushes, she shivered and pressed her face against his chest to muffle a cry.

He welcomed her and held her up with one arm, but didn't stop stroking her. She was indeed very receptive, and he loved how open to new experiences she was, how much she trusted him.

"That's..." She panted on his chest, her shoulders lifting and lowering.

He brushed his lips against her temple and inched a slow finger inside her. Carefully, he moved, watching her face for any signs of discomfort, but her flushed cheeks and bright eyes showed only pleasure.

The moment she gripped him, she breathed faster and shivered in his arms again. Another scream was ruthlessly suppressed by his waistcoat.

Perfect moment. He only wished he could see her face. After he withdrew his hand, he held her and gave her time to recover. Her legs quivered, but he supported her.

She gazed up at him. Not an ounce of shame clouded her face. "I had no idea something like that was possible."

"There are more pleasant ways to achieve the same result."

"I don't believe you. What can be more pleasant than this?"

"I'll show you, and you'll change your mind."

"I accept the challenge."

He adjusted her skirts as best as he could although he wanted to do the exact opposite and undress her completely.

"Can't we continue?" She wrapped her arms around his neck, and he laughed.

His body screamed, '*Yes,*' but he didn't want to rush, and she needed to learn a few things about him first.

He kissed her lips, lingering until his heartbeat returned to normal. "We don't want to get caught. But there will be other occasions. In a more private place. I don't want to take you on a table in the library." Not that he hadn't done that before. Some of his ladies had peculiar tastes. But with Emma, he wanted a proper bed, warm and safe.

"Of course there will be other occasions." She hugged him tightly, and the fear of losing her—no, the certainty of losing her soon—choked him.

Another sleepless night awaited him.

twenty-eight

That morning, Marcus's puff tie didn't want to cooperate.

He'd been standing in front of the wall mirror in his bedroom for a while, trying to fix his attire with little success. His encounter from last night with Emma had calmed nothing and fuelled his inner turmoil. A turmoil that didn't need more fuel.

His determination not to be involved with her was threadbare and flimsy, like an old cobweb. The truth was he couldn't stay away from her.

Leaving Emma's house would be the right thing to do, for her sake. With Lady Beaumont and Lady Redfern pestering her and rumours circulating about her, he should find somewhere else to live. At least the ladies would pester him directly, instead of talking to Emma.

He gave a sharp tug at the tie and sod it. The fabric was all askew, but he didn't care.

"Sir." Neil, the footman, entered the room. "You asked me to tell you if a message arrived for you." He handed him an envelope.

"Thank you, Neil." He opened it, already dreading what it might be.

It was Lady Beaumont, as he'd feared. She wanted to see him alone, or she would barge into Emma's house and demand to see him immediately. She'd given him a place and a time.

The park wasn't the spot he would have chosen. Anyone could see them.

He worked his jaw. He hated having to be at Lady Beaumont's beck and call, but it was better to confront her outside of Emma's house.

Jesse entered the bedroom. Flour stained his shirt.

Marcus brushed it off. "Helping Mrs. Daubney in the kitchen?"

"I want to earn my keep." Jesse finished the job, brushing another flour stain from his trousers. "Is there any news about Sir Horace?"

"Not yet." He undid the tie for the umpteenth time. "Why do you ask?"

"Just curious." Jesse waved him down. "You seemed worried about him."

"I am." He bent over.

Jesse knotted the tie quickly. "If things go well with Sir Horace and turn bad for us, what will happen to us?"

He straightened and checked his reflection. Jesse had done a good job. "Don't worry. We'll never go back to Seven Dials."

"But what will happen?"

"We'll find a nice place to live." He ruffled Jesse's hair. "I have to go now."

"May I come with you?"

"It's better if you stay here."

Jesse didn't ask questions. Habit, likely. "I'll go back to the kitchen then."

"Don't get too tired."

They went down the stairs together. At the bottom, Jesse headed for the kitchen. The boy was preoccupied. So was he, but with the money he would earn from his job for Trevor and Emma, they would never have to return to Seven Dials.

He was donning his coat in the hallway when Emma and her lady's maid came down the stairs. She looked beautiful in a tight pink gown that turned her hazel eyes green.

He could still feel the softness of her skin under his fingers and her sweet taste on his lips. His body tightened with desire in an instant.

A light flush coloured her cheeks. The smile playing on her lips held the secret of a night encounter in the library.

"Are you going out as well?" she asked. "Lovely. We could go together. I need a walk. Where are we going?"

Damn. He was shocked back to the present. "I have a private errand to do. Apologies, but it's important."

Her expression lost some of its radiance. "I'll see you later."

"My lady." Feeling like a scoundrel, he bowed and left the house.

Hiding his former profession forever wasn't possible, but he'd be damned if he let Emma learn the truth from someone else. He had only to wait for the right moment to reveal the truth. Then she would be horrified and order him to leave her house.

A chilly gust blew to his face like a quick slap. Maybe it was a sign he should talk to Emma. But on the other hand, his work was almost over, and after that, he wouldn't need to tell her anything about his past because he would leave anyway.

He rubbed his forehead, wishing he could wipe all those thoughts from his mind. The constant back and forth on his decision was consuming him.

He found Lady Beaumont sitting on the bench under a weeping willow with her lady's maid. When Lady Beaumont saw him, she talked to the maid, who stood up and walked a few yards away.

"I knew you would come." Smiling, she patted the empty spot on the bench.

"You blackmailed me. I didn't have a choice." He didn't sit down.

She narrowed her large eyes. "We're starting this conversation on the wrong foot, and you're standing."

"What do you want?"

"A short time ago, you wouldn't have dared talk to me with that tone."

"A short time ago, I wasn't as tired as I am now."

"Fair enough. I'll go straight to the point. Is Lady Emma your sole client now?"

"No." Just thinking about Emma paying him for a tumble made him sick to his stomach. "I don't work in that field anymore."

"Don't talk about work! Don't you care about me? A little?" Her voice quivered.

He had to be honest. "You've always been kind and generous to me, and I appreciate that, but I don't feel anything for you aside from gratitude."

She leapt to her feet, cheeks reddening. "Is it Emma? She put you up against me."

"Lady Emma has nothing to do with you." Keeping himself calm required effort. "It's me. Just me. I'm done with that life. I'm not going back." He was growing tired of repeating it.

Without a word, she pivoted and strode away, followed by her maid.

He exhaled, hoping that was the last time he had to deal with Lady Beaumont. He had barely time to turn around when his heart skipped a beat.

Emma was watching him from the path.

WHEN MARCUS HAD TOLD Emma he had an errand to do, she'd thought he would head towards the city, not the park.

Instead, he'd finished a rather spirited conversation with Lady Beaumont—judging by the way she'd marched away from him—and now he showed a stunned expression like a thief caught red-handed as she watched yards away from the path.

To his credit, when he noticed her, he didn't pretend not to see her but walked over to her, straight and proud.

He was magnificent. The way he carried himself, his grey eyes, and his midnight hair were a powerful combination of charm and beauty. Their last kiss had changed their relationship forever.

Even though she was a bit annoyed by his behaviour—he'd claimed not to know Lady Beaumont—she couldn't deny the warm, fluttery feeling in her chest as he walked over to her.

"I didn't follow you," she said, regretting it immediately. But seeing him talking with Lady Beaumont had been a harsh surprise.

"I didn't think you did." He offered her his arm, but the lady's maid cleared her throat before Emma could take it.

Yes, probably walking arm in arm with him in public might be too much, considering rumours abounded. She nodded at Gibson for a bit of privacy. They walked side by side along the busy path.

"So you know her," she started, finding it difficult to organise her thoughts and keep them separated from her intimate reactions. "Not a simple bowing acquaintance, I gather."

She had no idea she could be such a wanton woman, but whatever beast Marcus's kisses had awakened inside her, it didn't want to go to sleep.

"I do know her," he said. "I lied, and I apologise."

She'd better be blunt. "Are you her lover?"

"No." He stared straight at her when he denied that. "But the situation is complicated."

"How did you meet her?" She didn't need to tell him not to lie to her. She trusted him that much to understand she wouldn't tolerate it.

He took his time to answer. A tendon of his neck stood out in sharp relief under the skin. "I worked for her. I don't need to work for her anymore, and she has trouble accepting that."

Finally, Lady Beaumont's words made sense. More or less. She believed Emma had forced Marcus to work exclusively for her.

"Why didn't you tell me the truth when I asked if you knew her?"

"I was ashamed," he whispered.

"Why would you be? You weren't doing anything illegal, were you?"

He flashed a sad smile. "Nothing of that sort."

"I hope you'll trust me from now on."

"I do trust you." He removed his hat, and the breeze ruffled his hair.

"Then why don't you tell me the truth?" She couldn't completely remove the annoyance from her voice.

"I will. Later today, if you have the patience to wait." He sounded honest and a little desperate as if he were frightened by her reaction.

"Of course. We'll talk later."

He exhaled in relief and bowed. "Now if you'll excuse me, I have some research I must do."

The conversation wasn't over. "Don't let me keep you."

"I'll see you later." He sped up along the path until he rounded a corner and disappeared from view.

Gibson glowered as she walked next to Emma. "Someone might have seen him with you, my lady."

"You don't approve of Marcus," Emma said.

"It's not my place to say, my lady."

"But I'm curious. Why are you upset?"

"I simply think a lady ought to be careful when dealing with a man like Mr. Kingston."

"What kind of man?"

"He's obviously a rake. Why would a married lady like Lady

Beaumont talk to him and become so upset at him if not because she's involved with him?"

"He told me he wasn't her lover."

"Begging your pardon, my lady, but isn't that what rakes always say?"

twenty-nine

Emma didn't know what to think anymore.

After she'd returned from the walk, she'd retired to her study, but found it difficult to concentrate.

Could Marcus be a rake? It wasn't difficult to imagine him pursued by ladies, but it was difficult to imagine him taking advantage of that. Considering he'd been starving and living on the streets for years, when would he have had time to seduce women and have one assignation after another?

He hadn't lied to her that morning in the park, but he hadn't been honest either.

She pushed aside the letters she needed to answer. Besides, with her precious typewriter broken, she had to write pages upon pages by hand.

Her concentration was so low a headache started to bother her. She propped her elbows on the escritoire and rested her forehead on her hands. Everything was going so well with Marcus until that moment.

"Emma?" Marcus's deep voice made her lift her head. "May I talk to you?"

She straightened, ready for whatever he had to confess. "Take a seat."

He exhaled before closing the door behind him and sitting on the sofa in front of her. "I suppose you have questions after today."

She shifted towards the edge of the chair. "I do"

He ran his palms over his thighs but didn't say anything. She waited, a nagging feeling at the back of her neck. He must have had many lovers.

"Let's start with Lady Beaumont," she said to help him talk. "You said you weren't her lover."

"I wasn't. Not exactly."

There was a long pause, and she didn't prompt him. The way he ran his palms over his thighs and his shifting gaze made her realise that was the first time she'd seen him so nervous.

He cleared his throat. "In the past years, I did everything I could to survive." He gave her a pointed look as if she were supposed to figure out everything by those few words.

"Do you mean stealing? I don't blame you for having stolen a wallet."

"No, it's not stealing although I tried that, and it didn't work. I'm a terrible thief." He chuckled nervously. He was always so confident that watching him fidget upset her.

"What is it then? You didn't kill anyone. I'm sure of that."

"No, not that either." He sucked in a deep breath. "I was such a disaster at thievery that I found myself starving for long periods when I couldn't find any leftover food behind the restaurants."

She put a hand on her chest. Thinking of Marcus rummaging through the waste container for food was as painful as a punch. "I wish I'd been there for you in those moments."

"You were with me," he said with such certainty she released a breath. His unsure voice was replaced by pure steel. "Always."

"You can tell me anything. What happened to you?"

"I was desperate. Those were dark days. I thought I was going to die of hunger a hundred times. Once, I fainted when I was crossing a railway, and by chance a train didn't kill me. So I had to do something not to die. I..."

She reached out to touch his hand, but he stiffened. "What is it?"

"It's difficult for me. I don't know how to say it in a polite way."

"Be blunt then. I'm not made of glass. You can tell me everything. I won't judge you. You know that."

He took a deep breath and said in a low tone, "I got paid to bed women."

"What do you...oh!" She remained frozen for a moment. Even her thoughts were still.

He didn't add anything else, giving her time to fully understand the implications of his confession. The fire crackling filled the silence for a few moments.

"In a disorderly house?" she asked.

He shook his head. "I did everything on my own."

"I didn't imagine that."

All the thoughts that had crammed her mind a moment ago vanished. Her mind became blank.

He swallowed hard a couple of times. "Neither did I. But when the opportunity presented itself, I took it." He lowered his gaze. His voice lowered as well. "What are you thinking? You can tell me everything, too."

She licked her dry lips as visions of Marcus in bed with other women flashed across her mind. They hurt for many reasons. Not simply because she was jealous, something she'd just learnt about herself, but because those women had taken advantage of a starving man for their own pleasure.

"Was Lady Beaumont one of those ladies?"

"Yes. She was one of the repeat customers. She was actually my first one. I met her at the market when I found a temporary job as a vendor's helper. She fancied me for some reason and proposed a deal to me. I refused at first, but I needed the money."

"And Lady Redfern?"

He gave her a grave nod. "She was one of my ladies, too."

"Oh dear." She pressed two fingers to her temples. Now Lady Beaumont's words made a lot of sense. And Lady Redfern's, too. "They think I keep you here as my exclusive mister. They think you're here only to..." She couldn't complete the sentence.

The thought of her taking advantage of Marcus's precarious situation made her want to cast up her accounts. If those ladies thought her capable of something like that, then they would do that themselves. But another terrible thought worked its way through her mind.

She swallowed a couple of times. "So what happened between us, the kisses..."

"No." He pressed his lips together. "I wasn't trying to make you pay for that. I swear on what is left of my honour, my attraction to you is genuine. Try me. Ask me to do anything you want to prove myself. I'll do it. But please do not doubt my feelings. They're the only things that kept me sane through those moments because they separated who I was from what I was doing."

"I know, sorry, I didn't mean...I shouldn't have thought that." She exhaled, rubbing her brow. His words struck something in her heart and let it hum. The longing she felt couldn't be mistaken for simple attraction. "I was wondering if you enjoyed those moments as much as I did."

"I did. Do not doubt that. That life took away a lot from me, including my dignity, but not my honesty, and I'm the master of my heart."

She stretched out her arm to hold his hand, but he didn't take it.

His grey eyes became distant. "I understand if you don't want to have anything to do with me after that. I just ask you to let me stay until we solve the situation with Sir Horace, and Jesse—"

"Marcus, I don't want you to leave. Never."

Disbelief hardened his features. "You don't care about my past?"

"I do, but not in the way you think." His sorrow had cleared her mind, and it didn't take much digging on her part to know she wanted him in her life. How could she let him go when the thought of not seeing him again caused her such pain? "I'm sorry for everything you've been through. It must have been horrible."

"Sometimes it was. But I have to be honest. There were times when I could have said no, but I didn't. It was my choice."

"No," she said. "If the choice was between dying of starvation and being paid, it wasn't a choice at all. Those women took advantage of your poverty."

"Yes, but had I been a better thief, I wouldn't have taken that path."

"How does that make any difference?"

He scratched his forehead. "I'm not sure. I'm talking nonsense. As I said, it's difficult to explain how it was. It wasn't pleasant but not extremely repulsive, either. Sometimes it was, but not always."

She rose and sat next to him. He stared at her with scared eyes. She'd never seen him so worried, aside from the night of the storm.

"Nothing has changed for me," she said.

He was shivering. "But you understand what it means, don't you? If my past comes out and you're seen with me, it will reflect badly for you. They'll make rumours about you, nasty ones. I'm used to that, but it's a fate I wouldn't ever wish upon you. Emma, I think it would be better if I left this house."

"No." She gripped his hands tightly. "No one wants a scandal like that to spread. Lady Beaumont and Lady Redfern would never blabber about you."

He laced his fingers through hers, a shiver going through him. "I can face anything as long as I won't lose you."

"That's never going to happen."

"You can be honest. If you want me to leave, I understand."

"I don't care what you did to survive. I mean it. I'm just sorry for what you had to endure." She drew in a shaky breath. "The thought of you starving and desperate horrifies me." Only compassion filled her heart. "I understand now why the night you arrived here, you jumped to the conclusion I wanted to use you like they had."

He worked his jaw. "Yes. I'm used to paying for food and shelter with a tumble."

She stiffened at the crudeness of his words.

"You need to know the whole of me before you make a decision. Compassion is one thing, but you might change your mind about kissing me again."

Could she renounce him and the way he made her feel? No. "Knowing what happened to you is a shock. I'm not going to lie. But that part of your life is over. You won't have to do that anymore."

"As usual, you're hopeful and certain the future will only hold good things." He smiled but sadly.

"I don't want to hear words of caution. We'll find a way to be together."

He kissed her knuckles, lingering with his lips on her skin. The usual flutter in her lower belly flickered and spread warmth through her body. She wondered if Lady Beaumont had felt the same way when Marcus had kissed her. That thought was squashed immediately.

She didn't want to think about that, about all the women who had been with him. He was with her now, of his own free will. He wanted to be with her. That was all that mattered.

"I'm glad you told me the truth," she said.

He kissed her fingers. "Thank you for not throwing me out."

"We have a deal, remember? I break things, you repair them."

He stroked her hand with the rough pad of his thumb. "By the way, your typewriter is as good as new. I repaired it this afternoon."

"Good." She caressed his hand in turn, wondering how his strong fingers would feel on her naked skin. "I'll inspect it later in the empty library to make sure everything works when no one is around."

"Sensible choice."

thirty

In the library, Marcus pressed a key of the typewriter to check it worked properly. The type bar shot forwards to print its letter on the paper. Repairing the device hadn't taken too much time; it'd been easier than he'd thought.

Like talking with Emma.

When he'd entered her study to tell her the truth, he'd believed she would have asked him to leave her house immediately. Her compassion and understanding had truly given him a new chance at life.

Her soft footfalls filled the silence of the library. His heart answered by pounding faster.

She stopped next to him in front of the typewriter. "Such a beauty. So strong."

"It didn't work properly for a while."

"Just a fleeting moment of difficulty." She pressed a few keys. "As I said, strong."

He trailed a finger over her hand, up her arm, and to her neck. "There's nothing I want more than to be with you. I've never felt like this with anyone. Only you." He caressed her cheek with his knuckles.

She quivered under his touch. "There's a small sitting room at the end of the corridor. Trevor never uses it."

He was more than tempted to gather her in his arms, carry her to the study, and not let her out until she was thoroughly satisfied.

"Are you sure?" he whispered, wishing with all his heart she said yes.

"I'll show you." She took his hand and led him down the aisle.

They passed rows of old books and ancient knowledge that added a solemn air to the moment.

A door opened to the left. A tufted red sofa and a low table were the only furniture in the small study smelling of worn leather and rich wood. When she closed the door behind them, only one diamond-paned window let the light from the street lamps in.

His situation hadn't changed. He would never be able to marry her. They could be nothing more than lovers until she found a husband. Then they wouldn't even be friends. He would be an embarrassing memory she wouldn't want to remember.

Moments like that would be everything he would ever have, and he accepted his fate. He would make those moments last for a lifetime.

She lit an oil lamp; its flame glowed over the brown wainscoting and the curtains. She sat on the sofa, bathed in the golden light. He knelt in front of her and took her lovely face in his hands. He opened his mouth to ask her again if she was sure, but she spoke first.

"Don't think too much." She stared at him, reading his thoughts. "This isn't the time to think about the future."

It was. But their futures were different—her future was safe and certain; his depended on too many things out of his control. But he wanted to make her happy now, in that moment, in that small room.

He kissed her.

The kiss had never the chance to start slowly. She parted her lips and stroked his with her tongue, and he couldn't contain his passion. She kissed him hard as if she wanted to prove to him she didn't care about his past. He replied in kind, feeling every one of her breaths on his skin.

Forgetting about the future was easy as she kissed him deeply and moaned softly. Only that moment existed. Even his past vanished. She wasn't the daughter of an earl anymore, and he wasn't a disgraced engineer, broken by an injustice. They were Emma and Marcus, and it was perfect. He was free to be himself with her. No tumble for money. And that made all the difference because he'd never experienced the wave of wonderful sensations going through him.

They shared heat and breath as he lifted her skirt and petticoats to bunch them around her hips.

He broke the kiss, needing to see her face. "I want to kiss you."

"You are."

He shook his head and slid a hand up her inner leg. "Here."

"Oh." She didn't sound shocked at all, but curious.

He caressed her thigh. "Do you want me to? Your wish is my command."

ALL THE EMOTIONS Emma was experiencing couldn't be normal.

Marcus had said they were, but as her blood was boiling and her body was pulsating, she wondered if she was just too wicked.

As she sat on the sofa, his hand stroked gently her inner thigh and didn't make her think straight. He was nestled between her legs, his large build barely fitting, and she couldn't help but hug him with her legs, lest he escape.

Did she want to be kissed? Yes.

He pulled apart the opening of her drawers and waited for her answer. "I'll stop if you don't like it."

He shouldn't have doubts. Just the thought of him kissing her started that delicious quiver through her body. She was more than ready. She would need only a light touch from him before she screamed out his name.

"Yes." It came out all breathy and husky.

He placed her legs over his shoulders, and her pulse spiked at the scandalous pose.

He stared at her adoringly before dipping his head, and her muscles clenched.

He kissed her, and it was shocking, delightful, and too powerful to stay quiet. Energy burst through her as if a hidden furnace had been lit inside her.

She had to trap her bottom lip between her teeth not to scream. He'd barely started, but she was already pulsating with pleasure, her head light and her chest heaving. She had no idea a kiss would be incredibly better than his touch.

He kissed her deeply and teased her with his tongue, and she couldn't believe the build-up of energy was starting all over. Her body must have waited all that time before releasing the hunger taking her over. Not one of the men she'd met so far had tickled the lurking desire within her.

She clenched her fists, squirmed, and curled her toes, but only Marcus could soothe the ache burning her.

When the second wave hit her, it was as if she were diving into a pool of warm water. She'd never experienced anything so liberating, powerful, and pleasurable.

He scattered kisses on her inner thighs, knees, and calves as she lay back, boneless and spent. Maybe she was too sensitive, but she adored every single brush of his lip on her heated skin.

He cupped her cheek, a mischievous light in his gaze. "I guess you liked it."

She threw herself at him, wrapping her arms and legs around him and kissing him madly. She kissed every inch of him available to her lips. They fell to the hard floor in a froth of fabric, but he laughed as she kissed his face.

"Take me, Marcus. Now." She straddled him, already anticipating the sensation of feeling him inside her.

The fact she had never done it didn't matter. Her instinct would tell her what to do.

He brushed a curl of her hair from her face. "Here? Now?"

"Yes."

"No. Not like this."

"I want you to feel what I feel."

"But I do." He stared at her in awe. "For the first time in years."

"That's surprising." She put her palms on his chest.

He took her hand and placed it over the falls of his trousers. "This is new for me as well. Emotionally, that is."

She gasped, and curiosity won. She opened the falls of his trousers and touched him. The deep groan rumbling from his chest was a great reward for her curiosity.

Indeed, as she stroked him, his breathing sped up, and he arched his back exactly as she'd done. The fact she was the one who made him feel that way pleased her to no end. With all the women he'd been with, she was the one who pleased him the most.

He shuddered and held her to his chest, and she returned the hug, lying on top of him on the cold floor. She pressed her cheek against his chest. His heartbeat thumped strong and steady, and his body shivered.

"I'll never forget this moment," he said. "Whatever is going to happen—"

"We don't talk about the future here. It's just us and just now."

He nodded solemnly. "You're my first one, too," he whispered. "Before you, being with a woman was only a physical act. With you, my body isn't the only one involved. My heart and soul are with you. I feel what you feel."

Out of nowhere, a sob remained trapped in her chest. All the pain and loneliness he had to endure hurt her intimately because she could have done something to spare him the pain.

She hugged him again. He wrapped his arms around her and held her. But that time, she wasn't seeking to satisfy her body ache. Only her heart.

thirty-one

Emma was glowing. She was convinced that if she closed the window shutters of her bedroom, her skin would appear luminous in the dark.

After she and Marcus had hugged on the floor, he'd escorted her back to her bedroom and had kissed her again. A sweet, good night kiss she still felt on her lips.

Contrary to what she would have thought, she'd slept soundly through the night and awakened rested and full of energy and full of thoughts of Marcus.

She'd spent the morning in the library typing letters for Trevor with her recently repaired typewriter. Her glance kept drifting towards the small room where she'd shared wonderful moments with Marcus.

She'd told him they wouldn't discuss the future, but the more time she spent with him, the more the future worried her. Her papa had always told her she was too naive, that life was a battle of nasty surprises, and for the first time, she'd wondered if he'd been right, if she would lose Marcus before she had the chance of being with him.

"My lady," Stewart said.

She hadn't heard him coming. "Yes?"

"Hid Lordship wishes to see you in his study."

The interruption bothered her, but she didn't want another argument with her brother.

She knocked on the door to Trevor's study, her mood shifting from hopeful to concerned, which was something new to her. Her hope had always been a faithful companion.

"Come in," Trevor said.

He wasn't alone. Marcus was sitting next to him.

"Afternoon, gentlemen." She stared at him for a moment too long, and her body tingled with sensations, remembering the kisses and touches in the moonlight.

They stood up when she entered.

"There you are." Trevor studied her. "You're still flushed."

"I'm fine. Truly." She sat on the chair in front of his desk. Marcus showed a fleeting smile. "What did you want to tell me?"

Trevor gave her one last sceptical look. "Marcus studied the documents from other construction sites of Sir Horace. I had to ask a few favours to get them, but never mind. He found the same pattern we've seen in St. Giles, repeated across each one of his works. He uses the same suppliers at every site although the costs he declares don't match the costs reported in the suppliers' catalogues. So Marcus was right. Sir Horace is a thief."

"He's a polyhedric fraud. Still a fraud," she said. "Tell the truth and shame the devil."

"That's the plan." Trevor smiled with a smug look of triumph she'd rarely seen. Usually, he was never satisfied with anything unless it was a stallion. "But I want to be cautious. I won't attack Sir Horace openly, not yet."

"Why not?" She couldn't remove the disappointment in her voice.

Trevor lifted a shoulder. "He's friends with a few powerful politicians. I want to find the right way to attack him without having it come back on us."

She frowned. "I disagree. We should bury him with everything we have."

"Patience."

"Cowardice," she rebuked.

"Still, it's great news, isn't it?" Marcus said, likely tired of another argument.

"Yes, in fact, a celebration is in order." She tossed a challenging glance at Trevor before facing Marcus again. "Would you and Jesse join us for dinner?"

Trevor's smirk vanished.

Marcus remained serious. "We discussed that many times."

"Yes, but I think we could indulge in a small celebration after what you discovered about Sir Horace. Trevor? Jesse would be incredibly happy to have dinner with us."

Trevor straightened a pile of documents. "It's too early for a celebration. This is but the beginning. As I said, I don't want an open war against Sir Horace."

"Where's your optimism?" She returned the attitude.

"I've never had it. That said." Trevor stopped tidying the desk. "The boy has been quiet and well-mannered. Mrs. Daubney told me he helps in the kitchen every day and is a hard worker. I have no objection."

"Thank you, Trevor. I knew you would change your mind." She hugged him, and he smiled.

Quick footsteps approached. Mrs. Ferguson rushed into the room. Her chatelaine clinked when she stopped. "My lord."

"What is it?" Trevor quickly lost his good humour.

Mrs. Ferguson swallowed between quick pants. "My lord, Jesse is gone."

"What?" Trevor and Marcus said together.

Mrs. Ferguson composed herself. Her dark gown made her cheeks look very pale. "Mrs. Daubney left him in the kitchen. He was peeling some potatoes while she went to the costermonger. When she returned, the potatoes had been peeled, but the kitchen was empty and the back door was open. No one saw him. We searched for him everywhere. He isn't in the house. It's been a couple of hours now."

"It's not possible." Marcus walked around the desk.

"He's probably hiding somewhere," Trevor said. "No need to panic. We'll search the house again."

"I'll check the garden." Emma ran downstairs, followed by Marcus.

"He would never leave without telling me," Marcus said as they took the path weaving through the garden.

"Perhaps he was bored and left for a walk." She searched around the bushes.

"Jesse?" Marcus called. "Come out!"

"Let's take a look at the shed."

The door screeched when he opened it. Garden tools and bags of seeds competed for space. No trace of Jesse.

"Where could he be?" Marcus raked a hand through his hair.

She walked along the hedgerow. "Did something happen? Did Trevor scold him?"

"Hey, I'm here, and I did not!" Trevor stood behind her. "I barely spoke to him, and every time he walks past me, he lowers his head and speeds up."

"I wonder why. Why would he leave then?" She paced on the path.

"I didn't tell him anything." Trevor held up a hand.

"Well, maybe that's the reason he left. You've been quite harsh to him."

"I don't think it was Trevor," Marcus said. "He decided to go somewhere for some reason."

"He's a clever, resourceful lad," Trevor said. "He knows how to survive the streets, does he not?"

Emma skidded to a stop, crunching the ground with her boots. "What is that supposed to mean?"

"That he has more experience than an earl's son his age." Annoyance was etched on Trevor's face.

"He's an eleven-year-old boy, alone in a big city, convinced that you don't want him here!"

Trevor's nostrils flared. "I didn't mean it as an insult."

"So it was a compliment, wasn't it?"

"Yes!"

"I know you too well. You never pay a compliment to someone."

"Well, maybe Jesse deserves it!"

"Please." Marcus stepped between them. "Let's split into groups and search the neighbourhood." He turned to Trevor. "If you want to, of course."

"I bloody want to, all right? I'll ask the footmen to help." Trevor marched towards the house with angry strides.

"I apologise for his words," Emma said.

"I think he was honest when he said it was a compliment."

"If Jesse left the house because of him, I'll give him some compliments."

Marcus smiled. "Let's go."

thirty-two

After two hours of walking up and down Mayfair without finding any traces of Jesse, Emma sat exhausted on a bench in Green Park with Marcus next to her.

The day had changed drastically from brightness to darkness, and she found fewer and fewer reasons to be hopeful.

"I'm sorry, Marcus. I feel responsible for Jesse's disappearance. I shouldn't have promised anything. Maybe he felt disappointed and left."

"It's not your fault. He was likely bored. I haven't spent a lot of time with him."

She rubbed her arms. "It's getting dark. Where could he be?"

"We'd better return home and see if the others have found anything."

They walked home in silence, checking every corner for Jesse. The shadows lengthened until the lamplighters turned on the street lamps. Carriages drove past as people returned home from their engagements.

She shivered as the dusk brought a chilly wind. "Trevor and I haven't been welcoming to you and Jesse."

"You saved Jesse's life. One can't be more welcoming than that."

"You know what I mean."

He draped his jacket around her shoulders. "I know, and you've been wonderful."

She gazed up at him. "You'll get cold."

He stared at her fondly, his grey eyes melting. "No, I won't."

She snuggled into the warm jacket that smelled like him. The scent brought her back to last night when she'd lain in his arms and they'd shared kisses and laughter. Guilt came right after. Jesse was missing, and she had other thoughts.

"I still think Trevor had a role in Jesse's disappearance. He's worried about his reputation," she said. "The way Mama was treated angered him, and now, instead of fighting that attitude, he shows it towards others. I don't understand it. Trevor and I don't have pure aristocratic blood. He should be more sympathetic towards Jesse."

"The strongest hate is the one towards oneself. He probably hates the fact he isn't a pure aristocrat. But he loved your mother dearly, so I guess he doesn't want someone like Jesse or me to remind him of your mother's origin."

"That's not an excuse." She craned her neck to check a dark alleyway.

"Emma." His tone became serious. "We can't live happily together under the same roof. Trevor is right. Your family shouldn't be attached to my name. As much as I don't want to think about the future, I have to."

"But we can prove Sir Horace is a fraud. That would clear your father's name, and you can start working again. Everything will be fine."

"Proving Sir Horace is a fraud now won't change my father's verdict."

She sped up, anger fuelling her steps. Everyone around her only saw horrible outcomes. "So it's all decided then. Your life is ruined forever, and we won't see each other ever again because that's our fate, and there's nothing we can do about it. Fighting is useless. Why don't you leave right now then?" She regretted the last words the moment they left her lips and hoped he wouldn't take her seriously. "Marcus..." she whispered.

He closed a hand around her arm. "I don't like it either, but pretending the problem doesn't exist won't make it go away."

She trapped her bottom lip between her teeth not to let it quiver. "I don't want to lose you again."

His eyes became two silver pools as he stared at her with his usual adoration. "You won't."

She hooked her arm through his. "That's all that matters to me."

They walked back to Hart House in silence, but inside, her thoughts were speaking loudly. Fear pressed against her chest, despite her wanting to be hopeful. Marcus could be right. They might not have the chance to be together, but if she didn't fight for him, then for what?

The stars hid behind the clouds by the time a footman opened the front door for her.

"Is he back?" she asked the moment she stepped into the entry hall.

"Not yet, my lady," the footman said, taking Marcus's jacket and her coat. "Mrs. Daubney is quite upset."

Trevor was in the drawing room, talking with Stewart and Mrs. Daubeny.

"If you'd been more understanding with the boy, my lord," Mrs. Daubney said, "he would be here now. He's scared of you."

Surprisingly, Trevor took the scolding from the cook with grace, nodding.

"A sweet boy like Jesse deserves only love," the cook went on.

Trevor hung his head.

Instead, Stewart had a pinched expression. "That's quite

enough, Mrs. Daubney. I believe you should return to the kitchen."

"But—"

"Mrs. Daubney," Stewart said in a warning voice.

The cook bobbed a curtsy and left, muttering, "Apologies, my lord."

Trevor held up a hand. "It's all right."

Emma stepped aside to let Mrs. Daubney pass and walked over to Trevor.

"News?" they asked each other at the same time.

Trevor released a breath. "Nothing. No one found him."

"We should go to the police." Emma glanced out of the window at the thickening darkness.

"I went to the police station," Trevor said, "and reported him missing. If they find anything, they'll send an officer here."

"Good thinking." She sat on the armchair with a sigh. "So we have to wait."

"Would you like a little supper, my lady?" Stewart asked.

"My appetite is gone." She shook her head.

"You need to eat something." Marcus looked out of the window as well. "I want to search for him after supper. I'll be in the kitchen if you need me."

"Stay here," Trevor said before Marcus left. "We can have a quick supper together, and then I'll go out with you."

Marcus remained speechless for a moment. "Thank you."

Trevor gave an easy nod. "It's nothing, and if we don't find the boy, Mrs. Daubney will probably stop cooking for me. It's a joke, of course."

She smiled at him.

The dinner was a restless affair with them checking the windows every now and then and jumping every time someone walked past the house.

"Where do you want to go?" Trevor asked once they finished eating.

"My old flat. Maybe Jesse went there for some reason."

"I want to come as well." Emma rose from the chair.

Trevor stood up. "You should stay here in case the officer comes."

"I don't want to stay here, and Stewart can talk to the officer."

"For once, can't you do as you're told?"

"I'm worried," she said through her teeth.

Trevor was about to say something when loud voices and footsteps came from outside the corridor.

Mrs. Daubney rushed into the room, holding up her apron to wipe her tears. "Jesse is back, my lady. Back door. Right now."

"Thank goodness." Emma headed towards the servants' entrance.

"Finally," Trevor said, following her.

They hurried towards the kitchen. At the back entrance, a small group of footmen and maids was gathered.

"Jesse!" Marcus made his way towards the door.

The servants moved out of his way, opening a path, and she finally caught a glimpse of Jesse.

His pale face was tense, and a corner of his mouth was twisted in a grimace. Aside from that, he was in one piece.

"Jesse!" She, Marcus, and Trevor spoke at once.

"Where have you been? We were worried about you." Marcus crushed Jesse in a hug, but the boy groaned and disentangled from him.

"I'm sorry. I left for a walk and got lost." Jesse gazed anywhere but at Marcus.

"Why didn't you tell us you were leaving?" Trevor asked, not without kindness.

Jesse twisted the hem of his jacket. "You were all busy."

"You gave me a fright." Mrs. Daubney kissed his cheek. "You disappeared."

"I didn't mean to stay out that long." Jesse shuffled his feet.

"We are never too busy for you." Emma hugged him but withdrew from him when he cried out.

"You're hurt," Marcus said.

"I'm fine. I'm fine. Never been better." Jesse's voice cracked.

"Show me."

Jesse clenched his fists. "I'm fine, but I'm a little hungry."

"Why don't you go and sit down with His Lordship and Her Ladyship in the dining room?" Mrs. Daubney said. "So you can eat something. I'll have a nice supper delivered quickly."

Jesse didn't need to be told twice. Wincing, he walked to the dining room with a small limp. They followed him with Trevor leading the group.

"You aren't well," Trevor said. "Tell us the truth."

"Let us see." Emma caressed Jesse's head. "What happened?"

Trevor bent over to stare at Jesse in the eyes. "You won't be punished. I promise. Just tell us what happened. Did a carriage hit you?"

He burst into tears in the middle of the dining room and hid his face in the crook of his elbow.

Emma hugged him gently, careful not to squeeze him too tightly. "You know no one will throw you out, don't you? Tell us where you're hurt."

Jesse leant against her, exhausted. "I was beaten," he whispered.

"What?" Trevor roared.

"By who?" Marcus demanded.

No answer.

"I think for now it's more important to assess the damage than to know who the culprit is," Emma said. "Let us see, so we can send for the physician if needed."

"Show us, Jesse," Trevor said. "We aren't angry with you."

Slowly, Jesse left her embrace and turned around. He winced and sniffled as he lifted his jacket and shirt to uncover his back. He revealed three long red areas, likely the result of the lashes of a walking stick.

There was a collective gasp and a grunt.

"Good Lord." Emma clamped a hand over her mouth. "Stewart, send for Sir Paul."

"Immediately, my lady." The butler ran out of the dining room.

"Who did this to you?" Emma hugged Jesse again.

He shook his head. "I can't tell you."

Marcus crouched in front of him. "Who was it?"

"You'll be angry."

"Yes, but not with you. Tell me."

Jesse shook with another sob and stared at the floor. "Sir Horace."

There was a cold moment of silence when they heard that name.

Jesse wiped his face. "I heard you talking about him and the horrible things he did, and I wanted to be useful. So I sneaked inside his house to search his office to find something to help you, but he caught me and thought I was a thief. He chased me. I ran, but he hit my back with his walking stick before I escaped." He touched the top of his head. "He grabbed my hair and pulled it, and I cried because it burned so much."

"Oh, Jesse." Marcus kissed the top of his head.

"You shouldn't have gone there," Emma said.

Jesse sniffled. "I wanted to help and not cause trouble. I wanted to show you I can be useful, that I can stay here and help you."

Trevor stood petrified, his eyes unblinking.

"My lord," Stewart said, "Sir Paul is here."

"Show him to Jesse's room. We'll be upstairs in a moment." Trevor exhaled and turned towards Jesse. "You don't cause trouble." He took the boy's trembling hand. "Let's go upstairs so Sir Paul can examine you. After that, we'll have dinner together. What would you like to have for dessert? I'm sure Mrs. Daubney will be happy to prepare anything you want."

Jesse wiped his tears again and said something she didn't catch.

"What?" Trevor asked.

"Nothing. Anything is fine. No need to cook something special. Every day here is a feast for me anyway."

"What about ice cream?" Trevor's smirk of triumph was back. "Would that be all right?"

Jesse's eyes flared wide. "Is it a trick? Will you punish me if I say yes?"

Trevor narrowed his gaze. "Blast it all! That's a great idea."

"Trevor!" Emma huffed.

"I'm joking. No, Jesse, no punishment. It was an honest offer."

Jesse nodded. "More than all right, my lord."

Trevor nodded back. "Then ice cream it is."

thirty-three

Marcus tucked Jesse in bed. After Sir Paul's visit and the dinner, Jesse had been so tired he'd fallen asleep the moment his head touched the pillow.

Emma sat next to him. She'd kept smiling while Jesse had been awake and giving him reassuring words, but now dark shadows crossed her face and tears hung on the tips of her eyelashes.

Seeing her worried was like a blade twisting in his chest. She had hope for them, and he wished he could share it with her. But life had taught him different lessons.

"Jesse took a huge risk." She lowered the flame of the oil lamp on the nightstand.

"I shouldn't have talked to him about Sir Horace, but we're used to sharing everything. Well, almost everything." He exchanged a meaningful look with her.

"We should let him sleep."

They left the room and quietly shut the door.

"As if I didn't despise Sir Horace enough," he said.

"At least he wasn't aware of who Jesse was. Had he known Jesse was your friend, he would have been more cruel."

"I'm going to see him." He headed towards his room, anger seething in his veins.

"Who?" She followed him.

"Sir Horace." He put his jacket on, but she touched his arm.

"Don't go."

"I don't care if he mistreats me, but Jesse is another matter. If he wants to fight someone, he should fight me. He deserves to be punished."

"He does, but barging into his house and confronting him won't make the situation better. And Jesse would be in danger after because you would make his connection known."

He worked his jaw. "Jesse is my charge. I promised him I would keep him safe."

"What happened isn't your fault. We shouldn't have talked about Sir Horace in front of him. It's remarkable that Jesse found Sir Horace's address and broke into his house."

"He must have found the address on my desk. It's full of documents about Sir Horace. As for breaking into his house, Trevor was right. Jesse grew up in the rookery. He has many skills."

"We'll fight Sir Horace by dragging him to court and exposing him. If you confront him now, you might compromise all the work you did."

He leant against the bedpost, releasing some of the tension with a long breath. "I hate this."

"What?"

"Being useless, feeling powerless and having only to suffer the blow and wait. After the incident, I couldn't help my father. Then he was accused, and I couldn't defend him. When he died and they came to confiscate everything I owned, I had to stand aside and let them take away the furniture my mother had chosen, the house my parents had lived in, and even my clothes. I had to bow my head and stay quiet. When I was starving and getting paid for tumbles presented itself, I bowed my head again and endured what I didn't want to do. And now, I can't help Jesse. What kind of person can't protect those he loves?"

Emotion tightened his throat. He'd never talked about his discomfort with anyone, not even with himself. Surviving had been his only goal in the past years. Every compunction he might have had about doing certain things had to be squashed immediately and never to be thought about again.

But he was thinking about them now. And it felt as if he were covered in dirt, as if he'd been a coward, choosing not to fight for what he'd wanted.

"That's not true." She put a hand on his chest, and the shot of energy going through him made him feel powerful for a moment. "You're working to protect Jesse and children like him."

He put his hand over hers on instinct. "I was powerless when I wanted to court you. I knew I wasn't enough for you…"

"That's not true either."

"I wasn't enough for my father." That hurt him intimately. "We were going through our most desperate moment, and instead of staying with me and helping me fight, he chose to leave me. My love wasn't a motivation strong enough for him to stay."

"He wasn't himself." Her voice thinned as if her throat were so tight she couldn't speak. "He loved you very much, but he must have been ashamed of himself for what had happened. Don't take his desperation for lack of love. That wouldn't be fair."

Something hollow ached within his chest. "Staying here, not having to worry about my next meal, made me think about my choices, and I'm not talking only about the ladies. I'm disgusted with myself."

"Don't." She took his face. "How can you be disgusted with yourself when I love you?"

All the breath was flushed out of his lungs as if someone had punched him. He searched her face for any signs she might be joking or regretting her words. But her hazel eyes stayed on him, unwavering. Her expression remained serious and determined. Her touch showed only care. Yet he couldn't believe it.

"Emma…" He couldn't even speak.

"I love you, Marcus, because you're kind, clever, and brave, and I don't care what the rest of the world says, and I don't want to lose you. And I hate that you don't consider yourself good enough for me. Because you're the best man I've ever met."

He hugged her, holding her close to his chest. For years, he'd dreamt of hearing those words from her, and now that she'd told them, he didn't know what to say. No, that wasn't true.

"I love you, Emma. I've always loved you, even when we were apart."

She squeezed him tightly. "You have to promise me you won't give up hope. I understand what you've been through has discouraged you, but this is a new start for both of us."

"I promise."

"You must mean it."

"I do." He gathered her in his arms and laid her on his bed.

She snuggled closer to him and tucked the top of her head under his chin. "I want to be your wife."

Happiness climbed up his throat and burst out with a funny noise halfway between a laugh and a sigh of relief.

"There's nothing I want more than to be your husband, build a house for you, and live with you for the rest of my life."

"It's a wonderful plan." Her voice came muffled as she pressed her face to his chest. "Just be quick. I don't like waiting."

He caressed her head and back. "Patience is a virtue."

"Then I'm not virtuous." Her eyes fluttered, and she drawled something with little meaning.

He held her as her body slackened against his.

She was wrong. She was the most virtuous person he'd ever met. Untouched by the ugliness of life. A dark side of him envied her for that, but his heart ordered him to protect her exactly because she'd lived almost all her life sheltered—what she'd seen in the river would stay with her forever—and her uncommon kindness and disarming hope came from that, from the belief life could be fair.

And he was starting to believe that, too.

EMMA WOKE up with a start before dawn. In Marcus's bed. In his arms.

Perfect, if not for the worry of someone realising she hadn't slept in her bed.

The flame-keeper would soon light the fireplace in her bedroom and might give the alarm at the empty bed, especially after Jesse's disappearance.

"I have to go." She disentangled from Marcus's arms and the covers.

He groaned and stretched out his arms. "Good morning."

She kissed him, searching for her slippers. She didn't remember having removed them. "I must go."

"Yes, yes." He rubbed his face and sat up on the bed, looking handsome all ruffled and dishevelled.

She exhaled when she found her shoes. "I'll see you soon." She kissed him again, feeling his stubble against her skin. And the stubble deserved another kiss.

He chuckled, and the sound was so charming she gave him another kiss.

Soon, they were kissing each other sloppily and laughing for no reason.

"I must go." She caressed his jaw.

"And I want to see Jesse." Another kiss. "Sleeping with you was beautiful."

"One day, we'll do that every night."

He didn't lose his radiance as he usually did when she mentioned their future.

He blew her a kiss, opening the inner door to Jesse's room. She wiggled her fingers and slid out of his bedroom.

His scent was all over her, and a sense of peace washed over her.

She turned around on her tiptoes to go to her room and gasped. Trevor, fully dressed in his riding habit, watched her, standing in the middle of the hallway.

She didn't speak or move as if by remaining silent and still, he wouldn't see her. But then again, there was nothing to say.

He pressed his lips hard and strode away. His heavy footfalls said everything he hadn't. But it didn't matter. She wouldn't change her mind about Marcus.

After she changed into a fresh gown, she helped Marcus apply a numbing ointment to Jesse's back. The angry red lashes had swollen, but they were less painful, or so Jesse kept saying.

A new peaceful atmosphere had settled between her and Marcus after last night's conversation. She loved him and wanted him in her life, but above all, she wanted to make him understand how important he was to her.

His smile was serene when he met her gaze, but she wasn't deluded. He wasn't hopeful about their future. She was ready to leave her life behind to be with him. Trevor would understand with time. He would be grumpy at first, but then he would accept the fact she loved Marcus.

Jesse muffled a whimper with his pillow as Marcus finished applying the ointment.

"Is it better?" She wiped her hands on a cloth, smelling the lavender oil.

"Much better. I don't feel anything." Jesse smiled, but unshed tears welled in his eyes.

"Tell the truth." Marcus buttoned Jesse's shirt. "I don't believe you don't feel anything."

Jesse lowered his gaze. "It stings a bit."

"It has to be more than a bit," she said. "Your back is swollen."

"If I sleep on my belly, I barely notice it." Jesse forced another smile.

"Tell the truth," Marcus repeated. "We can't help you if you pretend not to feel anything."

Jesse's smile vanished. "I'm sore and achy everywhere and tired of being sick. But don't tell the earl I said that."

Emma adjusted his shirt. "Why not?"

"I don't want him to think I'm trouble."

Speaking of the devil, Trevor poked his head inside. "May I come in?"

Jesse wiped his face quickly and smiled brightly. "My lord."

Trevor shot her a glance that lasted a second. His expression changed when he turned towards Jesse. He showed a smile so wide that wrinkles appeared at the sides of his eyes. "How are we this morning?"

"Spectacular," Jesse said in a flat tone.

Emma folded her arms over her chest. "What is it?"

She didn't think Trevor would vent his annoyance at her on Jesse, but she wouldn't tolerate any rebuke.

Trevor scrubbed the back of his neck. "I have a surprise for Jesse."

Marcus tilted his head, a crease between his eyebrows. "What surprise?"

"For me?" Jesse sat upright, grimacing.

"You'll see. But we need to go to the park." Trevor's smile worried her. "Take a break, fellas, and come with me."

"Can you walk, Jesse?" Marcus asked.

"Ye-yes." He gingerly climbed off the bed. "If the earl asks me to go with him, I'll go."

"You should stay here." Emma narrowed her gaze at her brother.

Jesse stood up. "No. I want to go."

"Then come. You'll be surprised," Trevor said.

Half an hour later, Emma, Marcus, Trevor, and a very suspicious Jesse entered Hyde Park. Trevor was beaming and walking with confidence towards the field while Marcus frowned, and Emma was confused, especially after her brief encounter with her brother. Jesse was the most nervous in the group, dragging his feet and fiddling with his hands.

"You'll see," Trevor said. "It's a big surprise."

"I'll be good. I promise," Jesse whispered. "I won't leave the house again without telling anyone. I'll do everything you ask me, my lord. Quiet as a mouse. You won't realise I'm around."

Trevor stopped in the middle of the path. "This isn't a punishment. Trust me." He stretched out his arm and withdrew it. Then he stretched it out again, and she wondered what he was doing. Finally, he gave Jesse his hand. "And I know you're a very good boy."

Emma gasped. What had happened to her brother?

Tentatively, Jesse slid his hand into Trevor's large one as if Trevor were a wild bear he didn't trust.

She exchanged a glance with Marcus. He looked as astonished as she felt.

They walked down the path towards Route de Roi where Emma and other Londoners were used to riding their horses in the morning.

"Surprise!" Trevor stopped in front of a brown pony already saddled and ready to go. One of their grooms stood next to the animal. "This is Button."

"Nice beast," the groom said.

"And Button is all for Jesse." Trevor stroked Button's muzzle.

Emma let out a delighted squeal. Marcus muttered something under his breath.

Jesse's mouth hung open. "A pony. For me?"

"Yes, and George here will teach you how to ride him." Trevor stroked Button's ears. The pony half-closed his eyes and neighed in pleasure. "He's a sweet-tempered boy, young and strong. The best pony for an inexperienced rider. I'm sure you two will become great friends."

"I didn't expect this," Marcus whispered to Emma.

"Neither did I."

Jesse burst out crying. He hid his face in his hands, his shoulders shaking.

Trevor patted his shoulder. "There. There. No need to cry." His eyes were suspiciously shiny as well.

Jesse threw himself at Trevor, hugging him tightly. "Thank you, my lord."

Trevor swallowed hard a couple of times. "It's all right. Now start getting to know Button."

"Can I ride him?" Jesse asked.

Trevor looked lost and shifted his gaze to Emma. "Can he? Isn't he still recovering?"

"You said you were sore," Emma said.

Jesse wiped his face. "Yes, but I want to try. Only a few minutes, please."

Trevor held up a hand. "I'm not going to say anything, or it will be used against me. Marcus, you decide."

Jesse tugged at Marcus's jacket. "Please. If it hurts too much, I'll stop."

"I'll be careful," George said.

"Only a few minutes." Marcus gave a nod to Trevor.

"Yes!" Jesse pumped a fist in the air.

"Also..." Trevor fished out a shiny red apple from his pocket and handed it to Jesse. "For you."

He took the apple and pressed it against his chest as if Trevor had given him the most precious gift. "Thank you."

For a moment, they stared at each other. Then Trevor cleared his voice. "Off you go, then. Button is eager to get to know you."

"Put your foot here and grab the pommel of the saddle." George explained to Jesse how to climb on the pony.

They sat on a bench as, a few yards away, Jesse slowly rode

Button under the watchful eye of the groom. Jesse didn't laugh, focused solely on following George's instructions, but excitement radiated from him.

Trevor nodded his approval. "You're doing very well, Jesse. Considering you don't feel well."

"Thank you for making him happy," Marcus said.

"He went through a lot, and what Sir Horace did to him was despicable. I understand he believed Jesse to be an intruder, and well, he was, but beating a child like that..." Trevor heaved a sigh charged with annoyance. "My solicitor will visit us this afternoon. We're moving onwards, aggressively so."

"So we're openly going against Sir Horace," Emma said.

"Yes." Trevor turned serious. "Before what happened to Jesse, I didn't plan to attack Sir Horace openly, but after that, I will not hide."

"You're wonderful." She squeezed his hand.

"Yes, and remember that the next time you start a conversation with me, saying *'listen'*."

Marcus stretched out his hand towards him, and Trevor shook it.

"Marcus won't be mentioned, will he?" Emma asked.

"Not if we can avoid it."

"If you don't hide, neither will I," Marcus said.

"But Sir Horace will retaliate," Emma said.

"I have nothing. He can't threaten me. He's already taken everything I have, and if the choice is between protecting myself or the people in the rookery, I choose the latter."

Emma covered his hand with hers.

Trevor glanced at their hands but didn't say anything. The harsh expression from that morning returned.

thirty-four

The study was so quiet Emma could hear Jesse playing with his brand-new set of wooden trains on the floor above. A gift from Trevor, another surprise after the pony in the park. Trevor was spoiling him, which was fine with her. The boy deserved it.

Mr. Carr, their solicitor, was examining the documentation Marcus had painstakingly collected. They waited in silence for the solicitor to give his opinion. The rustle of the pages was the only noise.

Mr. Carr removed his glasses after he finished reading. "I think there are enough questionable circumstances to open an inquest. The barrister will likely send the police to investigate Sir Horace's activities and inspect his building sites and registers."

"What will happen then?" Marcus asked.

"While the investigation is ongoing, every construction site supervised by Sir Horace will be blocked, and the workers will be dismissed, causing delays and disruptions, and I must tell you, investors won't like that."

"Dismissed?" The word caught Emma's attention. "What will happen to all those people who work for Sir Horace?"

"They'll find themselves unemployed, at least for as long as Sir Horace's position hasn't been cleared up."

"I thought dismissing workers wasn't easy." She angled towards her brother.

"It depends on who the workers are," Trevor said. "They won't be dismissed immediately, but if the construction site is declared condemned, they'll have to go."

"How long will it take for the workers to get their jobs back?" She hadn't thought about that problem.

"Alas, it depends." Mr. Carr put his glasses on. "It could be a couple of weeks or months. And if Sir Horace's building sites are permanently closed, then the workers will need to find new employment."

She exchanged glances with the others. "Those workers need to support their families. How can they survive for months without work?"

Mr. Carr exhaled without looking very sympathetic. "It'll be difficult for them, and if Sir Horace is found guilty, they will be jobless."

Doubts gnawed at her. "Maybe we should think of a solution for those people before denouncing Sir Horace."

"We must think about the people who are going to live in those houses," Trevor said. "The workers' situation is unfortunate, but we must make a decision."

"Can't we set up a reimbursement for the workers?" Marcus asked. "We might be facing a massive riot if those workers don't receive any pay."

"If they were a handful, yes, but we're talking about hundreds of people to be sustained for months." Trevor spread his arms. "I don't have the funds for that."

Emma leant back in the chair, wondering what her father would have done in that situation. She'd been ready to condemn him for being insensitive and for lacking compassion, but perhaps he'd faced one too many of these choices.

"I need to know your decision," Mr. Carr said. "Do you need time to think about this, or do you want me to proceed immediately?"

She opened and closed her hands. "We should take more time to find a solution for those workers."

"Emma." Trevor shook his head. "I thought you wanted a quick attack on Sir Horace."

"But we can't let families starve."

"I would like to proceed now," Trevor said. "You accused me of cowardice, and I think you were right. Whatever we do, no matter how we do it, there are going to be risks. So let's close this case and brace for the consequences. The longer we wait, the worse it will be."

She sank her teeth into her bottom lip. "Heaven."

It seemed that whatever she chose, someone would suffer. But then again, Trevor had a point. Sir Horace might be the reason so many buildings and structures weren't fit for living.

"I agree with Trevor," Marcus said. "It's better to start the inquest now. I'm hopeful that we'll find a way to help the workers."

She nodded, smiling at him. "All right. Let's proceed."

AFTER MR. CARR LEFT, Emma was about to leave the study with Marcus, but Trevor called her.

"I need a word," he said in a serious tone.

Marcus waved at her before going upstairs.

She sighed and closed the door, fearing he wanted to talk about that morning. "If it's about Sir Horace, no, I won't accuse you of anything this time."

"Not about him." He gestured at the chair next to him and sat down when she did.

"What is it?"

"You and Marcus are very close." He raised an eyebrow and gave her a pointed look.

"Well, this morning—"

"No." He held up a hand. "I don't want to discuss what you were doing this morning in his bedroom. No details, thank you. I want to know what's happening between you and him. Is it a passing infatuation, odd friendship, or something else?"

She straightened and prepared for a battle. "That doesn't concern you."

"You're my sister, so yes, it concerns me. It concerns me a lot."

She lifted a shoulder. "And?"

"You're behaving wantonly with him."

She was, and it was delicious. "What if I am?"

"Bloody hell, Emma." He rubbed the bridge of his nose. "We aren't playing a game. Your reputation is at stake."

"I love him." There. She'd said it. She wasn't ashamed of her feelings, and Trevor should understand she was serious.

"Oh, great." He threw a hand up. "Very sensible."

"Love isn't sensible."

"Exactly!" He exhaled through his teeth. "He has nothing to offer you. I had doubts about him when he had a promising future, but now? I don't have any doubts."

"He has everything to offer me. It's my life, Trevor, and I'm ready to renounce my position here—"

"And your dowry?"

"And my dowry to be with him. I'll do my best not to damage your reputation. I could live somewhere far from here, not to bother you."

"Great plan. Congratulations. And when Marcus is penniless, and no one wants to talk to you, what will you do?"

"Marcus and I will work together. I won't beg you for money, and I believe in Marcus's talent. I have hope for him."

He clenched a fist. "Hope won't feed you. Forget hope. Hope is dead, all right? There's only the real world, and it's brutal."

Why did everyone have to be so grim? Her hope wasn't a baseless dream. Marcus was a great engineer. He would find a good job and start again. "If you don't want to help me, fine, but at least you could avoid being so cruel."

"I'm not cruel."

"Don't worry. I won't ask you for a farthing. If my future is to starve next to Marcus, I'll accept it."

"Your self-sacrificing spirit is completely unnecessary and over dramatic. I just want you to make the right decision, which is to marry sensibly, not unreasonably."

"No, enough." She leapt to her feet. "You can't order me how I should lead my life only because you're the earl. I thought we loved each other. I was wrong." She strode out of the study, ignoring him calling after her.

thirty-five

After dinner, Marcus arranged the papers, documents, and articles he'd used for his research and stacked them into the folders in his bedroom.

His job was done. He'd proved that Sir Horace was a fraud, and Mr. Carr would make sure there would be an inquest. His permanence in Hart House was coming to an end. In fact, Trevor had already paid him.

Once he finished tidying his desk, he took a good look at it. Everything was in order. The pencils and pens were stashed in their boxes, the books he'd used were back on the shelves, and the documents were ordered by date. He couldn't have been more meticulous than that.

Dusk covered the city with a black cloak. He would miss the view of the large diamond-paned windows of the houses limned with golden light. In the rookery, darkness fell quickly, and light occasionally lit the windows at night. Oil and wax were expensive.

He ran a hand over the polished wood of the desk. He would miss this study, the warmth of the stove, and Mrs. Daubney's sandwiches. Above all, he would miss Emma.

He wasn't giving up on them, but objectively, he didn't have a reason to stay, and his presence in Hart House posed a problem for her.

As if summoned by his thoughts, she entered the study, beautiful in a light green gown and the natural radiance only rainbows had. He'd always thought he couldn't have her. But the hope of them being together made his need for success personal. He wanted to be an engineer again, to make her proud and give her the life she was used to.

"Are you packing your things already?" A note of alarm crept into her voice.

"Yes. My job here is finished."

She laced her fingers through his. "You aren't leaving, are you?"

"No. Just tidying everything."

"You're sad."

He caressed her cheek. "There's nothing I want more than being with you."

"I hope you mean it."

"I do. Completely." He frowned. "Do you doubt me?"

She tugged at his hand. "Follow me."

The corridor was quiet. Not even the voices of the maids cleaning up the dining room could be heard. Jesse was asleep, exhausted again after Button and Trevor's gifts, for once completely happy and satisfied.

Nostalgia for the house and that moment with Emma caught him. How was it possible to miss the very instant he was living?

The semidarkness of the house, the silence, and the smell of wood polish would forever remain in his memory, along with Emma's soft touch, her smiles, and her stubborn hope.

Emma opening the door to her bedroom brought him back to reality.

"What are you doing?" he asked when she locked the door behind them.

She released his hand, smiling shyly. "I dismissed Gibson early, and Trevor is out to his gentlemen's club. No one will disturb us." She walked backwards to the bed.

His first instinct was to roar *yes*. Energy already pumped through his body, and his fingers itched to remove her clothes and replace them with his naked body. But he forced himself to be rational and didn't rush to her.

He focused on the consequences of his choices on her reputation. "Do you realise what will happen if we're together tonight?"

"Yes." She started to unbutton her tight shirt. "I'll be thoroughly happy, and I'll do my best to make you happy, too, once we get married."

His sight sharpened. "You know your reputation might be ruined forever."

"I'll be careful then, and I believe my future husband doesn't care." She removed her shirt and dropped it on the bed. "What other objections do you have?"

He was sure there were many. "Well..."

She unhooked her corset, and with each hook yielding to her elegant fingers, his thoughts became more muddled. He was saying something about...

"Yes?" She put the corset aside.

Only her flimsy chemise covered her lovely breasts. Her nipples pressed against the fabric, attracting his attention.

"You might regret it," he finally said although he was focused on Emma untying her skirt.

"I'm sure I won't." She removed her shoes and slid the skirt down her legs.

As she bent over, she gave him a spectacular view of her breasts, and he didn't remember what she'd said. She stood up and unfastened her petticoats. He rubbed his chest as a powerful tingle started on his skin.

He shouldn't do that. Touching her was one thing. But compromising her irreversibly was another.

"Emma." He sounded weak to his own ears.

"Are you still protesting? Let me help you make a decision then." She tossed her garter away and rolled down her stockings, revealing inch upon inch of creamy skin.

His pulse drummed so loudly he couldn't hear his thoughts.

Her drawers were next, and her chemise followed. And somehow he was standing less than a foot from her, having no idea how or when he'd crossed the room. Her scent teased his senses, driving him mad with desire.

"I haven't finished." She undid her chignon and let her long blonde curls fall to her waist. "What do you have to say?"

"You're a goddess." He took a curl and rubbed it between his fingers. He'd never touched anything so glorious and silky.

He held her by the waist with one hand and with the other he traced the curve of her jaw, neck, and shoulder to cup her breast.

She inhaled deeply as he rolled her nipple gently. Her hushed moan destroyed the last shred of determination not to bed her. He kissed her, but not as gently as he would have wanted. He thrust his tongue in her mouth and took possession of it as he fondled her breast.

She unbuttoned his waistcoat and shirt with impatient hands, but he barely paid attention to that, busy tasting her deeply and touching her softness.

"Remove it," she whispered among pants.

He obeyed without thinking. Between her hands and his, he was naked in a second. He allowed her only a moment to caress his naked chest before laying her on the bed. She was a vision with her hair spread around her head and shoulders against the blue bed cover. The soft light turned her skin the colour of pearls.

He kissed her again, savagely, and when she was wheezing and writhing, he trailed his mouth down her neck. Her back arched when he sucked her nipple.

Many women had been with him, more than he would care to admit, but Emma obliterated all the memories of those encounters. The powerful emotions she stirred within him cleansed him from the shame and humiliation he'd endured. He was a new man, free from his past.

She wrapped her legs around him and urged him closer. He did as she ordered but paused before it was too late.

They stared at each other in an intimate conversation that didn't require words. She caressed his cheek gently and lifted her hips to meet him. A groan reverberated deep in his throat because the small contact with her set a fire in his body. She rolled her hips, and he couldn't remain still any longer.

A gasp tore out of her when he inched forth.

"Hurt?" he said among pants.

"No." She tightened her grip around him, effectively trapping him.

He barely started moving back and forth before she quivered underneath him. She was stunning with her cheeks flushed and her eyes half closed. He kissed her parted lips before moving again.

Her nails scratched his back. Her legs hugged him, and her scent was on his skin. But above all, she spoke to his soul. She was the radiance he'd searched for in his life.

They shared the moment of giving themselves to each other as something sacred. There wouldn't be anyone else after her.

They found a rhythm together, and together they reached their releases. But he had to pull away before it was too late.

One day maybe they would build their family.

She wrapped her arms around his neck, her eyes lit with thousands of stars. "Don't leave."

"I won't."

She pulled him down until he lay stretched over her. He hugged her, and she closed her legs around him as well. They lay entwined like English ivy as if they needed the contact to live. Maybe it was true.

thirty-six

Marcus couldn't stop kissing Emma's neck as she tried to type a letter in the library. It wasn't his fault if her skin was so tempting and the sound of her laughter made him dizzy with happiness. After last night, he wouldn't doubt her hope anymore. She commanded his heart, and his heart was a willing subject.

"Marcus, I can't finish a sentence." She giggled. "You're distracting me."

"You can finish it later." He lingered on a lovely, soft spot under her ear.

He loved it when she trembled and sighed, sagging against him.

"The letter is for a new charity event. I want to raise money for the workers in Sir Horace's sites in case they lose their jobs."

"Good idea." He kissed the curve of her neck.

"I want everyone to donate generously."

"Hmm, hmm." He lowered her neckline an inch, just enough to kiss another spot on her skin.

She closed her eyes but kept typing blindly and pressed a key too hard. The sound of metal snapping jolted her.

"Bother." She stared in horror at the broken key. "You're my witness. I didn't do anything wrong. This typing machine hates me."

He laughed and hugged her, wiping the worried expression from her face with his lips. "I think you and devices aren't good friends. I'll fix it. Don't worry. I'll mend everything you break."

She kissed him back.

Footsteps came from the other side, and he reluctantly stepped back from her.

"My lady?" Stewart's voice came.

She cleared her throat and pulled her neckline up. "I'm here."

Stewart came into view. "Sir Horace would like to be received."

Emma stiffened. "Did he ask for me or Trevor? Trevor isn't here at the moment."

"Sir Horace asked specifically to talk to you." Stewart dabbed his forehead with a handkerchief.

Marcus shook his head. "You shouldn't see him."

Mr. Carr, the solicitor, had quickly set up their case. Sir Horace was going to face a tall pile of charges, and his presence there didn't bode well.

"I think it's better if we hear what he wants to say." She nodded at Stewart. "Show him into the drawing room. I'll be there in a moment."

Stewart left, but his frown suggested he agreed with Marcus.

"I'm not sure his presence here will have legal consequences," he said.

"I'll send a message to Mr. Carr afterwards to inform him of my conversation with Sir Horace."

As they walked to the drawing room, nervous energy stirred up Marcus's blood. The last time he'd seen Sir Horace had been when he'd signed the documents to cede his share of the company to him. After that, Sir Horace hadn't bothered to see how Marcus was faring.

"Do you want to wait for me upstairs?" she asked.

"I won't leave you alone with him, and hiding is pointless now. I signed the reports on his building sites. He knows I'm here."

"It must be difficult for you."

"I've seen worse, and it would be more difficult leaving you alone."

Sir Horace entered the drawing room still wearing his coat and hat, meaning he didn't plan to stay long. The years hadn't changed him. Aside from a few more grey hairs and plumper cheeks, he was the same man who had greedily taken everything from him. As if time hadn't passed.

Marcus's anger hadn't changed either.

"What's the purpose of your visit?" Emma asked without preamble.

"I won't be long, Lady Emma." Sir Horace shot a glance at Marcus but didn't acknowledge him. His cold eyes didn't betray any emotions. "You decided to go after me."

"You decided to put people's lives at risk," she said.

Sir Horace didn't deny that. "I'll give you the opportunity to think again about your accusations. Withdraw the charges, and I'll spare you in turns." He glanced at Marcus again.

She let out an impatient huff. "We aren't afraid of you."

"I don't care about what you fear or don't fear, my lady." Sir Horace tugged at his kid leather gloves. "I'm well aware of the fact you care more about people than money, and that you care about one person in particular." He tilted his head towards Marcus.

Emma's cheeks flushed. "I think whom I care about is none of your business."

"You are right. I don't care whether Marcus stays here or on the streets, but you should know his past carries a few stains society won't forgive easily. You don't want those secrets to come out, do you?"

Marcus suppressed a comment. He didn't care about society's disapproval; he'd dealt with that years ago, and now it couldn't hurt him. But Emma would be crushed.

Sir Horace's cold expression sent goose pimples down his neck. "Do you think you're strong because you lived on the streets? Do you think life owes you justice and success because you were left with nothing?"

"By you," he rebuked.

"I come from nothing," Sir Horace continued. "From a family of eleven. My father drank himself to an early grave, and it was up to me and my elder brother to help my family survive. Yet I don't complain."

He folded his arms across his chest. "Are we supposed to feel sympathy for you? Whatever your past is, you made choices that have consequences. I seek justice. You seek revenge on society. We have nothing in common."

"No, we haven't," Sir Horace said. "I'm not the only one who comes from the rookery. You would be surprised to know how many politicians share my same past. As Marcus knows, surviving the rookery is all about cooperation and compromises."

"I think you should leave." She opened the door. "Stewart, Sir Horace is leaving."

Sir Horace touched the rim of his hat. "I hope you'll think about my words."

When he left, Emma paced across the length of the room, looking as if she needed even more space. "How dare he! And what does his family and friends have to do with anything?"

"He made friends during those years when he rose from the streets to become a successful businessman. The bonds forged on the streets are powerful."

He'd seen gangs rising and falling because of those strong bonds. People who became successful after living on the streets didn't forget their friends.

She waved a dismissive hand. "I don't care about his friends. I already knew about his connections to Parliament. So what? Trevor has his own connections in the House of Lords."

"He isn't wrong about the damage your reputation might suffer because of me."

"We've discussed that many times, and I've always told you that I'm not afraid of that. When I was younger, I sometimes resented the fact I would never inherit my father's title or part of his legacy. But I changed my mind. The lack of a title means freedom to me. I can do what I want." She tilted up her chin, and he couldn't help but admire her courage and determination.

"To an extent. You're always an earl's daughter and an earl's sister."

"I'm not going to withdraw the accusations and risk people's lives for fear of gossip and society's snub. Sir Horace would need to find something better to threaten me with." She stopped pacing. "Does he know about you?"

He rubbed his aching temples. "He shouldn't. But I underestimated my skill to keep my job quiet. I thought Lady Beaumont didn't know the names of my other clients, and I was wrong. I might be wrong even about Sir Horace."

She lowered her gaze, and seeing her dejected pained him because she'd always been the hopeful, strong one between them.

"If he knows," he said, "the truth can damage you and your project."

"I can't pretend Sir Horace didn't do anything wrong and let him work on the houses in St. Giles. That would be wrong. Even if he spreads what he knows about you and my reputation is damaged, the important thing is that he will be out of the job and stop building precarious houses. That's what matters the most."

His heart burst with love and hope. Without her, he wouldn't dare to dream of a better future.

"You're truly a wonderful woman." And he would do his best to make her proud of him.

thirty-seven

Marcus spent the afternoon working on the broken typewriter in his bedroom. Again. Only that time, the work required more attention because one of the bars had snapped. He would need to solder it with tin and lead, being careful not to join other bars together.

Emma was busy organising the charity event, shut in a room with several matrons and ladies, while Jesse sat on the floor, playing with his train set next to him.

"Button makes a funny noise when I scratch his neck," Jesse said. "And he loves apples, but only if you slice them for him, and I don't mind doing it. He tickles my palm when I feed him."

"I'm happy you like him so much." He frowned at the typewriter.

The broken key was stuck in the machine harder than he thought. There was no easy fix for the damage. He would need to pull the machine apart, but putting it back together didn't guarantee it would work as it did before. Sometimes fixing a damage required causing a bigger one.

"George told me that if I keep growing tall at this rate, I'll need a new horse." Jesse stopped playing. "I don't want to leave Button."

"If he's your friend, you won't." He slid a pair of pincers to seize a metal fragment.

There was a quick knock on the door before Trevor entered; he looked pale and tense, but his expression softened when he smiled at Jesse.

"My lord." Jesse shot up. "Thank you again for Button. He's the best person I've ever met. After Marcus, Lady Emma, and you, of course."

Trevor's eyes widened, and his chest rose. "Why, I understand your sentiment. We should have a morning ride together."

Jesse beamed. "Yes, my lord."

Trevor returned serious as he angled towards Marcus. "Marcus, I need a word. My study."

"Of course." Tension charged the air when Marcus entered Trevor's study. "What is it?"

"Close the door."

He did as told and sat in front of Trevor's desk.

"I met Carr to receive news on the charges against Sir Horace." Trevor exhaled, rubbing his forehead. "There are allegations about you that discredit your credibility in regard to the evidence you collected against Sir Horace, and they have nothing to do with the fact he ruined your father."

He shifted on the chair, already having a hint. "What are these allegations exactly?"

"They're about you having solicited yourself for years for money." Trevor huffed. "I'm sure this is all poppycock, but if the allegations start to become stronger, our credibility will grow weaker."

Marcus reclined his head. "Is it known with whom I'm supposed to have solicited myself?"

"No, but it doesn't matter because I'm sure you can prove the allegations false." Trevor raised an eyebrow, waiting for a reassurance that would never arrive.

"I can't," he whispered. "They're true."

"Not again." Trevor swallowed a couple of times. "What the bloody hell were you thinking?"

He clenched his fists. "Desperation and hunger aren't the best advisers during difficult times. I did it for the same reasons as everyone desperate enough to work in a disorderly house did."

"You're missing the point. The women you were with won't hesitate to blame you if their names should come out. They'll say that you interfered with them," Trevor half-hissed, half-whispered. "You might face more than society's scorn."

"I didn't force anyone. If anything, sometimes it was the other way around."

Trevor closed a fist in front of him as if he wanted to grasp something. "I don't want to discuss your personal choices. My only concern is, actually, my *two* main concerns are Emma and our case against Sir Horace."

"Yes."

"I believe you'll agree that not talking to Emma is unavoidable," Trevor said. "I won't do it. This is something you should take care of as soon as possible. On the other hand, how can we go around this obstacle? Is there anything you can say that will convince the barrister to take the case seriously?"

"What happens if I simply deny the allegations?"

Trevor grimaced. "I'm afraid it won't work. We both know Sir Horace is behind the sudden surge of these allegations. The battle will turn ugly, especially for you."

"I can make a statement and explain the circumstances of my past while reinforcing the importance of the evidence presented against Sir Horace. Besides, what does my past have to do with hard evidence?"

"It's a matter of credibility." A ring of tension showed around Trevor's mouth. "Your situation is already compromised by the history between you and Sir Horace. You might have attacked him out of spite. That's a reasonable doubt we've taken into account, and which I'm fairly sure we can argue against because we have evidence. But add to that your past, and our work is demolished."

Marcus didn't say anything. He'd always thought the ladies who had been his clients would never expose him for fear of exposing themselves. Sir Horace starting the rumours had never been an option he'd contemplated, but he must have learnt the truth from one of the ladies.

"Talk to Emma, please." Trevor's tone was glacial.

"She already knows," he said. "And she doesn't care."

"She already knows?" Trevor's voice rose. "So I'm the last one to know? Wonderful." He thumped the desk and stood up. "You could have bloody told me before embarking on this operation."

"I didn't think it mattered."

The hard stare Trevor shot him made him feel rather stupid. "No need for secrecy then." He pulled the rope, and Stewart opened the door. "Tell Emma I need her here."

The butler bowed his head. "Lady Emma is entertaining her friends in the drawing room for the charity event."

"It won't take long. It's an urgent matter."

Stewart pressed lips before leaving.

A few awkward minutes passed with Trevor standing next to the window, as rigid as a statue. It would be better if he paced or yelled.

Emma entered the room, frowning. "What is it? I have only a few minutes. It was difficult to convince those ladies to come in the first place with all the rumours about me. We have almost finished with the preliminaries of the organisation."

Trevor clasped his hands behind his back. "Sir Horace is using Marcus's past as a paid rake to discredit his allegations, and it seems you already knew about Marcus's past but didn't think it was right to inform me."

She remained straight, her chin up. "Because I didn't think it was important."

Trevor shifted his index finger from her to Marcus. "You two are perfect for each other. You both live in your own world where actions have no consequences. I think it was an important detail to be aware of before we involved our solicitor in a situation where credibility is everything!"

Marcus had to agree with that. "You're right, but it's done. I can leave today if that will make things better."

"No." Emma closed her fists on her lap. "I disagree."

Trevor sat down again, dropping on the chair hard enough to make it rock. "This disaster was completely avoidable if you had talked to me, but yes, I expect Marcus to leave my house at this point."

"No," Emma said as Marcus said, "I will."

"It won't change anything," she said, "and if we send him away, that will only prove to everyone we believe the allegations are true. And I don't care about his past. I want to be with him forever, and I don't care what you think, either. You can keep your scruples and morals to yourself. They'll keep you company when you are here alone."

"Emma," Marcus whispered.

"I won't stay quiet." She flushed. "The only thing he cares about is his reputation. He's the earl, and I understand he has to think about the family's name, but I want to marry you, and he won't stop me. I will not consider him my brother anymore if he forbids me to follow my heart."

Trevor's nostrils flared. "That's a passionate speech, if I've ever heard one."

"Exactly. Passion is what you deny yourself." Emma leant closer. "I'm not surprised Ophelia left you." She gasped and put a hand on her chest. "I'm sorry. I didn't mean to say that. It slipped."

Marcus could sense the change in the air; it turned colder and heavier.

Trevor pressed his lips together. Then his words exploded out of his mouth in a rush as if they'd waited a long time to be spoken. "Ophelia didn't leave me. I left her when she confessed to having worked in a disorderly house for a short time."

Emma drew in a breath, and Marcus's jaw dropped open.

Trevor's expression didn't change. It remained hard and cold. "Shocking, isn't it? After she told me, I broke the engagement and told her I didn't want to see her again. She left London. So you see now why not knowing about Marcus's past is problematic for me."

Emma shook her head. "How could you? She loved you."

"Let me finish." Trevor clenched his jaw. "Not a day passes without me regretting my actions. That's why I didn't court anyone else. I miss her every day."

"I'm sorry for your pain, but you should understand what I feel because of it." Her voice became shaky and thin.

"I think he does." Marcus touched her arm. "I think he won't oppose us being together. Am I right, Trevor?"

"I'm still debating." Trevor swallowed a couple of times. "By giving you my blessing, I would partially atone for what I did to Ophelia. But either if I will or not interfere with your life, that doesn't mean the allegations aren't going to be a serious problem or that Emma's reputation won't be ruined. I regret how quickly and harshly I dismissed Ophelia. I don't want to make the same mistake again with my sister."

"Why don't you send Ophelia a letter and ask her to see you?" Emma's tone was sweet.

"Why would she want to see me?" Trevor flashed a sad smile. He seemed aged in a second. "She must hate me. I would if I were her."

"Is she married?" Marcus asked.

Trevor shook his head. "No, she lives with her aunt in a cottage near Bath and grows irises of all flowers. They represent hope."

She frowned. "How do you know?"

"I have a book on the meaning of flowers. I'm not a brute, you know."

She shot a glance at the ceiling. "How do you know where she lives and what she does?"

Trevor lowered his gaze and fiddled with a pencil.

"Trevor?" Emma narrowed her eyes.

"I paid an investigator to keep an eye on her."

"You didn't!" She huffed. "You complained and fought me when I wanted to hire an investigator to find Marcus."

"Because I'd already hired one to follow Ophelia!"

"This is wrong and hypocritical of you. You treated her like a criminal and then you set a hound on her tail. Send her a letter and ask her to see her." She was flustered. "Honestly. Every time I feel sorry for you, you do something that makes me regret it."

"I don't like surprises." Trevor gestured between Emma and Marcus. "Or secrets."

She chuckled. "Funny. I was about to say the same."

"I just wanted to make sure Ophelia was safe, and I was ready to intervene in case she needed my help." Trevor lifted a shoulder. "A romantic gesture. That's all."

Marcus cringed inwardly. "It's not as romantic as you might think."

Trevor held up a hand. "Enough of my personal life. I want you both to think about a solution for this damage."

That was one damage Marcus wasn't sure he could fix.

thirty-eight

Sitting on a bench in Hyde Park with her maid, Emma found it difficult to enjoy watching Jesse with Button.

He'd become a good rider in a short time, but the most incredible thing was Trevor, riding next to Jesse and laughing with him. Her brother patiently showed Jesse how to manoeuvre the pony and how to trot without hurting his back. She would have never thought Trevor would show the same affection he did for horses to a boy.

Worries piled up in her mind faster than sand in an hourglass as she waited for the reaction to the rumours Sir Horace spread about Marcus.

"Do not worry, my lady," Gibson said. "The charity will raise a fortune in no time."

"Hopefully, if people don't get frightened by the rumours."

"I think you'll raise a fortune exactly because of the rumours. People will want to know the truth."

Lady Beaumont promenaded towards them, followed by her maid. She paused at their bench and nodded. "Good morning, Emma."

"Good morning." Her voice was as sweet as rat poison to her own ears.

Marcus's past was behind him, but she couldn't completely forget Lady Beaumont had been with him on more than one occasion.

Lady Beaumont gazed around. "I'm afraid I'm in a hurry, but I just wanted to tell you that I'll support your charity event, whatever you choose it to be."

"Thank you. That's generous of you." She sounded as if she were choking, but considering the annoyance boiling within her, she was doing a good job.

"I trust that everything else is all right."

"It is, thank you."

Lady Beaumont loitered, glancing around. "Well, I guess that's all."

"I really think it is."

The change in Lady Beaumont was immediate. Her gaze sharpened, and she straightened her spine.

"We don't have anything else to say. Have a nice day, Emma." Lady Beaumont hurried again along the path as if the police were after her.

Lady Beaumont had changed her manners, which Emma didn't mind. Her attention towards Marcus wasn't welcome. Or maybe Lady Beaumont was worried about the rumours spreading and that might involve her. So far, there was nothing clear aside from a rumour about Marcus having worked in a disorderly house, which wasn't true. But that was the reason why he'd decided to stay home and not show himself in the park.

The barrister would establish if the evidence brought by Marcus against Sir Horace was to be considered valid or not, hopefully before the rumours became unmanageable.

Jesse followed Lady Beaumont with his gaze before climbing off Button. He rushed towards Emma, holding his flat hat in place with a hand.

"Are you tired, dear?"

"Lady Emma," he said, breathing quickly. "I have something that might help you with Sir Horace."

"Please. You aren't going anywhere near him."

He shook his head. "It's not that. I don't have to go to his house, but there's something I didn't tell you about that night."

"What is it?" She prompted when he didn't talk. "You know you can tell me anything."

He scrubbed the top of his head. "When I entered his house, he was arguing with a lady, that lady." He nodded towards Lady Beaumont.

"Are you sure it was her?" She checked the path, but Lady Beaumont had already vanished.

"Very. I had to wait for them to finish before coming out of my hiding place, and they argued a lot. I took a good look at her, and it's her."

"And what did they argue about?"

He blushed. "They had an affair, but it ended. She ended it. She told him not to ruin her. She didn't want her name to come out, and if it did, she would tell everyone he went to a place called..." He paused. "I don't remember the name, but it was a town with a bridge up north. Port something. No, I can't remember."

A sharp quiver went through her. "Newport-on-Tay?"

"That one." He nodded. "He got angry when he heard that name and told her to stop talking. She said that everyone will know he was the one who inspected the bridge."

"Sir Horace was the one to inspect the bridge." Emma took a moment to ponder the news. "As Marcus's father always claimed."

"Was that important?" he asked.

She hugged him. "You're brilliant."

∽

MARCUS WASN'T sure Emma's idea would work. Seeing Lady Beaumont again was nothing short of unpleasant for him, and having to deal with her and recruit her help against Sir Horace would be difficult.

Emma didn't seem happy either. She kept looking out of the window of the drawing room as they waited for Lady Beaumont to arrive in Hart House.

"We can't be sure Lady Beaumont will be willing to talk against Sir Horace," Marcus said. "She must be the person who informed Sir Horace of my past."

"I don't think so. She wouldn't risk her reputation by exposing your past to Sir Horace. She has very little to gain. I think Sir Horace learnt about your past from someone else, and Lady Beaumont became outraged and worried that the rumours about you might lead to her."

"I don't trust her, but you're probably right."

She slid her hand into his. "I know it's difficult for you. But we must try to turn Lady Beaumont into our strongest ally."

He smiled. "Always the hopeful one."

"Well, so far, so good."

The sound of a carriage stopping in front of the house caused them to tense and shortly after, Stewart came into the drawing room.

"Lady Beaumont."

"Show her in, please." Emma smoothed down her blue gown, and for a moment, he indulged himself in looking at her beauty and the sense of freedom and peace she so easily set into his heart.

Lady Beaumont walked in, wrapped in a cloud of flowery perfume. The scent brought him back to their encounters and her demanding attention. Her lady's maid glanced at Marcus for a fleeting moment.

"Emma." Lady Beaumont's gaze lit up when she saw Marcus.

He bowed. "My lady."

"Thank you for coming, Lena." Emma's tone could cut glass. "Please take a seat."

Lady Beaumont didn't sit down. "May I ask what this is all about? After all the rumours circulating about you, I don't want to spend too much time here. You surely understand."

She cleared her throat. "You know Mr. Kingston, don't you?"

A moment of awkward silence thickened the air.

"I need to talk to you," Marcus said.

Lady Beaumont was flustered. "Then I want privacy. If we have to talk, I kindly ask Emma to leave the room."

"Excuse me?" she said. "This is my house."

Marcus gave her a nod. "I think it would be better if you weren't here." He didn't want her to listen to details of his former job with Lady Beaumont.

"Just because you asked me." Tension flickered in Emma's face. "I'll be in the sitting room."

"Thank you, Emma." Lady Beaumont turned to her lady's maid. "Walker, take a walk." She laughed at her own joke.

The maid curtsied, her gaze flying upwards for a moment. "My lady."

Before leaving, Emma paused at the door and gave him a warm smile only for him. There was no possessiveness in it, only love.

When he was alone with Lady Beaumont, he faced her, his hands clammy.

"What did you want to tell me?" she asked, sitting on the sofa.

He sat in front of her. "I know you and Sir Horace were lovers."

She paled but collected herself quickly. "I don't know what you're talking about."

"My lady, please. We can be honest with each other. Do you think I would judge you? Or do you think I'll gossip about that?"

She fiddled with a fold in her skirt. "It was before I met you, and I didn't like it. I was young, just married, and unhappy, and he made me feel adored. For a while. Then he became demanding and jealous."

That reminded him of someone.

"As I said, I'm not going to judge you. I mentioned that because I don't think it was you who spread the rumours about my past. I think it was Sir Horace, but he didn't learn the truth from you, did he?"

She shifted on the sofa. "Well, I didn't tell him anything, but he discovered it."

"What do you mean?"

"You were one of the reasons I didn't want to keep my affair with him going on. He didn't take it well. As the possessive and jealous lover he is, he had me followed. I guess it wasn't difficult for him to be informed of who my new interest was."

"Did he promise he would keep quiet about your involvement after you confronted him at his home?"

"How do you know that?"

"By chance."

She gazed around, losing her composure for a moment. "He did, but I didn't believe him."

"So you blackmailed him."

That got her attention. Colour leached from her face. "I had to protect myself. My marriage isn't perfect, but Jonathan and I are much happier now. We respect each other. I can't have my reputation tarnished by such a scandal."

He didn't care about that, either. "You were with him in Newport-on-Tay one year before the bridge collapsed." He could barely contain his eagerness to hear her answer.

"I was. It was his idea of a romantic escapade. We pretended to be married during the trip. Once there, he did his work, and we saw each other in the evening only. Quite boring for a romantic escapade. So yes, I know he inspected the bridge."

A weight lifted from his shoulders. He'd never doubted his father, but hearing the same story confirmed by someone else quietened some of his hunger for justice. He swallowed past the lump of emotion in his throat.

"Why didn't you tell me?" he asked, not without kindness.

"First, I didn't want you to know I had an affair with Horace. And second, I didn't link your father's identity to the bridge incident until later on. Until you talked about your father. I'm not heartless. I swear it."

"Again, I'm not here to judge you. I want your help to stop Sir Horace from spreading rumours about us, and I want him to face justice."

Her eyebrows shot up. "Justice?"

"You must have heard he's facing charges of negligence."

"Yes, but when I asked him about that, he minimised the whole affair."

"It would be to our mutual benefit if you would help me put this rumour to rest. You can end it while discrediting Sir Horace. Can you do that?"

She smiled. "I think I can."

thirty-nine

Marcus needed a distraction, and the charity carnival in South London they were visiting was perfect. Emma had managed to involve many ladies to set up the large festival. Her hope was her strongest suit; it allowed her to overcome many obstacles. The air was thick with the smell of toffees, nougats, and sugar plums. Happy music and laughter drifted from the crowded stands, and most importantly, no one stared at him or whispered behind his back.

Jesse pointed at a stand with a sign reading *'palmistry.'* "What's palmistry?"

"It's a form of fortune telling," Trevor said. "Someone will read your past and your future by examining the palm of your hand."

"What?" Jesse stared at his palm. "I want to try."

"Why? You know your past, and you'll know your future." Trevor waved a hand in dismissal. "Wasted time."

"Let him go." Emma poked him with her elbow. "He wants to try new things."

"I want to try the ball in a basket, the ring toss." Jesse rose on his tiptoes to see past the people in front of him. "And the shooting game, and Sir Horace!" He grabbed Marcus's hand.

"Where?" he asked.

"Over there. He's coming towards us."

"How does he know where we are?" Emma stepped closer to Marcus.

"He must have asked Stewart. It's not a secret." Trevor straightened his jacket before moving closer to Jesse, and Marcus wrapped an arm around him.

A sudden lash of anger cut through his chest. One day, he might look at Sir Horace and not feel anything aside from disappointment, but for now, a furnace of fury burned inside him, especially after Lady Beaumont confirmed his father's words.

Sir Horace walked against the flow of the crowd, gripping his walking stick hard.

He stopped in front of them. "I was looking for you. I demand —" He stared at Jesse for a long moment. Darkness spilt in his gaze. "You! The little thief. I should have guessed you sent him." He reached out to grab Jesse, but Marcus, Trevor, and Emma moved at the same time.

Marcus pushed Jesse behind him, and Trevor blocked Sir Horace's arm with surprising agility.

"What do you want?" Trevor asked.

"You sent that boy to steal from my house." Sir Horace pointed a finger at Jesse.

"Don't be ridiculous." Trevor huffed. "Why would I ever do that? And to steal what? That horrible green vase you're so proud of? Or that disgusting portrait of you with a fake sword, in a fake suit of armour?"

Sir Horace shifted his gaze over all of them as if considering how much time he would need to kill them all. "You spread false, nasty rumours about me."

"Believe it or not, we don't spend our time thinking of you."

Trevor gestured at him to move aside. "It's actually the opposite. We try hard not to think of you. Now move out of my way. We need to have our palms read. I want to know if we'll ever get rid of you."

Sir Horace grabbed Emma's arm, and she let out a whimper.

"It was you," he hissed.

"Let her go," Marcus said at the same time as Trevor said, "Don't touch my sister!"

Marcus was faster than Trevor and shoved Sir Horace, forcing him to release Emma.

She rubbed her arm. Jesse held her hand, his eyes filled with fear.

"You inspected the bridge." Marcus moved closer to Sir Horace, not caring about the sheer anger flickering behind his eyes. "My father told the truth."

Something in Marcus's tone or attitude must have scared Sir Horace because he stepped back. "Your father didn't understand that making money means to make compromises."

"Thank goodness for that."

"Your pathetic attempt at ruining my reputation won't change anything." Sir Horace shook his stick.

"Then you have nothing to worry about." Trevor glowered. "Why all this fuss then? For the last time, move or I'll give all the people here something to gossip about."

"You tell him, my lord." Jesse remained half-hidden behind Marcus. "I bet he doesn't like horses."

"Leave," Marcus repeated.

Sir Horace gave them one last glaring look before he strode away.

Jesse released a long breath. "Thank you, Lord Pembroke."

Marcus rubbed Emma's arm. "How are you?"

She touched her arm. "Glad he's gone."

"We'll make sure he's gone for good," Trevor said, offering his hand to Jesse. "Now, who wants to have their palms read?"

EMMA WOULD NEVER UNDERESTIMATE the power of gossip. She drank her morning tea in the sunroom, skimming through the scandal sheet.

While she hadn't been fond of the idea of Marcus having to deal with Lady Beaumont again, she was impressed by how the lady managed to spread some vicious rumours about Sir Horace. Although she wondered if they were rumours or not.

Sir Horace was now branded as a liar and a man who enjoyed harassing young ladies. In every fashionable parlour, club, and tearoom, Sir Horace was the main topic of conversation.

No one remembered that Marcus had been at the centre of another scandal a couple of weeks earlier. Exactly what she wanted.

Sir H is rumoured to have tried to steal the virtue of young Lady M...Rumour has it Sir H enjoys pursuing married ladies, as Lady J confirmed...Lady R accused Sir H of inappropriate behaviour...

The scandal sheet was an avalanche of gossip, nasty allegations, and rumours that bordered on cruelty. But without that, he would never face justice.

On the other hand, donations for the workers had poured in steadily at the fair they'd organised. They were still far from covering the salaries of everyone, but she was hopeful. Of course she was.

Trevor entered the sunroom, carrying a wide smile and twinkling eyes. He regarded the pristine table and stopped smiling. "Where are Jesse and Marcus?"

She lowered her cup of tea. "What do you mean? They're where you sent them, in the kitchen."

"No, I asked them to be here." He turned towards the footman. "Neil, call Jesse and Marcus."

Neil left as Trevor sat at the table.

"You're happy," she said.

"Very much."

"Does it mean you're a fool?"

"I wish you had never studied philosophy." He exhaled. "I have news, but I'll wait for Jesse and Marcus to be here."

"Why?"

"Impatience is unappealing."

She scoffed. "You're impossible."

Jesse rushed into the room, followed by Marcus.

"My lord, are you going to give the announcement?" Jesse asked, shifting his weight from one foot to another.

"Yes, more or less." Trevor looked nervous. "Please have a seat."

She stared at Marcus, and he gave her his lopsided smile.

"Are we having breakfast here?" Jesse took in the bacon, scones, butter, and kippers.

"Yes, from now on, if you like. Sit down. I have news." Trevor cleared his throat and waited for everyone to be seated. "The police found evidence of Sir Horace having exaggerated the expenses and bought cheap construction materials. My solicitor is confident Sir Horace will end up in prison." He paused dramatically. "We won. Almost, but I'm hopeful."

"Yes!" Jesse celebrated by filling his plate with bacon.

"That's wonderful." Emma took Marcus's hand.

"But that's not the good news. The police reopened the investigation on the Tay Bridge disaster." Trevor became serious, but his face softened at the same time. "I'm sure your father's name will be cleared once the investigation is over, and you can rebuild your company if you want."

Marcus's smile dropped. His expression became deadpan, and he didn't seem to breathe. "What..." The word came out strangled.

"Marcus." Emma stroked his knuckles. "You can start working as an engineer again. That's wonderful."

"It's not all sunshine, though," Trevor said. "Starting a new company at the moment isn't an easy business. But with my help, we'll get Marcus's company back up on its feet as soon as possible. What do you think?"

Finally, Marcus blinked. He swallowed a few times. "My father would be happy. He would want that. Yes, I want to restart my company."

Emma hugged him, and he hid his face in the crook of her neck. "I'm so happy for you."

"Thank you," Marcus said. "Without you, I would have never started again."

Trevor grinned. "You're welcome."

"What about the other announcement?" Jesse asked, spreading butter on his scone.

Trevor coughed into his fist. "Yes, well, Jesse and I will take a short holiday together. Now enjoy breakfast before it gets cold."

"Wait a moment," Emma said at the same time as Marcus said, "What holiday? Where?"

"Boring details." Trevor waved dismissively. "We'll leave next week, and we'll be back soon."

"Trevor, you must tell us more." She glanced from Jesse to her brother. "Since when have you gone on a holiday? You've never taken a day off if not for riding a horse. Well?"

"May I?" Jesse asked.

Trevor sighed and nodded. "If you must."

"Lord Pembroke wants me to go with him to a town close to Bath to meet a lady called Ophelia."

"Oh, Trevor." She touched his hand. "That's lovely."

"But why is Jesse coming?" Marcus asked.

"Company." Trevor waved again. "Where's my tea? Does anyone want more kippers?"

"Trevor." She nudged him. "Tell the truth."

Jesse gave him an encouraging nod. "Lady Emma will discover everything anyway. It's better to be honest, my lord."

"Ophelia likes children very much." Trevor paused. "So I thought to take Jesse with me."

"And?" she insisted.

Trevor's brow lowered. "And we're leaving. Where's the newspaper?"

Jesse wiped his mouth. "I'm the poor, wretched orphan Lord Pembroke saved from the streets. That's what I'll tell Miss Ophelia so His Lordship can win her heart back. I'm practising my crying." He started to wail and sob, mumbling unintelligible words. "Lord Pembroke told me to cry a few times when I meet Miss Ophelia."

"Trevor!" Emma shot him a glare.

Marcus chuckled, lowering his cup of tea.

Trevor avoided meeting her gaze. "It's true. Marcus meets Jesse first, but he lives here, does he not? And he's an orphan. No lies there. And the palm reader told me that my love enterprise would be successful."

"You said you didn't like secrets," she said.

"When I'm the one who doesn't know the secret, not the other way around."

Marcus craned his neck towards Jesse. "Do you agree with this farce?"

"Lord Pembroke will give me three pounds." Jesse smiled. "And we'll go riding in his estate in Devon."

"Oh, Trevor." Emma shook her head, but Marcus laughed.

Trevor didn't flinch. "Somebody told me love isn't rational. I agree."

Marcus went through the house designs again, walking across the open construction site.

The house would be fully detached but not particularly large, at least not as big as Hart House. Emma was used to wide rooms and plenty of space. The house where they would live once married was more modest but made with the finest materials he could find, and it would be warm and comfortable.

"...and the kitchen has been planned as well, sir," Edward, Marcus's foreman, said. "As you can see, we're on time. Unless your bride-to-be has changed her mind again and wishes to speed things up?" A note of panic quivered in his voice.

He smiled. "No, she hasn't. We agreed to get married as soon as the house is completed."

Edward sighed. "Good to know."

Speaking of which, a carriage stopped at the rough drive, and Emma jumped out of it to run to him.

He hurried to take her hand, lest she trip on the discarded building material cramming the drive.

"So? How are we doing?" Her smile dropped when she tilted

her head up and looked at the skeleton of the house and the scaffolding. "It's the same as it was two weeks ago. I don't see any difference."

He kissed her hand. "Trust me, we made a lot of progress. Invisible progress to the untrained eye. We finished the foundations, the connection to the main sewer, and the plumbing. Those are the most complicated structures to build."

She stuck out her bottom lip. "What about the walls and windows?"

"They are next."

"I've already chosen the tiles and the furniture. Can't we speed up the construction?"

Edward focused on a wooden beam in the room that would be the drawing room and pretended not to hear her.

Marcus shook his head. "Always so impatient."

"I want to marry you." She hooked her arm through his. "As soon as possible. I had to wait a whole year already, and with Trevor seeing Ophelia again, I want to get married soon so I can help her organise their wedding."

"We waited a year because I needed to rebuild my company." And he couldn't have done it without Trevor's help.

Surprisingly, even Lady Beaumont offered her help, and the new construction company, Kingston & Hart, was born and going well. The financial scandal that had engulfed Sir Horace had gained such proportions that not even his friends in Parliament could protect him. He'd been charged with negligence, and Father's name had been cleared. So Marcus's company was slowly thriving. The fact his former clients hadn't gossiped about him—to protect themselves—had helped his reputation.

Even Trevor was thriving to an extent. His visit to Ophelia had at first been a disaster. But being a persistent chap, Trevor had slowly rebuilt a relationship with her. But she didn't make it easy for him.

"We should leave." He guided her towards the carriage.

"But I want to talk to the foreman and ask him if he can speed up the construction. I want the walls. What's a house without walls?"

Edward paled and glanced around, likely searching for an escape.

"That's why we need to leave." Marcus took her hand and they got into the carriage.

She looked out of the carriage window at the house until it disappeared behind a curve. "It's a dream. A dream that seemed impossible a year ago."

Since Marcus was engaged to Emma, he didn't live in Hart House anymore but in a nice flat not far from her. He and Jesse still spent a lot of time with her and Trevor.

In fact, at Hart House they found Jesse and Trevor confronting each other across a chessboard in the sitting room.

Trevor was scowling while Jesse smirked.

"What's happening?" Emma kissed Jesse's cheek.

Trevor narrowed his gaze. "He beat me at chess."

"It's all about using the knight properly." Jesse picked up the pieces and rearranged them on the board.

Trevor made a funny noise.

"You aren't used to losing." She kissed his cheek as well.

"No, I'm not. But it's not my fault. I'm distracted." He drummed his fingers on the armrests, gazing around. "This house is going to be empty and silent once you leave, and who knows if and when Ophelia will agree to marry me. I'll be alone for a long time. Are you in a hurry to build that house?"

"I'll come every day," Jesse said. "And we'll keep riding together in the park, won't we?"

Trevor smiled. "Of course."

Emma wanted the construction of the house to speed up; Trevor wanted it to slow down.

Marcus, instead, was happy.

Whatever happened, however it went, he had everything he'd wanted or needed right in that room.

He and Emma had built the most beautiful life ever.

about me

Love stories have always captured my imagination. What's better than two people falling in love with each other? I write steamy romance, usually with a paranormal twist in an historical setting. Add a touch of suspense and mystery and a pinch of darkness. I love stories with  strong, sexy heroes and mischievous heroines who pull no punches.

I live in the City of Sails, New Zealand, drinking tea (coffee gives me anxiety) and devouring books.

Join my newsletter for exclusive content and the chance to receive an ARC copy of my books. Just copy and paste this link into your browser:

Barbara's Newsletter: https://bit.ly/39yZ4Lw

also by barbara russell

If you want historical romance:

<u>Victorian Outcasts</u>

If you love steamy paranormal romance set in Victorian London, my Royal Occult Bureau series is for you:

<u>The Royal Occult Bureau Series</u>

Are you into shape-shifter romance? Check out my da Vinci's Beasts series, set in WW2:

<u>da Vinci's Beasts Series</u>

For more Victorian paranormal romance with witches and sexy warriors, see the Knights of the White Blade series:

<u>The White Order Series</u>

A small press bound by the belief that every voice matters.

Sign up for our newsletter to learn about new releases and more.
https://oliver-heberbooks.com/subscribe/

Follow us on social media:

facebook.com/oliverheberbooks

instagram.com/oliverheberbooks

amazon.com/oliverheberbooks

youtube.com/@OliverHeberBooksPublisher

www.ingramcontent.com/pod-product-compliance
Lightning Source LLC
Chambersburg PA
CBHW020244010826
48973CB00006B/1644